"I should've been there." He followed her into the kitchen, regret welling up like blood from a wound that should have long since healed over. "I should've fought harder for you..."

"I only wish—" She turned around to face him, looking startled to see how close he stood behind her.

When she splayed her hand across the center of his chest, he thought she meant to push him back, to give herself some breathing space. Instead, she gave him a look that seem to bore straight through him. "But why waste one more second regretting what either of us might've said or done half a lifetime ago?"

He grasped her upper arm, his gaze dropping to her lips before returning to a pair of beautiful brown eyes in what felt like a homecoming.

"Maybe I'm not thinking at all about the past right this second—not when the present's standing right in front of me, looking a hell of a lot better than anything I've seen in years."

Dear Reader,

Have you even lain awake during the darkest hours of the night regretting some long-ago past event and wishing you could get a do-over? I believe that most of us have had that experience. But no matter how much sleep such thoughts have cost us, for the most part, we have little choice except to learn to make peace with our pasts and forgive our younger selves.

Every once in a blue moon, however, the universe gifts individuals with the chance to go back to where it all started. There, they are given the rare opportunity to see if—with time, maturity and hindsight—they might overcome whatever obstacles prevented them from putting the puzzle of their lives together in a way that will bring joy instead of heartache. When long-ago lovers turned bitter rivals Hayden Hale-Walker and Kate McClafferty find themselves unexpectedly faced with such a prospect, neither has any interest in reopening past wounds— or working together one minute longer than it takes to complete a life-and-death search-and-rescue mission in a remote canyon in Texas Hill Country. But a heart-twisting set of circumstances—including a deadly ambush—changes everything...and reveals that buried beneath the years of hostility between them, embers lie waiting to be rekindled if they can find the courage and the will to try.

Ambush at Heartbreak Ridge is set in and around a section of Texas Hill Country a couple of hours northwest of San Antonio. The towns and rivers of this beautiful area are real places, but some geographic features are fictional or altered slightly to serve the needs of the story.

Colleen Thompson

AMBUSH AT HEARTBREAK RIDGE

Colleen Thompson

HARLEQUIN®
ROMANTIC SUSPENSE™

Recycling programs for this product may not exist in your area.

ISBN-13: 978-1-335-73800-4

Ambush at Heartbreak Ridge

Copyright © 2022 by Colleen Thompson

For questions and comments about the quality of this book, please contact us at CustomerService@Harlequin.com.

Harlequin Enterprises ULC
22 Adelaide St. West, 41st Floor
Toronto, Ontario M5H 4E3, Canada
www.Harlequin.com

Printed in U.S.A.

The Texas-based author of more than thirty novels and novellas, **Colleen Thompson** is a former teacher with a passion for reading, hiking, kayaking and the last-chance rescue dogs she and her husband have welcomed into their home. With a National Readers' Choice Award and multiple nominations for the RITA® Award, she has also appeared on the Amazon, BookScan and Barnes & Noble bestseller lists. Visit her online at www.colleen-thompson.com.

To my mother, Lois Swartz,
who taught me the meaning of unconditional love.

Chapter 1

Though he had promised to join the equine search and rescue team at first light, the sun was already streaming over the horizon by the time Sheriff Hayden Hale-Walker's black-and-white department SUV pulled up beside the half dozen assembled pickups and horse trailers parked along the grassy hillside. With his jaw already clenching in anticipation of the coordinator's—his former fellow deputy Kate McClafferty's—snide remarks about his tardiness, he adjusted his black Western hat and zipped his jacket as he jumped out, his warm breath pluming against the sharpness of the early-morning chill.

With no one in sight, he jogged between vehicles and called, "Hello?" in the vain hope that he might find a straggler—anyone who could point him to his mount and let him know where he might catch up with the searchers.

His spirits plunged, however, when his voice echoed in the mountain air. Worse yet, the only living thing around turned out to be the groomed and saddled animal that his former colleague had evidently left tethered for him beside the four-horse trailer behind the blue pickup he recognized as Kate's.

"You've got to be kidding me," he said, drawing a curious stare from the tall, well-muscled bay mule.

Chuckling to himself, he shook his head, figuring that her decision to stick him on a jackass—a sight she'd undoubtedly be sure to photograph and share far and wide—had been in no way accidental. When he unclipped the animal's lead and moved to mount up, he began to wonder if she was trying to punish him with a few bruises, too, for the mule declined to stand still, spinning in circles and braying loudly, refusing to allow him to get a foot in the stirrup, much less hoist himself up onto the broad, brown back.

"Son of a— Hold still, will you?" Hayden said, grasping the reins more firmly as he attempted to take charge. Though he'd ridden little over the past few years, he'd learned his way around a horse on his family's cattle ranch before he'd learned to ride a bike. Still, every time he tried to climb aboard, the animal snorted, sidled away or—on one particularly frustrating occasion—managed to rip the reins free and start bucking so hard that Hayden had no choice but to back off before he ended up sporting a set of mule-shaped hoofprints on his rib cage.

"Whoa, whoa! What are you doing to my Jasper?" came a familiar—and decidedly outraged—voice behind him.

Face burning, he turned to see Kate emerging from a lingering whorl of dawn fog aboard a powerfully built dapple-gray quarter horse, who pranced nervously in response to the mule's histrionics. Wearing a safety orange jacket along with a helmet, with her hair tucked out of sight, she glared at him, her big, dark brown eyes accusing.

"I was *trying* to ride out to look for you," he said, "since I figured you'd left *this* for me as some sort of punishment."

"Punishment?" she scoffed, head shaking as she dismounted. "You should be so lucky as to have Jasper for a mount. He's the smartest, most sure-footed trail animal I've ever ridden—as well as my personal pet."

Passing him the gray's reins with her gloved hands, she crooned to the mule, "My poor boy. What did the mean man do to scare you?"

Hayden made a disgusted face. "Other than dodging his damned hooves, *nothing.* Or was I just supposed to stand there and let your jackass kick me when I tried to mount?"

"You were supposed to be *on time*, as promised," she reminded him, scratching the now perfectly placid mule's neck. "If you hadn't been so late—as usual—then I wouldn't have had to ride out alone to show the other searchers their route into the canyon."

Adjusting his black hat, he shrugged off the criticism. "Just as I was heading out, I finally got a call back from the investigator handling the Kessler family's missing persons case back where they live in Memphis. Figured I'd better talk where I could take a few notes instead of trying to hold a conversation on the fly."

Ignoring his excuse, she went on to explain, "I thought it might be a good idea to burn a little energy off your mount. He tends to get a little rambunctious on chilly mornings like this, and I wanted to make sure he wouldn't be too much for you to handle once you finally got here."

"He won't be too much for me." Hayden frowned, annoyed at what he took as a dig, her way of implying that when his family had lost the ranch they'd owned for generations, he'd reverted back to greenhorn status. "That is, if he's any better trained than that long-eared whirlwind of yours."

"Jasper, my love, *stand*." She prompted the mule, who'd had his neck stretched out while enjoying his scratch, to square up and go still as a statue while she swung aboard to look down on Hayden, imperious as any queen. "You were saying…?"

He rolled his eyes before just as easily mounting Banner—and noted with appreciation that the stirrups had already been adjusted to accommodate his greater height. *"Thank you,"* he forced himself to say, the Western saddle creaking, "for allowing me to join you, for loaning me the horse and tack and for riding back to meet me. Especially since I'm sure you would've rather sent me out with any passing stranger."

She didn't bother with a denial, instead responding in that same irritatingly prim voice—the one he knew to be sarcastic, "You're very welcome, *Sheriff*."

The emphasis was a reminder that after the county's former sheriff, Arlo Turner, had succumbed to a fatal heart attack, Hayden and Kate, both ambitious deputies at the time, had thrown their hats into the ring to run for his office. And that despite Kate's bachelor's degree in criminal justice, her undeniable talent and work ethic, the voters of the traditionally minded rural county had favored him three-to-one in the election. That result culminated in her calling him an "overrated good old boy" as she'd tossed her badge down on his desk—her glare strongly suggesting what he might want to do with it— before storming out the door for good.

"There's no need to *Sheriff* me. You know that," he growled, scarcely able to believe there had been a time, when they'd apparently been so delirious with hormones, they'd been completely obsessed with one another. Obsessed to the point that—

He clamped down ruthlessly on the thought, reminding himself they'd only been kids back in those heady days. Yet for an instant, a sixteen-year-old version of the still-disarmingly attractive woman before him blazed through his memory, her dark red hair streaming out behind her as she'd raced her palomino, Cloverleaf, around the third barrel to the cheers of throngs of rodeo fans…and the timer counted down the final hundredths of a second before—

No. He damned well wouldn't allow himself to go there.

"All right, then. You're welcome, *Hayden.*" Kate spoiled her otherwise pleasant tone by infusing his name with a touch of venom. "But let's go over the morning's plan, since we're already running behind."

"You've got it," he responded, forcing the echoes of long-faded screams out of his mind.

Riding up beside him, she pulled out a GPS hand-held device and showed him a satellite map of the area. Her expression sobered as she pointed out a spot by a tight curve Hayden recognized, poised as it was above a steeply wooded slope.

"This is the location where Nicolas Kessler was killed after the family's car broke through the guardrail and plunged off the highway." Kate settled her stamping and snorting mule with a subtle adjustment of her reins.

"We recovered his body last night just after sunset," said Hayden, recalling the complicated operation, which had involved rescuers in harness, "along with enough evidence to convince us there had been family members in the car who must have climbed down to the canyon floor below, since getting back up to the road was impossible."

He'd never forget the horror he'd first felt when the firefighters had radioed him about finding the woman's purse, two booster seats and clothing items clearly belonging to an adult female and children—individuals who were nowhere near the wreckage.

Her brow furrowing, Kate shook her head. "Last night, I know you weren't sure when the wreck happened, but have you gotten any more information that might help us figure out how far they could've gotten or what their condition might be?"

Hayden shook his head. "All we know for sure was that the last known sighting of the family—mother, father and their two elementary-school-age daughters—was three days ago as of this morning, when they checked out of the motel where they'd been vacationing in New Orleans."

"And no one's heard from them since?"

"Not a word," he said as his horse champed at his bit. "But getting back to our route…"

"Right," said Kate, before refocusing them on the task ahead. "To get down into the canyon, we'll ride over this hill ahead here and then down along a fairly narrow rock ledge. That's the trickiest part, but it's a short span—and we have nothing to fear aboard these mounts."

"I'll trust your judgment on that," he said, knowing that whatever his feelings were regarding Kate's people skills—especially her competitiveness with him—she knew her equines.

Nodding, she continued, "Once we get past that, there's a wider, more circuitous route we'll ride for another half hour or so to the lower canyon level to take us down below the crash site—"

"So the Kessler woman and her daughters—they could've actually walked out by this route on their own, right?"

She nodded. "*If* they'd been able to spot it. But I can't imagine them doing that without a map or GPS, especially from their lower vantage point—and there's no way a regular cell phone will have any signal way out here."

He shook his head and sighed. "Ada Kessler doesn't even have her cell. I received a copy of a police report from New Orleans this morning, too. Apparently, both the Kesslers' phones were stolen from their room while they took the girls for a swim in the motel pool the night before they checked out."

"What rotten luck," Kate said. "That data could've been so helpful tracking their last movements…"

"It's a bad break," he agreed.

Her brow crinkled as she made a face. "Weird, though, isn't it, that they didn't try to pick up at least one new cell before leaving New Orleans? Especially if they weren't intending to head straight back home to Memphis? With most people so dependent on their phones these days for everything…"

"That's not the half of it. They were both due back at their jobs and the girls—their names are Hazel and Charlotte—at school the day after they left Louisiana. But instead of heading north, toward home, they ended up driving ten hours *west*, into a wild section of the Texas Hill Country. And as far as any of their friends and family knew, they'd only been planning a quick New Orleans getaway."

"I take it they didn't mention this change of plans to anyone?"

He shook his head. "And no one saw or heard from them again after they left that motel."

"That phone theft…" Kate suggested, her dark eyes taking on a laser-like intensity he hadn't realized until this very moment how much he'd missed. "It wasn't just a random crime of opportunity, was it?"

"Makes you wonder, doesn't it?" he said, skeptical as well. "But getting back to our approach, are there any other routes Ada Kessler and her daughters could've taken to make their way out of the canyon on their own?"

"Realistically, it's unlikely, unless they were expert climbers."

"We're talking two traumatized little girls, eight and ten, with a newly widowed, reportedly none-too-athletic mom who works as the principal's secretary at the local high school."

Kate sighed. "The poor things. I can't imagine. And they could be hurt, too."

"If you'd seen the condition of the wreckage—" His stomach turned as he thought about the photos the rescuers had brought up to road level last night. "It's a miracle any of them could walk away."

"At least this allows us to focus only on this valley instead of having to spread out our people any farther," she said. "I only pray we're in time and we can narrow down their location quickly."

"I can't for the life of me imagine they could've gotten all that far, not as rough as this terrain is. And considering how bad the car looked, it stands to reason that one or all of them might be hurt as well, and fighting the overnight cold and probably hunger, too, by this time."

She nodded in agreement. "I don't think they've made it too far, either. That's why I've focused my teams close to the crash site. Team One is starting in this area." She pointed it out for him on the map. "Meanwhile, Team Two's concentrating on this sector, to the east. I have a dog and handler en route, too."

"How do you plan on getting them down into the canyon?"

"Same route we'll be riding, only Anderson will be driving an ATV with Gonzo." A smile sparked in her eyes as she shook her head. "I swear, nothing fazes that dog."

When Banner swished his tail, Hayden gave his neck a pat. "So what about us? Where will we be searching?"

"We'll check out this ravine here to the south, the one that runs along the canyon floor up against this steep bluff."

"Why there in particular?" he asked, interested in her thought process.

"The approach looks fairly accessible, for one thing," she said, "and if I had to guess from the geography, I'd say we'll find a creek running through there, though I don't see it on the sat map."

"Especially with the recent overnight rains," he agreed, troubled by the thought of the little family shivering their way through the last night or two, which had been wet. If they were even still alive to feel them. "And you're thinking they might try to follow it, right?"

She nodded. "Most victims stick close by water sources, and a lot of people believe that following a creek or river downstream is a good way to find their way back to civilization."

"Too bad that won't pan out for 'em here."

"No, and more likely than not, this'll end up being one of those waterways that runs above ground for a while before diving back underneath the limestone. But I have a hunch Ada still might've followed it as far as she could along the edge of what I'm calling Heartbreak Ridge, you know, just for mental reference."

"Heartbreak Ridge, huh?" he said, looking at the hill directly ahead of them, where tattered wisps of fog clung eerily to rocky outcrops that reminded him of tombstones. "Let's hope it doesn't turn out that heartbreak's all we'll find here."

Apparently catching his somber tone, she gave him an odd look as she tucked the handheld back inside her pocket. "Don't tell me you're getting superstitious, Hayden."

"Not *superstitious*, exactly," he said, frowning. "It's just—if you'd been up there last night, on the highway after we winched up the father's body in the basket... Poor man—he was a hell of a mess from the wreck... but he still had these photos in his wallet, pictures of his family."

He closed his eyes for a moment but couldn't force the images out of his mind. "Nice-looking blonde wife," he continued, "big, friendly smile. A couple of adorable blue-eyed girls, the younger one with freckles, kind of like you used to have back when you were that age..."

Silence fell between them, an awareness of the passing years and all the losses they'd tallied within them dawning painfully.

"All right, then," Kate told him quietly. "*Safe Haven* Ridge, we'll call it. Safe Haven and not Heartbreak. That sound better to you, Hayden?"

An instant later, the first, sweet notes of morning birdsong floated across the valley, and the two searchers' gazes solidly connected. Connected on a level that reached deep inside his chest and plucked a string some eighteen years gone still.

Kate nudged Jasper's ribs to ride ahead, knowing that every minute they delayed subtracted one more from their window of daylight search time. And if she had anything to say about it, Ada and young Hazel and Charlotte Kessler wouldn't spend another night, even another hour, cold, hungry and terrified as they struggled to survive a hostile wilderness.

Cases like this one, where a very real chance that her team was searching for living survivors rather than coyote-gnawed dead bodies, reignited the fire in her belly she'd first felt when she'd accepted this position, which often required her to work long hours in tough conditions, train and manage sometimes unmanageable volunteers and send out countless pleas to wealthy patrons and corporate sponsors for donations needed to stay afloat another season.

But Hayden's unexpected passion for this case truly stunned her, from last night's personal request, via phone rather than the usual web portal form, to marshal her resources and get them assembled at this location, a two-hour drive from her current home outside of San Antonio, to his highly unusual request that she provide an extra mount so he might join her team on the search. "Because I mean to personally be there when they're found," he had explained, the commitment in his voice as unmistakable as it was out of character for a man who normally spent his time directing the activities of the employees of the same small rural department where she had once worked.

Last night, she'd eventually convinced herself he was only angling to swoop in and grab the glory if a successful rescue happened. Considering how she'd burned her bridges—or rather blown them sky-high—following the election, she could easily imagine him downplaying her team's role to the local press, conveniently neglecting to mention her name. But thanks to his well-developed instinct for self-promotion, she had zero doubt he'd somehow end up on the front page of area papers, his smile handsome as ever as he posed with the grateful survivors or shook hands with whatever state official showed up to offer congratulations. Vintage Hayden, she'd thought—

Until just minutes ago, when she'd seen his stricken expression as he'd spoken of those photos from the dead man's wallet. It was a look that had reminded her all too sharply of the boy she'd imagined gone forever, the sweetly sentimental first love she'd once pictured the other half of her soul.

But the accident had stripped away that foolish notion, had shattered her certainty along with her body. By the time, years afterward, she'd found herself working with him, the grown version of Hayden had become an utter stranger to her. A stranger who'd attended to his duties competently enough, always saying the appropriate things to the right people and going out of his way to be seen making the right gestures. He'd even pulled it off on those days he'd shown up to work hungover following one of his biweekly out-of-town benders, where he was rumored to blow off steam in a big way before hooking up with the badge bunny of his choice for the night.

Yet she told herself—or tried to—that it wasn't those activities that disgusted her, not half as much as the way he remained so coolly unaffected by those calls that she struggled with, from the fatal car wrecks to brutal domestic violence situations so reminiscent of her own earliest memories, before she'd been taken from her birth mother and put into the foster system prior to her eventual adoption.

When Kate had broken down one night over one particularly triggering case involving a couple of young toddlers, she'd never forgot how old Sheriff Turner had pointed out her "weakness" as one more reason he'd avoided hiring female deputies before her. But to her way of thinking, it was Hayden who'd gone wrong somehow, retreating in manhood to a place where nothing had the power to truly touch him any longer. Or maybe she'd been wrong before, a deluded teenager fooled into imagining that he had ever really cared for her—or had the emotional capacity to truly feel for anyone at all.

So what's so different about this case—or is it Hayden himself who's changing once again? And why did she find the idea that he might be so very disconcerting?

As they crested the hill, Kate had no issues getting the nimble Jasper up over the ridge and guiding him down onto the narrow shelf where the trickier rock ledge began. Once across, she held up momentarily, waiting for Hayden to negotiate the same descent, handling the larger, more muscular quarter horse with a care and confidence she couldn't help admiring. And damn him, he still looked better than he had any right to doing it, though he could clearly use a shave and a full night's sleep rather than the coffee and adrenaline she knew he must be getting by with. She was doing the same after spending most of the night on the phone making arrangements before setting off from San Antonio at 3:00 a.m.

Once they had safely crossed the ledge, she clicked to Jasper, leading them both into an easy lope over that gentle downslope that would take them into the search area. While the rhythmic drumming of their mounts' hoofbeats allowed them little opportunity for conversation, it gave her the chance to regain her equilibrium. And to tally the many reasons to be glad she no longer had to deal with him on a daily basis.

She was up to number fourteen when he called her name and signaled her to hold up for a minute.

By the time she reined in Jasper, Hayden was pulling out his phone, which must have satellite service, just as hers did, to allow him to maintain contact in remote locations. He spoke for a few minutes before thanking the person on the other end, his expression troubled.

"Everything all right?" she asked, circling back closer as he shoved the phone into his pocket.

Grimacing, he shook his head. "Far from it, I'm afraid. That was the medical examiner. Full autopsy's not finished, but he's just done X-rays on the body recovered from the accident scene last night, and he thought I ought to know—a bullet was clearly visible."

"Kessler was *shot*?" She felt breathless with this news, which turned what they'd been imagining a tragic accident on its ear. "Before he plowed through that guardrail?"

"We can't know for certain about what happened when," Hayden pointed out, "but it seems unlikely it would have been *after*. The entry wound was to the back of his head, which I don't believe would have done a damned thing for his driving."

Kate visualized the family, talking, maybe laughing or simply quietly looking out the windows of the car together when the bullet had come crashing through a window or punched through the car's sheet metal. Her stomach flipped as her mind conjured the burst of blood, the shrieks of terror—and that heartrending moment the car had plowed through the guardrail and plunged down through the trees.

Mentally pulling back from the imagined scene, she felt slightly sick to realize what she and Hayden discussed had been a murder. Or possibly the intentional execution of an entire family.

She couldn't understand how it could've been missed earlier. "Last night, how is it that you didn't notice a gunshot wound on the body—or any bullet hole in the vehicle itself?"

He scowled at her. "I know you live to second-guess me, but you have to understand. By the time we finally got a rescue team to that wreck, it was dusk already. And the firefighters who rappelled down were focused on the victim, along with the evidence there had likely been a woman and children in the car."

"I *don't* live to second-guess you," she argued, more annoyed than ever, "and do I take that to mean you haven't seen the car yourself at all?"

"Not personally, not yet," he admitted, "just a few drone shots initially followed by phone photos. And later, when the body was finally brought up, there was a lot of blood around the head and neck area, gore and matting of the hair and so on, like we've seen in all too many accidents along these twisting roads."

She thought of the multiple such scenes she'd worked during her tenure in the department, nearly all of them resulting from someone's inattentive driving, a blown tire or the sudden appearance of a fallen rock, an animal or another vehicle along these treacherous, winding roads.

"You're right. There was no reason for you to have suspected Kessler might've been shot," she said, cutting him some slack, as, by unspoken consent, they started their mounts downhill once again. "But the real question is, who killed him? Could it have been an accidental shooting, from someone being careless doing target practice—or maybe hunting on private property too close to the roadway?"

Though regular hunting season was long past, in this state, certain non-native species—from invasive nuisance animals like feral hogs to exotic deer—could and often were legally taken on private land year-round.

"No way on the target practice, and I'd have to say the

same thing about the hunting, too. Terrain's just too extreme, the grade too steep, along that stretch of road—"

"Unless the car traveled for some distance, maybe with Ada Kessler trying to control it, before they crashed through the railing."

He cursed softly and then sighed. "Sorry, I just— You hate to think about it. Those kids in that vehicle when it all went down."

Once again, she was struck, seeing this new, more vulnerable side of a man she'd written off as glib and self-serving. Was it possible he'd only been hiding his true nature before from her, afraid she might use it against him as they'd jockeyed for position?

Pushing aside the odd thought, she turned her mind back to the shooting. "Do you think it could've been a road-rage situation?"

"I can't discount the idea, though you know we don't see a lot of that way out here, so far from any real traffic. And I can't imagine that his wife would've been the one to pull the trigger, either. Even if she'd been upset enough to risk all their lives by shooting her own husband, the angle of the shot the ME described was all wrong."

"It's got me wondering, was someone intentionally targeting him—or trying to get rid of the whole family for some reason?"

"Targeting him, why?" Hayden wondered aloud. "I mean, the guy's not exactly James Bond. According to the Memphis investigator I've been speaking with, he's a CPA at an accounting firm, spends most of his days auditing corporations and most recently, nonprofits."

"My eyes cross just thinking about how dull that would be, and I *work* for a nonprofit," Kate said. "Though I suppose there's always the chance he stumbled upon some financial malfeasance."

"Killing a man's an awfully extreme way to cover up something like that, let alone wiping out his entire family."

"People kill for dumber reasons... Or who knows? Maybe Kessler was messing around where he shouldn't, say with his boss's or a best friend's or a neighbor's wife or girlfriend? Because, by and large, murder almost always comes down to sex or money."

"When there's a reason to be had, you're right," he said. "And the fact that the Kesslers' cell phones were stolen makes me believe this wasn't random."

"So you really think the two crimes were connected?"

"I don't like the coincidence," he said. "But if this *was* the same person, that'd mean somebody'd tracked them ten hours west of their last known location. How?"

She shrugged. "Maybe the car'll turn out to have a GPS locator on it—one the family didn't know about."

"I'll have to check it out. Because it may be a while before we get it hauled up—and I'll want to see that vehicle before then. But they wouldn't necessarily have been followed electronically. Could've tailed them the old-fashioned way."

"What *you* need is to find Ada Kessler," she said, "if you ever want more answers than questions."

Hayden nodded, saying, "Amen to that. I definitely do need to find her and her kids fast—before someone else decides it's worth any risk to track down the only three witnesses to Nicolas Kessler's murder, to make sure they're also dead."

Chapter 2

By the time they reached the ravine south of the crash site, the sky had brightened to a deep azure and the early-March temperatures had warmed enough that their breath no longer fogged the air. Squinting against the glare, Hayden was nearly to the point of digging out his sunglasses when he followed Kate back beneath the trees into the heavily shaded—and cooler—search area she'd pointed out earlier on the map: the entrance to the long ravine.

"Ho, Jasper," she said, prompting him to rein in his horse as well.

As the hoofbeats clattered to a stop, Hayden heard water trickling beyond the undergrowth closer to the rocky bluff that she'd initially called Heartbreak Ridge. Despite the way she'd tried to rename it, he couldn't shake the initial feeling of dread that had settled over him when she'd first spoken the name, the painful premonition that some horror awaited them ahead.

But he knew not to operate on fear, and even if it turned out the family was beyond the reach of help, their loved ones still deserved a prompt, respectful recovery effort, along with answers that would help them begin to deal with their grief. So he locked down his own emotions and gestured toward the splashing noise, telling Kate, "Sounds like you guessed right about there being water down here."

Nodding, she turned toward him, her expression thoughtful. "If we can hear it from this spot, the Kesslers might have, too. And by the time they hiked this far, they were probably pretty thirsty, so the banks up ahead might be a good place to check for signs of them."

He grimaced. "Would've been better, I'm thinking, without last night's rain to wash away their trail."

"The going hasn't been too muddy so far, so I can't think it's rained that hard. Maybe not all their tracks will've washed away. Before we head that way, though, I'd like to check in with my team leaders."

"You do that," he agreed. "But if you don't mind, I'm going to tie up Banner and hike ahead on foot to have a closer look at that creek."

"His lead rope's in the saddle pack to clip on to his halter."

"Thanks," he said, knowing how unwise it was to tie a horse by its reins.

"And be careful over there," she warned. "I don't want to waste time having to fish you out of some creek."

"I'm truly touched by your concern for my welfare," he grumbled before urging Banner into an area of deeper shadow and dismounting where the undergrowth grew thicker and more tangled.

After securing the gelding to a tree, he patted the gray's shoulder. "You've earned the breather, big boy."

Leaving the horse to nibble at a nearby bush, Hayden stepped up onto a rock before pushing his way through tightly spaced, slender trunks, cacti and vines—some of them thorny enough to catch at skin and jacket alike. Once he'd extricated himself, he paused, squinting at a trio of pale strands blowing in the light breeze at about the level of his chin. His pulse quickened as he realized they weren't cobwebs as he'd initially thought but instead wavy human hairs—blond like Ada Kessler in her photo.

Though he couldn't know for certain that these particular strands belonged to the missing woman—or even whether they were definitely human—he felt a surge of hope to have discovered a veritable needle in the haystack of this wild canyon. After replacing his warm gloves with a thin Tyvek pair, he carefully bagged and labeled the evidence before zipping it into an inner pocket of his jacket.

Unable to find more hair or any clothing fibers among the other nearby thorns, he peeled off the blue gloves before climbing a small embankment overlooking a rocky cliff face, out of which a geyser of clean, clear water spurted.

Beneath the small waterfall, an inviting-looking pool had formed, the head of a creek that chattered over a series of humped rocks like the gray-brown backs of turtles. Beyond those rocks, the water narrowed to a tree-lined channel that trickled along the ravine's lowest point before he lost sight of it in the shadow of the eroded base of a ridge that towered some thirty to forty feet above.

Climbing down to a patch of exposed bedrock, Hayden headed toward the creek bank while avoiding the softer sand, not wanting to add his footprints to any evidence he might find. He quickly came across animal tracks: older, deeper prints that looked as if they belonged to deer, though these were mostly melted into muddiness by the flow of the night's rain toward the watercourse. Some of the fresher tracks were clearer, but these had come from smaller creatures: birds, squirrels and maybe raccoons.

No signs of humans at all.

Huffing in frustration, he continued walking, keeping his feet on the rock shelf as he scanned for any sign. Then something caught his eye, a splash of sparkling pink—a reflection off a small, artificially cut crystal caught among the undergrowth about ten yards ahead and six feet back from the water.

Hurrying to investigate, he moved too quickly, his boot's sole hitting an unexpectedly slick patch of algae-coated bedrock and skating out from underneath him. With a shout of surprise, he came crashing down, the back of his head bouncing hard, the point of his left elbow whacking rock and his right foot splashing down and instantly filling with cold water.

"Hayden!" he heard Kate shout as she came running up behind him.

"Careful there. Rock's slippery," he said dryly, reaching up to cradle the back of his skull with his hand—and wincing in pain.

"I *saw*," she said, her brown eyes wide as she hurried to offer her hand. "Are you all right?"

Upset to have been caught in such an undignified position, he pulled his foot out of the water and pushed himself into a sitting position before retrieving his now-crushed hat. "Sure you don't want to snap a picture first? You know, something to add to your arsenal in case I need putting in my place later? *Again.*"

They both knew it wouldn't be the first time she'd gone out of her way to embarrass him.

Lowering her hand, she glared at him. "I see your *ego's* still intact, at least. But I was more concerned about the rest of you. That looked like it really hurt—and that's blood on your fingers, from your head, isn't it? Let me take a peek."

"I'm sure it's just a few drops," he groused. "You know as well as I do, scalp wounds bleed like anything if—"

She peered at his face, her eyes concerned. "There's blood around your mouth, too."

He shook his head, tasting coppery salt. "I bit the inside of my cheek when I went down—that's all."

He wiped away a reddish smear.

"Let me check the back of your head," she insisted, stepping nearer.

He went still as she bent over him, cupping his shoulder with a hand before gingerly moving her fingers through his thick, dark hair. Her touch had him catching his breath, all too aware of how many years it had been—*eighteen now*—since they'd been in such intimate contact. More than half a lifetime.

He hissed, jerking back as she found and pressed the sore spot.

"You'll have quite a bump, I'm sure, but the cut's not much," she said, pausing to study his eyes for a few moments. "I'm more worried about that hard crack to your skull, though. If you'd been wearing a helmet instead of that cowboy hat like a sensible person…"

She rapped her own helmet with a knuckle, her look annoyingly judgmental.

Rubbing his elbow, he said, "I would've just taken it off the second I dismounted anyway. You know that."

"I know *you*, yes. Which is why I'm worried you're hurt worse than you're letting on."

"Just give me a second, will you?" he asked, but regret—and something less familiar, *guilt*—had him avoiding her gaze. "Sorry I snapped at you for asking if I'm okay. I guess old habits die hard."

"For both of us, I suppose," she admitted. "Here. Let me help you to that log. Your pupils look the same size—isn't that one of the things they taught us to look for in that first responders' first aid training they made us take? But you still look pretty rattled."

"I can do it," he said, scooting over to the fallen tree she'd pointed out. Once seated there, he blinked repeatedly, trying to clear his vision.

Giving him a considering look, she asked, "How many fingers am I holding up?"

"More than just the one, which from you, I'm counting as a victory." He attempted to soften the statement with a smile.

"We're not playing around here, Hayden," she scolded, putting one hand on her hip. "What day of the week is it and what are we doing out here?"

Understanding she was checking to make sure he was alert and oriented, he got serious and carefully answered all her questions before pulling off his wet boot. He grumbled a few choice words as cold water poured out of it.

Giving him a sympathetic look, she suggested, "Maybe you ought to call it a day. If you feel up to riding, I'll have one of my people escort you back to the rendezvous point, but I'd suggest you take it slow and easy and call one of your deputies out to drive you back. If you're not steady enough to ride, though…"

"Don't be ridiculous. I'm not about to let you chase me off over a simple slip and fall and a soggy sock," he argued, telling himself he'd had plenty of worse headaches when he'd sworn off drinking after his election. And surely, his vision's fuzziness, along with Kate's tendency to blur and waver, would correct itself if he only gave himself a few more minutes. "We've barely started.

I answered all your questions right, too. Don't try to tell me I didn't to get rid of me."

She shook her head. "Let's not try to make this into some kind of personal thing, Hayden. I *watched* your skull bounce off that rock. You could easily have a concussion."

"If I thought I had a head injury worthy of the name, I'd listen to you, Kate. I promise. But I'm not wasting everyone's time over nothing, not when I'm almost positive the Kesslers came through here."

Her brow furrowed. "What makes you think that?"

He told her about the blond strands he'd found, caught among the thorns at about the correct height to have come from Ada Kessler's head. "I bagged those and secured them, but just before I fell, I thought I'd spotted something else."

"Where was that?"

"Right over there." He pointed toward the underbrush, scanning the low branches until he saw the same spot of color that had caught his eye before. "There it is again. Just let me—"

But when he started to get up, Kate speared him with a stern look, pointing at the log. "Don't you move from there, mister. Let me. But hand me another one of those bags if you would first. And a pair of gloves."

He produced both and passed them to her, trusting her to handle evidence appropriately. "You see that sparkly thing down there, in the weeds and sand? Careful of that slick muck, though. We don't need you falling, too."

Stepping gingerly around the spot where he had slipped, she squatted to peer at the vibrantly colored item. As she pulled on the blue gloves, she said, "I think you may be right about the Kesslers coming through here."

Rising, she walked over and showed him the item she'd retrieved: a child-sized bracelet with pink-and-purple beads and a silver, unicorn-shaped charm dangling from its center. Carefully brushing away some of the sandy mud that clung to it, she said, "It must've washed up under those branches in the rain. I'm amazed you even spotted it."

"I wouldn't have, if the light hadn't been hitting that crystal inset on the unicorn's body at exactly the right angle." He jammed his wet foot back inside his boot. It might be cold and uncomfortable, but it had the benefit of taking his mind off his aching head.

"And you spotted those hairs, too, in the thorns. You have a sharp eye for this kind of work."

Rising to his feet, he gave her a bemused look, grateful to be seeing only one of her at the moment. "Is that an actual *compliment*, coming from you? Or should I still be waiting for the punch line?"

She snorted. "It's a little easier these days when I don't have to sit around listening to Sheriff Turner brag you up every time you arrested some belligerent drunk or scabby meth head while he stuck me with a bunch of drudge work."

"I'll admit, the old man had a hard time getting used to the idea of a woman deputy at all. And I know it must've been frustrating, him treating you like a glorified file clerk and errand runner, what with that fancy degree of yours—"

"As I'm sure you pointed out many times while sucking up—"

"I *did* stick up for you, Kate," he said, knowing she would have been fired for her attitude on at least two occasions if he hadn't. But damned if he was going to tell her. "Let's not waste any more time on that old nonsense right now. Not while those poor little girls and their mother are out there waiting for our help."

"Then you're really all right to go on?" she asked,

handing the bagged bracelet to him. "I don't want you just saying so out of stubborn male pride."

He attempted to straighten his hat but sighed, seeing that the brim had split on impact and the crown was crushed beyond redemption. "My stubborn male pride's more dented than this Stetson at the moment—"

"May they both rest in peace…" she put in.

"But I'm not about to give up," he said, holding up the plastic evidence bag between two fingers, "not until we reunite the little one who belongs with this trinket with her treasure. So let's keep checking along here until that bend up ahead before we head back to grab our mounts. Deal?"

"And some dry socks for you, too," she offered, nodding. "I always pack along a few fresh extra pairs in different sizes for my team, because nothing's more miserable than wet feet on the trail."

"Thanks," he said. "That's kind of you, considering." He hadn't exactly pulled any punches during the campaign against her, either.

She slanted a narrow look in his direction. "Maybe I just don't want you slowing me down. Or *maybe*, I've had the opportunity to reflect over the past few years… and realize that the voters actually did me a favor, choosing you for sheriff."

"Oh?" he asked carefully as they walked, thinking he might need a pair of asbestos gloves to handle her response.

But to her surprise, she chuckled. "Heck, Hayden. I may be good with the law enforcement stuff, but we both know I'll never fit in with the area's old ranching families that hold so much sway in the county's politics. They'd always see me as that pathetic stray foster kid the Mc-Claffertys took pity on and dragged home."

"You've never been pathetic, and anyway, I'm not so sure it was ever that, so much," he said, thinking of her many suggestions to modernize department practices. Not gradually, with care and consideration of anybody's feelings about long-held traditions, but so bluntly and abruptly she'd left many in the rural community offended and more dug in than ever against even necessary changes.

"No? Well, I guess you never had to listen to the snide remarks during the election about my *opponent* coming from good ranch stock or heard people speculating about whether I might still have ties to the community's criminal element." Her brown eyes blazed with fury, and he knew she was thinking of the lowlifes who had once abandoned her, underweight and covered with bruises, in a filthy mobile home. There were scars, too, though she mostly kept them hidden: the small, circular scars he knew had come from cigarette burns.

She'd never spoken of the details of her abuse, and he had never asked for fear that if she ever told him exactly what she'd gone through, he wouldn't be able to prevent himself from hunting down and beating senseless whoever it was who'd done such things to the helpless child she'd once been. Even now, when he could no longer count her among his friends, much less anything closer, the idea that anyone would hold her childhood abuse against her made him want to punch somebody.

"I'm sorry if a few ignorant rednecks acted that way." His foot accidentally kicked a stone into the water at his right, where it plunked down with an angry splash. "I swear, Kate, I'd *never* allow talk like that to go unanswered—not if I heard of it."

"I know you wouldn't," she said, pushing aside a branch that was in her way. "From the time I came to live with the McClaffertys, you and your family never treated me like I was any different than anybody else."

"Mostly because my brothers and I figured out that you were just plain *better* than anybody else. Helluva lot more exciting than any of the other neighborhood girls, for sure, since you were always up for climbing trees and riding bareback, and jumping off the rope swing into the river—even in the *winter*, if anyone was fool enough to dare you. You were absolutely *fearless*."

"Not really," she admitted, "just desperate not to let anybody see how much I cared about the things those snooty girls at school whispered behind my back or why they'd never invite me to sit with them at lunch, to say nothing of joining their stupid little gossip parties. But the longer I pretended, the more fun you guys made things."

Always more fun with you, he barely stopped himself from saying, since in the end, she'd brought more misery than he had ever imagined possible… And if that weren't bad enough, she couldn't just move along and let him get on with his life the way that anybody else's ex would. No, she'd had to follow him, not only into the same profession but the same damned *department*, as if her solitary goal in life had been to find the burning ember she'd left him for a heart and crush it to ashes under her heel. By outshining him at every turn, proving to everyone that she was smarter, stronger, better.

Only it hadn't gone quite the way she'd hoped.

"Well, I'm glad you've found a job that's so well-suited to your talents." He turned his head toward her too quickly, bringing a brief eddy of nausea. Swallowing past it, he asked, "But you don't miss it? Law enforcement?"

"Sometimes," she admitted, "but I find my work so satisfying, helping families find peace by bringing home their loved ones," she said. "And doing it on horseback—or muleback, as the case may be—only makes it sweeter."

"Glad to hear you're happy," he said gruffly, but wondered if this new contentment of hers might mean she'd also found fulfillment of a more personal nature.

When she'd removed the nitrile gloves, he hadn't noticed a ring. But considering the risk of losing jewelry out here, or having it catch or transfer contaminants that might taint any DNA evidence, it wouldn't be surprising if she'd simply chosen not to wear one. Not that it was any of his business whether she'd married, lived with someone or even gone and had a kid since he'd last seen her, but for some reason he found it damned annoying to be left out of the loop.

Or maybe it was only the throbbing in his head making him feel so irritable.

"I am," she insisted. "But what about you, Hayden? Are you— Is being sheriff everything you wanted?"

"I guess it'd better be," he said, "for another four years, at least, since I was just reelected this past November."

"But are you…happy?" she asked in a way that made his skin prickle with annoyance.

Who was she, Kate McClafferty, the architect of his discontent, to ask him such a question, after everything she'd done to ensure that he could never be?

"No," he said, more sharply than he meant to. "Right this minute, as a matter of fact, I'm not, because we're wasting time with a bunch of foolish talk when I have an aching head, a sopping boot and a family out there somewhere that may be dead already."

Too angry to bear being so close, he walked ahead of her—or tried to.

She grabbed his upper arm. Hard. "*Hayden*, don't take another step."

Unable to disobey, he turned to stare a challenge. And saw the worry in her brown eyes.

"First of all, are you okay?" she asked him. "Because your cowboy charm has slipped a few dozen notches, and I'm still a little worried that I blew it, not getting you a medical assessment right after you took that fall."

"I'm fine," he said, his jaw clenched.

"Glad to hear you think so," she said, looking as if she didn't buy it for a second. "Then look down, right where you were about to stomp off."

He glanced down and then did a double take as he spotted the issue. "Wait a minute. Is that from a—" Stepping back so he wouldn't accidentally tread on it, he squatted down to study a perfectly formed paw print in the damp sand.

Stepping beside him, she nodded. "It sure is. I've heard rumors of mountain lions in this area, but the size of this one's—"

"Damn." Judging from the track, he guessed they were looking at a big male, which could easily be two hundred pounds or more of solid muscle—every bit of it adapted for stalking and bringing down large prey.

Kate's brown eyes bored into his, worry drawing her mouth tight. "Let's just hope it's been feeding well enough on all the wildlife this valley has to offer and hasn't decided to go after helpless human prey instead."

But when they heard the buzzing thrum of what sounded like a pair of engines in the canyon—coming not from the point where Kate's team had been assembling but from somewhere farther down this ravine—Hayden forgot all about the cougar. Instead, his mind flew to the more dangerous predator who had already murdered one member of the Kessler family and might now be back hunting more.

Chapter 3

"Those are ATVs, right in this ravine—and there's no way that's my dog handler." Kate was certain Anderson would've informed her that he and Gonzo were on scene, and he wouldn't be coming from that direction, either. "Whoever it is, they must've found another route into this valley that I didn't spot on my map."

Hayden shook his head. "It's definitely none of my people, either, which means it's most likely somebody we need to head off if we want to find the Kesslers before they do."

Already turning from her, he started back toward where their mounts were tied.

Kate still had concerns about his injury. Despite their longtime rivalry and his macho aversion to showing weakness, she knew him well enough to sense when something was off with him. His shortness of temper, the way he'd been so slow to get moving after his fall, indicated he was hurting worse than he wanted to let on.

Now, despite his obvious urgency, she saw him stagger and grab on to a low tree branch to steady himself, his face pale and dotted with perspiration despite the coolness of the morning.

"Hayden, you need to call for backup," she urged, grabbing at his arm. "It's obvious you're in no condition to—"

"Don't you hear? They're getting closer," he asked, shaking his head—before grimacing with the movement. "And you know as well as I do, any backup I call's a good hour away, at least. The Kesslers, if they're still alive, might not have an hour."

"Then let me," she said, but he was already jogging toward their mounts. To her relief, his gait smoothed out, and he made it back to where she'd secured Jasper next to Banner without falling. As she untied her mule, he unzipped his jacket, flipping the tail of it behind his sidearm in its holster.

"Are you sure you're okay to use that?" she asked, for the first time missing the weapon she'd once carried since deciding it was more of an encumbrance than an asset in her present role.

"If it's necessary," he said, undoing Banner's lead rope, "I'll take care of business."

"Maybe I should take that for you, Hayden. Since you're—"

Tossing aside his ruined hat, he gave her a look of disbelief. "Have you lost your ever-loving mind? I'm not handing you my gun. It might be your job to find these people, but I'm sworn to protect them. And you, for that matter."

"I get that, but I don't believe you're currently fit to make a life-or-death call or even to be riding."

Turning away from her, he grabbed a handful of Banner's mane along with the saddle horn and shoved his boot into the stirrup before swinging aboard the gray. If it were anyone else, she might have missed the way he slightly overbalanced and then hesitated, recovering for a beat or two, giving her time to mount her mule to face him.

"You're clearly dizzy. I can see it," she challenged. "So please, Hayden, you need to—"

The engines' noise abruptly dropped off, but they could still barely make out the low rumble of the motors idling. With the ravine's rocky face amplifying the sound, she knew it was tricky to judge distance. Though the vehicles couldn't be far, they might be just literally around the next bend in the creek or more than half a mile downstream.

Before Kate could regain her train of thought, shouts, followed by an anguished human cry—definitely a woman's—carried from the same direction. The terror in it had Kate's breath catching, her nerve endings standing at attention.

"Call for assistance, *now!*" Hayden ordered before kicking Banner's side and leaning forward.

As the gray galloped away, Kate was torn between her need to follow, to help if need be, and the directive he had given. Her law enforcement training kicking in, she forced herself to hold back Jasper to keep him from instinctively running after Banner while she put in the call, reaching a county dispatcher whose voice she immediately recognized as that of longtime department veteran Marta Clyburn.

Once Kate had briefly communicated Hayden's request and their location, she told Marta, "You'd better send EMS as well. I'm thinking we'll need at least two ambulances at the rendezvous point. And get people standing by—a medevac chopper if you can, too—because I'm likely to be calling for more support, depending on how this shakes out."

"You be careful out there," warned the older woman, obviously deeply shaken, "and please, Kate, I know you two didn't part on the best of terms, but you take care of our Hayden, too."

"I promise you, I'm on my way to see to that now," Kate said—flinching as the echoing cracks of the first gunshots reached her ears.

Three minutes earlier...

"Mommy, wake up. *People!*" Ada Kessler heard Lottie saying as her younger daughter jostled her where they'd been sleeping, huddled together on a grassy slope not far from the winding creek they'd spent the previous day and a half attempting to follow out of this beautiful but deadly Eden.

Though she'd barely slept throughout the long night, kept awake by churning anxiety, gnawing hunger and the pain of the injured ankle that had so badly slowed their progress, Ada woke, demanding, "What? What's going on?" her voice so sharp that the eight-year-old shrank back, her freckled face paling.

"I think it's motorcycles," ten-year-old Hazel insisted, her hair a nest of soft brown tangles as she pointed downstream. "They're coming toward us—I'm sure of it!"

Hearing the thrumming engines now, too, Ada jolted fully awake. Adrenaline flooded her veins, sending a welcome rush of warmth and energy through her cold-stiffened body. Yet she had no way to be certain. Was this the miracle she'd prayed for, or was death coming for them, too, bearing down on them as relentlessly as it had her husband?

Her last glimpse of the man she'd loved blasted through her mind, his blue eyes fixed and staring, his once-handsome face locked in a bloody grimace. She slammed a black door on it, walling herself off from shock and pain. She couldn't afford these indulgences now, not if she meant to succeed in the one thing she could do for Nic, the only thing that mattered: making certain the children he'd lived for made it out of this alive.

Using the stout branch she'd found to support her weight, she levered herself to her feet and looked down at the girls. Despite their knotted hair and dirt smudging their jackets and faces, they shook with excitement, blue eyes bright and alert. Seeing how strong they still looked, she decided she'd been right, foregoing her own share of the two granola bars and bag of trail mix she'd grabbed from her purse before they'd left the wrecked car and rationed out the meager supply between them. Though she'd begun to suspect that at least Hazel, the ten-year-old, knew better, Ada had fed them on a lie, too, that their father—mostly hidden from their view by airbags—had only been unconscious. The moment they found help, she'd told them, stifling a sob, they would send paramedics to get him to a hospital to see to his injuries.

Ada knew that neither their struggle nor even her best-intentioned falsehoods would mean a thing if she allowed all of them to be caught off guard now.

"I need you to hide," she told her daughters, anxiety knotting in her stomach, "over there, behind those trees. Lie down low and don't make a sound, not until I've made absolutely certain these people are friendly and I call out for you."

"No, Mom—I want to see them. I have to tell them about Daddy in the car," Lottie pleaded.

When Hazel's blue eyes found her mother's, Ada's

heart broke as she recognized the terrible knowledge in them. But she felt a surge of gratitude, knowing she had an ally in her elder daughter.

"Take her. *Now*," Ada demanded, pulling the pistol from her pocket with a shaking hand.

Whether it was the sight of it, or the unaccustomed firmness in her mother's voice, Hazel gasped. But she did as Ada asked, pulling her sister toward the tree. "Come on, Lottie," she insisted, "and keep *quiet*, or I'll give you the hardest pinch."

Blinking back tears, Ada breathed a silent prayer: *Forgive me—and protect them.* She then turned her attention toward the swelling sound of the approaching engines, her hands slick with sweat as she raised a handgun she had never fired in her life—but absolutely would, if it came down to it…

And did, only thirty seconds later.

Which still turned out to be a few moments too late.

Chapter 4

Jasper's long ears gave Kate an early warning, turning in the direction of the approaching hoofbeats before she made out their clattering over the wild pounding of her own heart. As desperate as she was to get to Hayden, she slowed the mule, aware that a mounted collision at this rate of speed could take them both out and fatally injure their mounts as well.

As Jasper slowed, she finally spotted Banner, and her heart stuttered to realize he was galloping riderless, parallel to the creek. Seeing the gray as well, Jasper called to his stablemate, his mulish bray-whinny ringing through the woods—and announcing their arrival on the scene with all the subtlety of flashing lights and sirens.

But at the moment, Kate was far less concerned for her own safety and more terrified that one of the shots she'd heard had been what had taken Hayden from the saddle. Was he lying somewhere, bleeding, or maybe even—

Stop it— If you let yourself think like that, you'll be no good to anyone.

Instead, she told herself it was more likely that Banner, who was a sure and steady trail horse but had never been exposed to gunfire, had spooked and thrown Hayden if he'd been forced to use his weapon. Or maybe Hayden had merely dismounted in a hurry, too distracted by his need to check on an injured person to worry about securing his mount. Whatever the truth, the gray angled toward Jasper, slowing when Kate called his name so that she was able to catch one of his reins and bring him under her control.

"That's a good boy, Banner. Ho," she said, eager to calm the quarter horse enough to lead him behind her own mount to a grassy slope overlooking the creek, where— since she and the animals had already made enough noise to alert anyone in earshot to their presence—she called out Hayden's name repeatedly.

Her own voice echoed back at her from the face of the rocky bluff across the water. Her throat tightened and her eyes burned when no one answered.

Urging Jasper forward, she convinced herself that Hayden must be preoccupied tending to an injured party, or maybe directing the Kesslers to stay hidden until he could be certain it was safe to come out.

But she'd only gotten a few paces farther when the bottom dropped out of her stomach as she caught sight of him lying facedown among the weeds a few yards ahead.

"No!" she cried, dismounting quickly and dropping Jasper's reins, telling him, "Whoa," to cue him and Banner to stand and wait, since both were trained to ground tie. Without checking to see if they obeyed, she rushed to Hayden, who hadn't stirred, and dropped to her knees beside him, her pounding heart in her throat.

Seeing no blood anywhere on the jeans or the olive-colored field jacket he was wearing, she tried shaking him again, pleading, "Come on, *please*, Hayden—you'd better not be messing with me!"

But even as she spoke the words, she knew he'd never do such a thing. It would be unthinkable for a man who always took his duties so seriously.

With a grunt of effort, she rolled him onto his side. Her hands shaking, she felt around his throat until she found the strong, steady bump of his pulse and saw that he was breathing. She saw, too, his gun, beside his hand where he had dropped it, but ignored it for the moment, more interested in checking him for injuries.

Aside from the still-oozing bump behind his head, she found no other obvious wounds—certainly not the bullet hole she'd been terrified of finding. Could his earlier fall on the bedrock have caused his current state—or was a tumble from the horse responsible? With fears of brain bleeds or even an undetected broken neck racing through her mind, she knew she needed to call for a medical evacuation helicopter right away.

As she reached for her phone, however, she felt the fine hairs behind her neck lift as a new sound sliced through her awareness. It was a child, softly crying—and the sound was echoing from somewhere nearby.

"Hel-hello?" she called, her body shaking. Still worried about whoever had been shooting a few minutes before, she scooped up Hayden's dropped pistol and came to her feet. "Hello there," she called again. "Are you hurt? Do you need help?"

No answer, but she heard someone's breath hitch—before the sobs intensified. Definitely a child's, Kate was now certain, jogging toward what she assumed to be a terrified, and possibly injured, little girl. "Don't be scared. I'm here to help," she said—only to cry out as a dirt-smeared, wild-haired child of about ten jumped out in front of her, her arms braced as she aimed a trembling gun straight at Kate's chest.

"D-don't come any closer!" the girl shrieked, her face mottled and her blue eyes red from weeping. "Don't think I won't pull the trigger!"

"No, please!" Kate reflexively lowered Hayden's gun—since she couldn't fathom the thought of firing on any child, particularly one of the girls she'd come to save. "I'm from search and rescue! My friend and I—" she nodded her head in Hayden's direction "—have been looking for you and your mom and sister. To get you someplace safe."

From behind the armed girl, a smaller, freckled version rose from the bushes, and Kate saw her hands were dripping red. "Help our mommy first! She won't wake up."

That was when Kate saw Ada Kessler lying a step or two behind her, her eyes closed and her chest dark with blood. Gasping at the sight, Kate nodded in answer. "Let me check to see what I can do for her. Then I'm going to take out my phone and call for a helicopter. That's the fastest way to get you all to a hospital."

First, though, she needed to make certain the girls' mother wasn't already beyond the reach of help.

His head pounding so hard he could barely stand it, Hayden attempted to push himself into a seated position, a movement that had him reflexively heaving and emptying his stomach. Crawling a few feet from the mess, he blinked, his vision swimming and unfocused. A roaring sound filled his ears, yet he made out the rippling trickle of flowing water. It served as a reminder of where he was and what he'd been doing, along with the last thing he remembered—drawing his weapon in response to the eruption of gunfire dead ahead and across the creek.

After that, he recalled nothing: whether he'd fired his pistol or taken fire personally, or how he'd ended up here on the ground. In spite of his throbbing head and some bumps and bruises from what he presumed had been a fall from his horse, he seemed to have avoided getting shot.

Sucking in a cleansing breath, he fought to clear his mind and vision. Where had Banner gone? And what had happened to the people who'd been shooting? Had they left him for dead or maybe ended up murdering each other?

An image came to mind—the filthy and rumpled but determined-looking blonde woman he'd spotted just before losing consciousness emerging from the undergrowth, aiming a pistol toward the approaching engine noises across the creek. In that single, jagged shard of memory, he'd recognized the awkward stance and wild aim that told him she was a complete novice with a weapon. Yet she'd clearly intended to defend herself against the threat she saw coming toward her and the two girls whose heads he'd barely glimpsed before they'd ducked behind some rocks.

Sitting up, he looked around for any sign of the Kesslers, but his vision swam, with objects doubling and forming ghostly afterimages whenever he moved his head too quickly, causing his stomach to pitch again. Rubbing at his eyes, he made another attempt. This time he spotted Banner, tied to Jasper's saddle, both standing about twenty yards away. Their ears were pricked forward, their attention turned toward something—or someone—on the ground, closer to the creek.

It was Kate, on her knees and leaning over a fallen body. As two sobbing young girls looked on, she appeared to be applying pressure to the blonde woman's bloody chest.

He needed to get over there to help her. But he barely made it to one knee before the world spun on its axis and he was forced to take a deep breath. He knelt there, waiting for the world to steady, and caught another movement from the left, out of the corner of his eye.

Turning to look in that direction, he spotted two white males in their thirties dressed in camouflage, approaching on foot, on the opposite bank of the creek. It came to him that he'd seen them earlier, on the backs of the same ATVs they'd fled on after appearing out of the brush.

The exchange of gunfire, Hayden remembered, had erupted so quickly—with Ada Kessler getting off only a single, wild shot before she went down—that there'd been nothing he could do but shoot at the two men to send them fleeing in order to protect Ada's daughters. But now the assassins were returning, apparently intent on finishing off the witnesses they'd left after Ada Kessler's shooting.

Desperate to stop them, Hayden reached for his weapon, knowing it was up to him to defend everyone against them. And panicking to realize that the gun he'd been holding when he'd fallen from Banner's back was gone. But where? Could he have dropped it before he'd tumbled from the horse?

With no time to waste looking, he bellowed a warning toward Kate. "Shooters're back! Get down, fast!"

Kate whipped around, assessing the threat before looking to the two wild-eyed children.

"Behind those rocks, now!" she shouted before snatching up a pistol and taking aim while the two strangers—thrown off by his and Kate's shouting—waved around their weapons, clearly trying to pinpoint their locations.

"Sheriff's department! Drop the weapons and put your

hands up!" Hayden thundered, meaning to give Kate an extra second or two—and the gunmen a chance to surrender.

Instead, two barrels swung in his direction.

As he flung himself to the ground, he heard the *crack, crack-crack* of gunfire as Kate fired on his assailants. Realizing she was shooting with *his* gun, Hayden was half outraged, half grateful that she'd clearly taken it without permission, with the needle swinging toward appreciation when one of the armed men went down, clutching at his throat.

With a roar of rage, the second man—whose thick, dark hair stood in a wavy ridge—fired toward Kate. She dived for cover behind the same rocky outcrop where she'd sent the children.

As she did, Hayden heard the whining zing of bullets ricocheting as they struck stone—followed by a cry from Kate that nearly made his heart stop. Had she been caught in the cross fire?

As he strained his ears for any sign of life from her, he caught a faint click from the direction of the man in camo. A click that told Hayden the shooter's magazine was empty.

Whether he had another ready to quickly load, Hayden had no idea, but he grabbed a couple of river rocks that were within reach and hurled them as hard as he could toward the man. He couldn't see whether he struck his mark—or anywhere close to it—but he was already feeling around for something else to throw, anything to distract the shooter from reloading. When he looked again, the man was running, abandoning his fallen comrade to disappear into the brush upstream.

"Kate!" Hayden crawled in her direction as the sound

of a retreating engine alerted him that the second shooter was fleeing aboard one of the ATVs. "Are you all right?"

"Hayden, you're awake!" she cried out, her pale face popping out from behind the outcrop, her brown eyes huge. "Are you—"

"Don't worry about me. What about you? Are you hit?"

Nodding, she said, "My hand." She raised her left just enough for him to catch a glimpse of dripping blood. "Ricochet tore—straight through it, but—I have to get back to Ada." Still looking pale but determined, she nodded toward where Hayden now made out the fallen woman, whose two girls were scrambling back beside her. "She's so much worse. If I don't keep pressure on that chest wound, she'll bleed out before the medevac helicopter gets here."

"They're en route?"

"I called earlier, asked Marta to try to line one up, but I need to call back again and— What about that man I shot?"

"Let me—let me go check on him," he told her, his vision darkening as he pushed himself to his feet.

"Hayden!" he heard Kate cry out before he sank back down into oblivion again.

Chapter 5

"So Kate finally cleaned your clock for you, did she?" Hayden's younger brother, Ryan, asked the following afternoon as he strolled into a private room at the same Kerrville hospital where Hayden, Kate and the Kesslers had all been transported. Dressed as usual in jeans and a Western shirt with the sleeves rolled to the elbows, his younger brother also wore a cap bearing the logo of the same brand of cowboy boots he wore.

Hayden knew he'd been lucky to reach Ryan on such short notice, since the tawny-haired six-footer worked as a ranch foreman when he wasn't off trying to break himself to bits competing in some rodeo or other. As a result of his most recent mishap, he was currently sporting a slightly chipped top front tooth.

To Hayden's way of thinking, it only made that taunting grin of his more annoying. But he suspected that his brother's flock of female admirers already had the kid—as he still thought of the thirty-two-year-old baby of the Hale-Walker family—half-convinced the flaw only added to his cowboy charm. As if his ego needed any more stoking.

"I told you on the phone, I slipped on a damp rock," Hayden said, in no mood for any razzing over his once more being forced to deal professionally with Hurricane Kate, as Ryan had started calling their former neighbor back when he was still a snot-nosed brat fighting to keep up with the older kids. "And before you start with the crap about how she probably pushed me and I surely had it coming, I know you're just trying to jerk my chain but *don't*. Not today."

Not after speaking to the doctor who'd stopped by to let him know that the subject of his investigation, Ada Kessler, remained in a medically induced coma until she could be sufficiently stabilized to remove the bullet from her lung: "Assuming she makes it long enough."

"She has to, for those girls' sake," Hayden had insisted, having already been informed that little Hazel and Charlotte had been picked up earlier that morning by a case manager who would place the physically unscathed but emotionally devastated sisters in an experienced foster home, at least until other family members could be located.

"We'll do everything we can for Mrs. Kessler, of course," the doctor had vowed, her dark eyes damp with compassion, "but if you're the sort of man who holds with prayer, Sheriff, it couldn't hurt to put a word in for her."

"I can do that," he'd agreed, and not only out of eagerness to interview the woman.

If Hayden's worries over the Kessler family weren't enough, he was also still grappling with the fact that Kate McClafferty and her team, who had followed the sounds of shooting to come to their aid, had been forced to save the day while he'd been out cold and utterly useless. The knowledge that Kate had been scheduled for surgery on her injured left hand this morning and he had absolutely no idea how she'd fared didn't help matters, either.

Light blue eyes sobering, Ryan gave him a once-over, appearing to fully take in how stiffly Hayden was sitting in the bedside chair in the darkened room, where he'd settled after dressing once the nurse had let him know he was due to be released within the next few hours. He hadn't even been able to leave the TV on to keep him company, since he was unable to tolerate either the sight or sound of it playing for more than a few minutes at a time.

"I've had my bell rung a time or two rodeoing." Ryan sounded sympathetic. "And I can see you're hurtin'. So what'd the doctors tell you? Grade 2 or 3 concussion?"

"Something like that," Hayden said, not wanting to get into the specifics, since there was no way in hell he had either the time or the inclination for the ridiculously drawn-out convalescent period the consulting neurologist had insisted he needed for recovery. He had a department to run and a shooter to find if he wanted to make certain that the Kessler family received the justice they deserved. "But it's not the head that's bugging me so much."

"I got here as fast as I could after you called me." Ryan sounded prickly. "Especially on the spur of the moment during calving season."

"Oh, believe me, I really appreciate your coming." Hayden made a face. "Apparently, Stacey heard about my accident and told my secretary to let everyone at work know that *she'd* be picking me up and driving me back to her place for some special TLC."

Ryan laughed at that, knowing Hayden had spent the

better part of the last six months trying to disentangle himself from the cute but clingy tax office clerk, even after he'd realized that, for all his emphasis on keeping things fun and casual between them, she had—in stunningly short order—set her sights on marriage. Despite the fact they had nothing in common whatsoever. "That woman *never* gives up, does she?"

"That's what I get for breaking my own rule about dating someone who works in the same damned building I do and lives in the same town for a change." He frowned, cursing the day he'd decided to ask out the curvy brunette based on what had felt like a promising, lighthearted flirtation. "I should've had my head examined for not sticking with situations I could just let naturally fizzle out after a month or two."

"It wasn't the geography that was working against you," Ryan told him. "It was picking a woman who had *needy* all but tattooed on her forehead. But I guess she would have had to've been wearing it across that chest of hers to get your attention."

"Trust me. I won't make the same mistake again," Hayden vowed. "But anyway, I owe you a steak dinner for saving me a whole heap of awkward. Or *more* awkward, anyway." He hated thinking of the way she'd wept when he had reminded her on the phone that the two of them were over, even though by now he recognized her tears for the emotional blackmail they were.

"Hey, what're brothers for?" Ryan asked, proof of how far their relationship had come compared to the years that all three of the Hale-Walkers had barely spoken to one another. Not that they still didn't have a long way to go to get back to the tight-knit bond they'd shared prior to the loss of the ranch that had been in their family for generations, but Hayden was grateful for the progress nonetheless. "But if it's not the head that's your issue, what is it?"

Hayden frowned. "I can't get anybody here to tell me how Kate made out with her surgery, or when she's going home or anything. It's frustrating as hell, since I can get information on the subject of my investigation, but when it comes to her, the nurses are holding firm on the privacy laws. And I guess you know Kate's mother isn't exactly my biggest fan, so I can hardly expect she'd stop by my room with a report."

"Not sure why she would, after the way you ditched her daughter after that barrel riding accident." Ryan eyed him with the same look of disapproval that always surfaced whenever the topic was broached. "I know you were pretty much a kid yourself at the time, but I've gotta tell you, man, that was a special brand of callous."

"It was also *eighteen* years ago." *As well as a total lie.* But Hayden didn't correct his brother's version of the story, the one that had gotten around afterward— probably leaked by Kate's parents in preference to a far more complicated truth that wasn't his to share. "I need to know she's okay—especially since she was hurt taking up the slack for me out there."

"You seriously can't blame yourself for what happened?"

"It's not about blame. It's about *responsibility.* And her welfare was mine, so I need to know she's all right, or that she's going to be."

"I'm sure she will be," Ryan said before attempting to lighten things up with an amiable smile. "No bullet's gonna stop the Hurricane."

"You don't know that," Hayden said, remembering the pain in Kate's eyes when she'd raised her bloody hand.

Ryan shrugged. "Maybe not yet I don't, but I'd be willing to bet that I can track down your information inside of ten minutes, and that I'll find out that she made it through her surgery with flying colors."

Hayden turned a skeptical eye on his younger brother. "So you're telling me you can somehow circumvent federal privacy laws based on, what? Because I seriously hope it's not what you imagine passes for slick talk and that busted smile."

Ryan only shoved a thick, golden brown forelock from his face and flashed that chipped-tooth grin again. Hayden would've rolled his eyes if the move wouldn't have spiked the headache he was barely keeping at bay.

Sticking out his hand, Ryan asked, "So are we on? A hundred bucks, right now."

"A *hundred*?" Hayden laughed. "You must be mistaking me for someone who hasn't figured you've been dating one of these nurses after your most recent rodeo dustup."

"Only one?" Ryan looked insulted. "You truly wound me, brother."

Though he hated encouraging his brother's cockiness, Hayden couldn't help but snort with amusement. "Or let me guess. You already ran into Kate's mom in the hallway five minutes before you walked into my room?"

"Aw, come on, man. Would I rip you off, my favorite brother?" asked Ryan, whose preferences, Hayden had noticed, shifted depending on his intended target.

"Of course, he would," Kate said as she was wheeled into his room by a fit-looking man with neatly trimmed, salt-and-pepper hair and a distinctly military bearing. With her long, wavy red hair brushed neatly behind her shoulders and fresh street clothes—a long-sleeved T-shirt over a pair of lightweight hiking pants and boots—rather than a hospital gown, she looked ready to go home as well, and better than she had any right to, considering the ordeal she'd been through. "My man, Ry-man's a born con artist. He just can't help himself. And we already chatted in the hall as I was being discharged."

"Way to cost me a C-note," Ryan griped at her before adding, "Good to see you again though, I suppose," and nodded a greeting to the man behind her before introducing him to Hayden. "This is Major Simon Corbett, Kate's assistant director from Central Texas Search and Rescue."

"Kate, Major Corbett…" Hayden rose to greet the visitors, only to regret the quick move when his vision darkened. By the time it cleared, Corbett—who was half a foot shorter than his own more heavily muscled six-three, stood stiffly but patiently before him, offering a firm handshake, which Hayden belatedly accepted.

"Good to meet you," he added, embarrassed by his slowness to respond and unshaven, undoubtedly rumpled appearance in contrast to the older man's crisp turnout.

"The *Major* part's unnecessary. I'm retired from the army," Corbett told him, "and Kate's told me a lot about you."

"Oh?" Hayden cut a concerned look in her direction.

She covered her blush by grinning and waving off the question. "Don't sweat it, Hayde. I've held back all the blackmail-worthy secrets."

"Glad to hear I haven't been payin' you off for all these years for nothing," he said, rolling with her jest before nodding toward her heavily bandaged left hand, which was wrapped all the way up to her elbow and supported by a sling. "How'd you make out? As sassy as you're sounding, I'm guessing that the news is good."

She made a face. "I've been warned the sass'll probably wear off along with the heavy-duty painkillers. I may still be a little loopy."

"There's a reason she's in that wheelchair. I promised I'd see her safely to the car," Corbett confirmed, a protective edge to the statement and the way he looked down at her. Though he must have a good ten—or maybe fifteen—years on Kate, Hayden got an inkling that his interest in her was anything but paternal.

Did Kate know how he felt? Or could they possibly be—

No, he was quick to assure himself. Kate knew better than to get involved with anyone she worked with. He remembered her saying, after a fellow deputy had repeatedly asked her out while they'd all served together, that a woman couldn't be taken seriously if she mixed business with pleasure. And being taken seriously meant more to Kate than any romance ever would.

"But the surgery was successful?" Hayden asked her. "You're going to be all right, aren't you?"

"So they're telling me," she said. "I'm told that over the coming months, I should recover most of the feeling and movement in my fingers, now that my palm's been put back together the way it should be."

His heart staggered as he once again imagined the bullet ripping through the delicate structures of a hand he still remembered holding in his own, caressing as though it were the most precious thing in all the world, so many years before.

"*If* she takes time off to rest and complete the physical therapy that's been ordered," Corbett added, sounding concerned—which made sense to Hayden, since as driven as Kate was, the odds of her taking the necessary time off were about on par with his own of following the neurologist's orders to the letter.

But she surprised him, saying, "Oh, I promise you, I'm

doing every bit of it. I'm a huge believer in PT— It's the only reason I'm walking today, for one thing."

"Damned straight," Ryan agreed, who'd been through his own share after a bull first threw and then fell on him before he'd given up trying to ride the beasts and switched to roping events years before. "Even though you cuss the therapist and the horse he rode in on at the time."

"Right." She nodded emphatically. "And I'm not about to lose the functional use of my left hand over a short-term inconvenience—even though I'll probably be tearing my hair out staying at Mom's recovering for the next month."

"Just down the road from Hayden's," Ryan couldn't resist pointing out, as if Hayden wasn't painfully aware of his proximity to her mother's ranch house.

"What made you decide to head home?" Hayden asked her.

"Partly, it was Simon," she admitted.

The older man confirmed it. "I knew for sure she'd jump straight back into work if she headed home to San Antonio. This woman doesn't know the meaning of off duty."

"But mostly," Kate said without denying it, "it was my mom's visit to the hospital last night. You know how she's been at loose ends ever since my dad passed last year."

"Again, I was so sorry to hear about that. Dr. McClafferty was a great vet and so well thought of in the community," Hayden said carefully, since Kate knew full well that the one person old Doc hadn't thought well of in return was him.

"I miss visiting with him out at Luna Roja," Ryan said, naming the ranch where he worked as foreman when he wasn't competing. "We used to have the best talks when he'd come to do a herd check."

"Thanks." Kate's warm brown eyes found Ryan's briefly before returning to linger on Hayden's. "And it meant a lot to Mom that you fixed her mailbox the way you did, without even being asked, after somebody mowed it down, and repaired that stretch of sagging fence so old Moonlight wouldn't get out."

Hayden waved away the praise. "It's no more than I'd do for any neighbor who looked like she could use help. And as I recall, your mom left some first-rate cookies on my doorstep and a pot of her good tortilla soup to say thanks, so the way I figure, I came out way ahead on the deal."

Each time she'd left the offerings, Rita McClafferty had slipped back inside her car afterward before honking her horn to get his attention instead of knocking, only to wave as she was leaving. Anything to avoid the awkwardness of an actual conversation after years of stony silence. The note she'd left with the soup, however, though appreciative, had reminded him that she was *perfectly capable* of seeing to her own place—or hiring a handyman the next time something came up.

Kate's smile was fleeting, quickly replaced by a look of worry. "Apparently, she's decided she'd like to get back into fostering. She's got this idea that she needs to *contribute* while she still has the health and stamina to do it."

"They'd certainly be fortunate to have her, with her experience," Hayden said honestly, "but isn't she a little… I know your mother's in great shape for her age. I see her out walking that big dog of hers all the time." A dog she'd probably trained to bare its teeth if he so much as waved in her direction. "Still, some of those kids can run you ragged."

"That's exactly what I tried to tell her," Kate said, "but you know my mom when she gets an idea in her head.

She accused me of calling her washed-up and telling her she should be relegated to porch sitting in her rocker."

"Sort of sounds like an ideal existence to me, to tell you the truth," said Hayden, who'd yet to make it through a day off since his election without at least three or four calls from work—which often ended up forcing him to concede defeat and head back to the office.

"With a cold six-pack and absolutely nothing on my agenda," Ryan mused, as if he could sit still for half an hour.

"It sounded good to me, too," Major Corbett put in, "but I only made it through three days of 'porch sitting' before I started to get stir-crazy—and less than three weeks before I began volunteering with search and rescue. Some folks just aren't cut out for retirement."

"Yes, but you're only forty-eight," Kate told him. "Mom's nearly seventy, with arthritis that flares up and makes her pretty miserable at times. And, as of this morning, she's fostering the Kessler girls."

"The *Kessler* girls?" Hayden had had no idea. "I hope you don't think I pulled strings to get them sent to your mom's house to make it easier for me to question them."

Kate shook her head. "Never occurred to me. If there's one thing I know about you and my mother, it's that odd jobs notwithstanding, you two normally avoid each other like the plague."

Hayden couldn't deny it.

"And besides, considering how rough you looked last time I saw you yesterday, I can't imagine you were in any shape to pull strings..." Kate made a face. "Which reminds me, I haven't even asked how you're feeling today. I see you're dressed to go home, so I'm hoping that means you're doing better?"

"I'm sitting upright without puking," Hayden said, realizing that, with the distraction of his visitors, his headache had also downshifted, from torturous to tolerable. "That definitely counts as better."

Looking concerned, she asked, "Pretty nasty concussion, though, I'm guessing?"

"Enough that I'll probably have to work from home for a few days," he said by way of answer, telling himself that if Ryan, who was younger, smaller and less muscular, could routinely exceed doctors' expectations, there was no reason to think he couldn't do the same. "But I'll be running the Kessler investigation, with a couple of my best deputies helping with the legwork until I'm ready to get back out there." He thought about the update his chief deputy, Clayton Yarborough, had given him over the phone before Ryan's arrival. "By the way, they're still working on trying to identify that John Doe you shot."

The skin tightening around her eyes, Kate flicked her good hand past her face to tuck her hair behind an ear. "Keep me posted on that, will you?"

"I will, and when you're ready, I'll need to get a statement from you, for the record," he said, softening his tone in response to what he recognized as understandable discomfort. "Of course, the DA's gotta look at the facts of the case, but listen, Kate. You shouldn't lose any sleep about this even going to a grand jury, considering the circumstances."

"From the sounds of it, she damned well ought to get a medal for putting down that menace," Ryan insisted before looking back down at Kate. "I only wish you'd knocked off the other fella as well."

She shook her head. "I'm not sure I do. In all the years I carried a gun on the job, I never had to use it. I'd shoot him again if that's what it took to protect us. Still—I've killed somebody, and I don't even know who he was or what he wanted."

"I should've been the one to do it," Hayden blurted, guilt returning to overwhelm him. "I'm so sorry I couldn't— And now you're hurt and have to live with—"

"Don't be ridiculous, Hayden. You were *unconscious*." She shook her head. "And even if you hadn't been, I could've still been caught in the cross fire."

"I told him, too, it's not his fault what happened to you or Ada Kessler," Ryan put in.

"He's absolutely right. No one's blaming you," she said.

Hayden could only grimace before his brother mercifully changed the subject. "Say, it sounds like we're all heading in the same direction. Could I maybe save your colleague here a long drive and give you a ride out to your mom's place, Kate? Unless you were planning on staying there, too, Major Corbett?"

Before Hayden could wonder if his brother was fishing for information for some reason, Corbett shook his head. "It's Simon, please, and I was just planning on dropping Kate off before heading back to San Antonio. Someone needs to see to the animals and keep the office running as long as she's out of commission."

"And I can't tell you how much I appreciate knowing you'll be there to handle things." When Kate smiled at him, Hayden felt a twinge that had nothing to do with his aching head, though he told himself that even if it were more than a friendly look between colleagues, he should only be happy for her, after all the years she'd spent alone. A woman as beautiful and vibrant as Kate deserved to have more than work in her life.

Turning to look up to Ryan, she added, "If you really don't mind, I'd love to take you up on the offer. That is, if it's okay with your big brother. I wouldn't want to contribute to Hayden's headache."

"I expect we can make the drive without arguing, just this one time," Hayden said.

"I'll hold you to that," his brother warned, "or *you* can ride home in the bed of the pickup, along with whatever loose hay and other nuts and bolts I've got rattlin' around back there."

Hayden smiled at Kate before firing back at his brother, "I dunno, man. Maybe the two of us'll form a pact just long enough to put *you* out on the side of the road and enjoy our arguing all the way back, the way nature intended."

"Better be careful, Ry-man," Kate teased as Major Corbett chuckled. "It could happen."

"I *might* worry," Ryan told them, looking skeptically from one to the other, "if one of you weren't too doped up and the other too soreheaded to manage the driving on your own."

"Thanks for saving me the extra miles." Corbett shook his hand before turning to point a finger at Kate. "And as for you, remember that your main mission in going to your mother's is to rest and heal, right?"

Kate peered up at him, her forehead furrowing. "And make sure my mother's all right to foster again, after losing Dad, yes. What else would I be doing?"

Looking down at her, he said, "If I know you, inside of twenty minutes, you'll be trying to horn in on Sheriff Walker's investigation. Or taking it over so you can track down whoever it was who shot you and Ada Kessler."

Chapter 6

Kate sat in the rear seat of Ryan's pickup as she'd insisted, mostly so no one could see the redness of her face. Or at least she imagined it was still glowing, considering how hot her cheeks were burning. Though she'd immediately denied Simon's statement, she'd seen the way Hayden had smiled in recognition, that infuriating look between two men who each assumed he knew how a woman of her temperament should best be *handled*.

She'd dealt with that nonsense all her life, men dismissing her abilities, or trying to keep her in her corner. A designated spot that wouldn't challenge their own God-given right to run the show without any inconvenient female interference. Even when she happened to be right.

When Ryan stopped at the pharmacy to pick up Hayden's prescriptions before leaving town, he turned in the driver's seat to ask her, "Sure you don't need anything from inside? A drink or something for the road, maybe?"

Taking a deep breath, she reminded herself he wasn't the problem before answering, "Some cold water would be great, thanks," since her mouth was dry from the medications that Simon had picked up for her earlier.

"I could use some, too," Hayden said, "in case I need to wash down a couple of those headache tablets on the fly. Thanks."

Once Ryan headed in, she said, "It's good to see you two talking again. And to see him here for you, the way a brother should be."

For years following the loss of their ranch to their eldest brother, Mac's, attorney's fees in the fight to regain custody of his children from their grandparents in Argentina, she knew the three Hale-Walkers had barely spoken to one another. Though none of them had been to blame, precisely, the loss of a legacy that went back generations, so close to their mother's passing, had broken down the once-close bonds—irrevocably, it had begun to look like.

Hayden swung his legs around so he was facing where she sat, behind the driver's seat. "We're working our way back, all three of us, since Mac's twins have finally come home."

"My mother told me she's seen them in town with him. It must be such a relief to have them back." Almost a miracle, more than eight years later.

"A miracle that nearly cost my brother his life." His deep blue eyes turned to capture hers. "I only wish our mom could've lived to see—to see that all the pain wasn't for nothing."

Remembering his mother, a tough, determined woman who had wholeheartedly thrown herself into the running of the family's ranch after her husband died years before her three sons came of age, Kate said, "I imagine she does know somehow, though, don't you?"

Hayden nodded. "Yeah, I do, and as far as my niece and nephew—I've never really been much of a kid person..." He hesitated a beat, an apology in his eyes before she urged him to continue with a wave of her good hand.

"But the more time I spend around Cristo and Silvia," he continued, "the more I get why Mac was willing to put everything on the line for them the way he did. They're pretty incredible."

She smiled at him.

"What?" he asked, reddening a little. "Am I gushing? Damn, I'm getting to be as bad as my brother, carrying on about how smart and amazing they are until we're about ready to dunk him in the river—or would be if it weren't such a relief to finally see him happy again."

She shook her head. "It wasn't that. It's just, out on the trail yesterday, I was thinking how affected you seemed by the case, how focused you were on the Kessler family. I get it now. Spending time with your niece and nephew must've made you think differently about there being kids involved. Or feel it more, at least."

"I expect you're right. I've been trying to make up for all the lost time, get to know them both some. And Mac's new wife as well. I don't know if you'd heard that he's remarried."

"The social worker, wasn't it?" A friend of Kate's who still lived in town had told her the story.

He nodded. "Yes, and Sara's done wonders, not only for the twins but with Mac, too. He's a different man these days. If he hadn't had an appointment with his lawyer that he couldn't miss, he would've come today to pick me up himself."

"With his *lawyer?*" Kate frowned at the thought of the legal problems that had already cost the family so much. But Hayden shook his head. "Don't worry. Whether or not he ever manages to collect a penny of the judgment he received against his in-laws in Argentina, he's put all the pain of the past behind him, now that he has a future with his family to think of. I'm so glad he's turned his life around."

When Hayden smiled, something lightened inside her. "Me, too—but I've got to admit something."

"What's that?"

"I'm still a little distracted, thinking about strangling Simon for making out like I'd try to commandeer your investigation back there." She gave a growl of frustration.

Hayden choked back laughter. "I swear, I saw your eyes *ignite* when he said that. I wonder if the major has any idea how badly he stepped in it."

"What? You think it's *funny* that I'm furious?" Forgetting herself for a moment, she unconsciously tried to flex her left hand, which surprised her with a jolt of pain that had her wincing.

"I think it's hilarious," he admitted, "especially since I'd been thinking there was something going on between the two of you."

Distracted from the discomfort, Kate laughed in surprise. "Between me and Simon? Are you serious? He's a good man and a great asset to the organization, but I'm *definitely* not his type."

"What's his type?"

She thought for a moment before making a face as she considered what little she'd surmised about his social life, judging from the insipid dates he brought to fundraisers for the center. "*Pliant*, mainly."

"That *definitely* rules you out." Hayden grinned. "But what about you, Kate? What's your type these days?"

She stared at him a moment before answering, "Two long ears, four shiny shoes and a nicely polished Western saddle. Seriously, between our missing persons cases, equine upkeep and fundraising, I really haven't had time for any—"

"Oh, come on. Surely, you can find a few hours here and there to squeeze in some kind of social life."

"What do you care?" she asked, the question coming out more bitterly than she meant. "It's not like you and I exactly parted on great terms."

He smiled, amusement glinting in his eyes. "That's quite the understatement. But maybe I've had time to think about the way that went down, to mull over my part in how things were between us. And to tell you that I'm sorry we couldn't have found a way to work together— because I believe the county lost a talented deputy the day you walked away. And I lost my chance at having an ally who could help me ease in at least some of those changes you suggested…because there were some excellent ideas in the mix there. I've done quite a bit of reading on them."

Feeling a lump forming in her throat, she eyed him with suspicion. "You aren't just saying that because the coast is clear now and you don't have to put up with my mouth any longer?"

"I'm not, which means that regardless of what your Major Corbett says—"

"He's definitely not *my* Major Corbett," she corrected.

"Regardless of what he says, I'd *welcome* whatever thoughts you might have regarding the Kessler case. Especially since you'll be living in the same household as those two little girls, and I could sure use your assistance getting information from them, considering how upset they must be."

She grimaced, thinking of the terrible things they'd witnessed, followed by the shock of being moved from the hospital into a foster home. Though she'd been younger the first time she'd been placed herself, her stomach still twisted with the memory of pulling up at a strange house and the terror of not knowing what hidden horrors might lie behind that door.

"I'm happy to help," she said, "but what you said before about yourself and children goes double for me. I'm *definitely* no kid whisperer."

Sure, a few of her friends had children, but other than showing up at the occasional baby shower or birthday party with a present, she tended to limit her socializing to adult-only meetups where people could unwind with a glass of wine or a beer while chatting if they wanted. Places where she'd never again find herself surprised by someone's auntie placing a baby-powder-scented bundle into her arms and asking her if it wasn't about time she thought of having one of her own.

As the pang hit, Hayden's somber gaze met hers, and in it, she saw deep regret—the pain of a loss now eighteen years behind them. A loss that had affected her in ways that he would never know, since she'd sworn that she'd go to her grave before she told him.

"You don't have to be into kids," he said gently. "All you have to do is care about putting away the bastard who killed the Kessler girls' father and maybe their mama, too—and shot you in the process. And finding him before he takes a notion to eliminate any remaining witnesses to his crimes."

Distracted when she spotted Ryan heading back to the truck with a couple of shopping bags in his hands, she swallowed hard before saying, "Oh, I care all right. I guess we'd both better, since we're among those potential targets, along with anybody who happens to get too close to those children—even someone just trying to be helpful like my mother."

* * *

As they made the hour-and-twenty-minute drive home, Ryan listened to music via earbuds out of consideration for Hayden's head while Kate dozed in the back seat after apparently succumbing to a combination of pain meds and the thrum of tires on the highway. Meanwhile, Hayden found himself staring out at horses, goats and flashy brown-and-white Texas longhorns grazing sprawling hillside pastures.

Glancing back to check on Kate, he wondered if her earlier worry for their safety was a natural reaction to their involvement in yesterday's shoot-out. Clearly, she'd been affected—to the point where he would've insisted that she see a counselor before being cleared for duty had she still been on the force.

But Kate wasn't under his command. And she wasn't necessarily wrong, either, he realized, to worry that the danger might not yet be over, especially to the children. Or anyone who happened to be too close to them.

Since Hayden would assume that the adult Kesslers had likely been the primary targets, it seemed a stretch to imagine that the surviving shooter would risk capture—or the same death that had befallen his partner—in an attempt to take out the children as well. But what if the man was known to the two girls, familiar enough that he worried they would point a finger at him? Could the fear of exposure, of losing everything if his crimes came out, push him to try again to make his problems go away?

The more Hayden thought about it, the less likely he figured it was that the Kesslers had met up with a pair of psychopathic thrill killers targeting victims at random. If the shooters had been strangers, they might've gunned down Nicolas Kessler before moving on to look for their next random victim. But by taking the time and trouble to hunt down their victim's wife, they'd given away that there had surely been some motive to their madness.

Hayden forced his sluggish brain to run through the most likely threats that might have followed the couple from their home. Perhaps he was looking for some business associate or neighbor who'd felt cheated in some financial dealing, an increasingly unhinged family member the pair had fallen out with or maybe either Nicolas or Ada had been sleeping with the wrong person outside the bounds of their marriage.

It made sense, too, to think the couple might have suspected they were in trouble when they'd left their home in Memphis. Perhaps not for a spur-of-the-moment vacation, as they'd told friends and coworkers, according to Lamar Robinson, the Memphis police investigator, but a desperate flight from some escalating threat they'd felt unwilling to report to the authorities for some reason.

That might well explain why, after their motel room had been breached and their phones stolen in New Orleans, they'd abruptly altered their plan to return home and headed west instead. Trying to outrun the death that already had them in its sights.

At the thought, Hayden frowned, realizing that this case was going nowhere until they had an ID on the dead shooter. With no wallet or identifying information on the body or the recovered ATV, he was praying the medical examiner would get a hit on AFIS. There, the deceased's fingerprints would be compared with the FBI's database. If no hit turned up, the job would grow exponentially more difficult, especially since the dead man was unlikely to be from the area…

Unless Ada Kessler woke up and started talking—or Hayden managed to gently extract the information from her traumatized girls…

As the afternoon glare brightened, the aching in his head intensified, slowing his thoughts to a crawl. Removing the extra sunglasses he'd borrowed from his brother's glove box, Hayden rubbed his eyes and leaned back in his seat, thinking through how to approach Kate's mother— a woman who could barely tolerate his presence—about speaking to her charges.

Sometime later, he jerked awake when Ryan hit the brakes and grumbled something about *damned spring breakers*.

Hayden cracked open his eyes and saw that they had slowed for traffic along the main drag of their two-light hometown of Leakey, a tiny city boasting just over four hundred year-round residents. Less than a half mile past the old limestone courthouse that was home to his own office, a glut of traffic clogged the normally uncrowded two-lane stretch containing various stores and businesses, including a small motel, a dollar store and several cafes.

"Sorry to wake you. This guy's apparently never heard of turn signals," Ryan said, nodding impatiently toward an RV whose driver's attempt to pull into the lot of an antique shop was impeded by a large group of motorcyclists rumbling past on the other side of the road. "Looks like the river rats and flower peepers are crankin' up early this year."

"What's a tourist town without its tourists?" Hayden asked, trying to sound resigned to the annual March holiday invasion, which along with summertime, was the busiest season for his department. But at the moment, he couldn't help but wish the onslaught would hold off until he'd put the Kessler case behind him—and preferably this concussion, too.

"Roads would sure be less clogged," Ryan grumbled.

Irritated by his lingering headache, Hayden sniped,

"Gripe all you want, but you know this town runs on the business they bring in."

"Maybe so, but I'm happy to leave seeing to their needs to Mac," Ryan said, referring to their brother's thriving river resort, "and keeping the rowdier ones in line to you."

"Here's hoping everybody pretty much behaves themselves so we can focus on the Kessler investigation—"

"Realistically—" from the back seat, Kate interrupted herself with a yawn "—when's the last time that happened? All the tourists behaving themselves, that is? Not even the locals can usually manage that when you're really counting on it."

Ryan glanced back at her. "How're you doing back there, Hurricane? Hand feeling all right?"

"It's hurting just a bit, but I can wait until I make it home to take another pain pill. Nap helped a little," she added. "I have to say, your driving's improved considerably from the days when you were running Jeeps up trees and drowning pickups in the river."

Ryan laughed at a memory. "I wouldn't've survived to maturity if I didn't get a whole lot better."

"If you call *this* maturity," Hayden popped off, and for just a moment, it felt as if they were all back in school again, as Ryan took a turnoff heading toward the area outside of town where all three had grown up. As they approached a crossing of the crystal clear Frio River, they were forced to slow for a small bus from one of the local outfitters as it unloaded a group of bare-chested teenage boys, each one holding an inflated tube while several also struggled to maneuver radios or coolers.

"You mark my words, those fish-belly-white fools are gonna be as red as strawberries by the time they come off the water," Kate said. "I didn't see so much as a T-shirt or a backpack for their sunscreen in that whole bunch."

Hayden smiled, remembering long ago spring breaks and summers from their own teen years, when one or the other of them—or sometimes all of them together—had sported sunburns of their own after a stolen afternoon on the river. He thought about how often Kate in particular, with her redhead's fair complexion, ended up slathering on aloe vera to soothe her skin's sting. Then, out of nowhere, he smelled sunscreen, a memory so sharply visceral that it almost hurt as he recalled rubbing its coolness into her heated flesh the first time she had asked him, "Catch my back, will you, Hayde?"

For a moment, he saw his own hand shaking, hovering beneath the delicate string tie that was the only thing keeping that cute little bikini top of hers on.

He was forced to turn away, to stare out the window until the river—and a cascade of memories too painful to revisit—fell away behind them. Though he could make himself be civilized around her—and only a monster would do any less after she'd literally been shot protecting him—it had been so much easier when he'd been able to think of her as the enemy, as unavoidable as she was insufferable in her attempts to put him in his place.

Not that he hadn't, he admitted, sometimes been a bit harsh with her as well. It had been easier to treat her like an unwelcome irritant and an intrusion into a career that had been stacking up pretty nicely without her there as the painful reminder of the very different goals he'd once had for his life…

For *their* lives, his and the girl he'd meant to make his wife, as soon as they could elope. He'd tried to talk her into cutting out and leaving with him earlier, but she'd told him it wouldn't be right after her parents had paid the entry fee for her in the biggest barrel racing event of the season. "This will be my last rodeo, I promise," she'd said after laying her hand over the faint swell at her middle, the one that she'd been wearing loose tops to hide and praying no one would notice until afterward. Flashing that fire-kissed smile he'd loved with everything in him, she'd added, *"Cloverleaf and I want to leave 'em a run to remember us by."*

His throat tightened as his vision blurred, and he wondered if the over-the-counter acetaminophen he'd taken—since he'd been warned that more potent pain-killers would raise the risk of a brain bleed—was doing anything at all against this headache. Soon, however, he was distracted when Ryan made another turn onto the dusty county road they knew so well.

Hayden still felt the old tug, just as he knew his brother must, to keep driving all the way to the big house they'd both grown up in, which lay behind the closed, brand-new gate of the vast ranch property their family had lost. Though over four years had passed since Hayden had purchased his own, far more modest home up the road, the sting of defeat often greeted him when he pulled into his drive. On the worst days, anger came, too, not so much at Mac any longer, but at himself for not having found some way to keep his family from losing the work of generations…for not having loved the ranch—and particularly the dirty, sometimes brutal cattle business—enough to fight to save it.

Before heading to Hayden's place Ryan pulled into the long drive of his closest neighbor. He passed an un-mown field brightened by deep blue wildflowers, where a somewhat swaybacked gray mare grazed. "Nice blue-bonnets, and I see old Moonlight's still looking fat and happy," Ryan commented.

But as the McClafferty family's big white two-story house and the old red barn with its paddock, small chicken coop and greenhouse came into view, Hayden, who hadn't set foot this deep on the property in ages, felt his spirits sag at the sight of the barn's badly peeling paint and the tall tangles of weeds growing up around the outbuildings and fence posts. Even the once-beautifully-maintained house showed signs of neglect, one of its blue shutters hanging askew and its dingy sides in need of pressure washing, though Kate's father had been gone for less than two years.

"Oh, Mom," Kate said. "Why didn't you tell me the place was going downhill like this, Hayden?"

"For one thing, your mother hasn't exactly invited me up to the house for tea," he fired back. "This is the closest look I've had in years, and anyway, if I *had* called you, we both know you'd have done the same thing your mother would've—told me to mind my own damned business and keep my nose out of yours."

"Come on, Hayden," Ryan urged.

"You still should have," Kate insisted.

"If you were so worried about your mother's welfare," Hayden asked, his head throbbing as his voice rose to be heard over the others, "why weren't *you* here, checking to see how she was getting along?"

"Because—because *Dad* was gone, and I couldn't bear to come back to the house, the farm, without him," Kate said, breaking down as she spoke of the adoptive father he remembered her tagging along with on ranch calls almost from the time that she'd arrived here at the age of eight.

"You're right," she burst out, sounding stricken. "It *is* my fault. I should have made myself come instead of always talking Mom into driving out to see me. I should have—"

"Let's not do this now, you two." Ryan turned to glare

at Hayden, looking mad enough to slug him. "And if you go and make her cry, I swear I'll—"

"Nobody's *crying*." Kate pulled herself together, disdain dripping from her voice at the accusation. "Certainly not over anything that *he* could ever say or do."

It stung Hayden, hearing her refer to him with such disgust. And realizing she was lying, just as he always was when he told himself that her words and opinions didn't matter to him.

They would always have the power to wound one another. The real question was, why did they feel the need to continue doing so, inflicting the slow death of a thousand cuts?

"I'm sorry," he said, meaning it—and feeling the ache in his head ease slightly.

"I'm sorry, too." Kate's brown eyes were sincere. "I shouldn't have put it on you. It's just so hard, without him, even now."

"I get it."

"If your mom needs any help," Ryan said, "I'd be happy to lend a hand, and I'm sure that Hayden would be glad to pitch in some more when he's able."

Kate shook her head. "She wouldn't allow it."

"She's made that clear enough," Hayden agreed, thinking of the note she'd left him. "But there's a youth minister in town I could talk to. He likes keeping his kids busy having them help out fixing up the property of older residents who're having trouble—"

"My mom would rather die than become an object of pity in the community."

"It's *not* pity," Hayden argued. "This place takes way too much maintenance for any one person to look after it all on his or her own. You know that even your dad hired out jobs when he got busy with his practice."

"Let me talk to her, try to figure out whether it's finances, pride or just plain old stubbornness that's been holding her back. Especially now that she's fostering again, maybe I can talk her into accepting help, to make sure the girls have a safe, well-maintained environment to heal in."

"That sounds like a good plan," Hayden said. "Let me know if there's anything I can do."

"Here's what you guys both can do," she said as Ryan pulled up front, around the corner from where Hayden spotted Rita McClafferty's vehicle parked. The older, dark green Grand Cherokee needed washing, but no more than most of the vehicles in the county, dirtied by recent rains and spring pollen. "Drop me off right here and let me walk up instead of coming inside with me."

"But you just had surgery this morning," Ryan protested.

"He's right," Hayden said, reaching for the door handle. "I'll need to see you safely inside, at least." Plus, he wasn't about to miss his chance to get a good look at the Kessler girls, whom he'd barely glimpsed the previous day, thanks to his own injury.

As he stepped out and opened the truck's back door, Kate emerged with her bag of belongings from the hospital, shaking her head emphatically. "You don't understand. I didn't text ahead to warn her it would be your brother and you bringing me home instead of Simon. And surprising her with the two of us together—I don't want to hear the dire warnings about how important it is not to go repeating the same foolish mistakes that cost me—"

"That cost *us*," Hayden corrected, speaking quietly but firmly as their gazes came together. After glancing back to make certain that Ryan had opted to wait inside the truck, he added, "Don't ever doubt that, Katie. No matter how you and your parents have twisted up the story in all the years since then, I swear on my life that neither of us walked away from what went down unscathed."

Chapter 7

Everything inside her tensed to hear him call her *Katie*, an endearment he'd lost the right to use the day he'd said the unthinkable to her parents.

I guess that lets me off the hook, then.

She still recalled how utterly shocked, how destroyed she'd been when they had finally told her, after she'd weakened enough to start asking for him again in earnest. Pleading, really.

Remembering the soul-crushing agony of knowing that he'd walked out on her, she turned away and started briskly toward the house's front porch so he wouldn't see it on her face. Wouldn't guess how even now, she hadn't completely gotten past it.

"Tell Ryan thanks again for the lift," she called back, adjusting her bandaged arm in its sling.

"Please don't do this, Kate," Hayden said, his longer strides easily matching pace with hers. "I'm sorry.

If that's what you want, I won't ever bring it up again, I promise. But let's not leave things—"

From inside the house, she heard the scrabbling of nails against the front window, followed by the booming barks of the furry, snow-white mountain of her mother's dog. The rescued Great Pyrenees had been purchased as a herd guardian by a nearby rancher. The oversize half-grown pup had been turned over to Kate's father in disgust after the young animal developed the dangerous habit of gulping down rocks whenever left outdoors unattended, resulting in him needing multiple expensive surgeries.

Fortunately, Thunder had since come to his senses, maturing into a loving companion for her mother, and Kate felt better knowing that his watchful and imposing presence would discourage any predators—either animal or human—from coming near the property.

Moments later, the front door opened, with Thunder bounding out ahead of her mother, a petite, attractive woman whose long, silver hair flowed halfway down the back of the soft, rose-colored tunic top she wore with a pair of jeans. Unlike the last few times Kate had seen her, she was even wearing a pair of small hoop earrings today, along with a bit of makeup, as if her recommitment to fostering had inspired her to take more pains with her appearance.

Before Kate could get out a compliment, however, her mom grabbed the dog's collar to keep him from jumping up in his excitement.

"Oh, Kate, let me look at you. Stay down, Thunder. Watch her poor arm." Reaching out, she lightly touched Kate's shoulder above the level of the bandaging, her brown eyes full of sorrow. "I can't believe that you were *shot*— That job of yours—I've had nightmares for years you'd end up hurt."

"I'm fine, Mom, or I will be soon," Kate assured her, knowing her mother had never been completely on board with her career choices. Probably partly because of the two years she'd spent supporting Kate through her struggle to get back on her feet after the accident.

"Your daughter was very brave out there," said Hayden, a few steps behind Kate. "I want you to know, her quick thinking and unhesitating action saved us all. You should be very proud of her."

Kate's breath hitched when their gazes collided: her mother's and her one-time lover's.

"I guess maybe *she* should've been the sheriff—" her mother's brown eyes went as flinty as her voice "—if she had to go and do your job for you anyway."

"Mom, please don't." Kate's face burned with embarrassment. "You know Hayden was injured, too, and none of what happened out there was his fault."

"It's all right," Hayden said. "And for what it's worth, Mrs. McClafferty, I'd give anything if I could go back and change things, see that your daughter and those girls you're caring for all came home safe and sound. Speaking of which, how are they?"

"He *doesn't* owe anyone an apology," Kate insisted, willing her mother to be the same kind and reasonable person she was with everyone else.

"Maybe not for *yesterday…*" Her mom buried her fingers in her dog's ruff to rub his furry neck. When Thunder, who'd been eyeing Hayden with suspicion, relaxed and sighed, she seemed to take it as a cue, grimacing as she shook her head. "I'm sorry, Sheriff Walker. Shall we start again?"

Hayden offered her a tight-lipped smile, though as

strained as he looked, Kate wondered how badly his head hurt. Or how much her mother's prickliness had gotten under his skin.

"I was glad to hear you're fostering again, Mrs. McClafferty," he said carefully. "I told Kate earlier, the system's lucky to have someone as good as you back again—and I'm sure you'll work your magic with those girls, if anyone can."

"I appreciate the vote of confidence," Kate's mother allowed, "but I'm afraid they need more than magic. They'll need time and patience and all the professional help they can get."

"I'm no expert," Kate said, "but I'll do all I can to support you as long as I'm here."

"And if I can help at all," Hayden offered, "I promise you, I'm up for it—"

"The girls are actually both out cold now in their bedroom," Kate's mother said. "I just looked in on them a few minutes before you drove up. I understand they scarcely slept at all last night at the hospital."

Kate's heart twisted to think of it. "I don't doubt it, after seeing the flight medics working on their mom as they were brought in."

"After they've had some time to rest, the social worker, your sister-in-law," her mother said, glancing at Hayden, "promised she'd be by to visit with them a bit." Lowering her voice, she added, "Sara told me they don't understand yet that their father's gone. You see, their mother apparently tried to shield them after the wreck."

"I heard the littler one asking the flight medic about her daddy as they were loading the girls and the mother onto the air ambulance yesterday." A lump formed in Kate's throat at the memory.

"She goes by Lottie," her mother said. "Make sure you call her that instead of Charlotte."

"I'll remember," Kate promised.

"But maybe hitting them with even more bad news now, when they're already so frightened for their mother, isn't the best timing," Hayden suggested. "It's a hell of a lot—excuse the language—for an eight- and ten-year-old to deal with. They may totally shut down."

"You're worried they won't be able to answer any questions," Kate guessed.

"You're wanting to *question* them? Now?" Her mother stiffened, already shaking her head as Hayden cut an irritated look in Kate's direction.

"Eventually, I will need to," he admitted, "once they're feeling a little steadier—"

"So you're suggesting we withhold important information from them now, information they have every right to know," her mother accused, "so you can barge in and retraumatize them by making them go over the most upsetting events imaginable?"

Hayden held up his palms. "I'm not out to do anything to hurt those little girls, I promise. But it *is* my job to make sure that whoever's responsible for what happened is held accountable—"

"*Your* job," she emphasized, "as well as *your* problem. Mine is making sure those two little ones are—"

"*Safe*, right?" Kate interrupted, running a hand over Thunder's ruff as he drew near her. "Isn't that *your* first duty? Well, it's Hayden's, too, Mom, which is going to mean that, sooner or later, he *will* have to find out what they saw, because right now, their mother's in no condition to answer any questions. And for all we know, she never will be— and so they're our only chance of making sure the children themselves don't end up the next ones in the killer's sights."

* * *

With her heart beating superfast and her knees so wobbly she could barely stay on her feet, ten-year-old Hazel Kessler flattened herself to the wall near the open front door to listen to the grown-ups talking on the front porch. The foster lady who was taking care of them had seemed nice, making them pancakes after they'd arrived and showing them how her giant dog melted into a furry puddle for an ear scratch, but Hazel assumed she'd been lying about their situation like everybody else. Her mom had been, too, when she'd told them help had probably gotten to Dad by now and he'd be feeling better before they knew it.

But Hazel had gotten a better look at him than Lottie after the wreck, and unlike her little sister—left sleeping in the yellow bedroom upstairs—*she* was old enough to understand what his glazed, wide-open eyes had meant. The memory of that last, quick look she'd gotten at her dad's face—what she now understood, a squirmy feeling slithering all around her stomach, would be her last sight of him ever—was the reason she couldn't sleep now. Well, that and what had happened when the bad men came back yesterday. The men who'd hurt their mom.

Thinking about the cracking noises and her mother falling, all that blood on her chest, the squirmy feeling got worse, the worms inside her wriggling so hard that for a few seconds Hazel was scared she'd throw up on the wood floor near Miss Rita's staircase. But she reminded herself she was made of tough stuff, not a drama queen like Lottie. Hazel hadn't cried when she'd fallen climbing out of their wrecked car or even when they'd gotten scared and cold and hungry, sleeping huddled together in the darkness. She couldn't because she'd seen how desperate their mom had been to keep pretending it was all some kind of crazy camping trip, asking wouldn't it be funny when they got home and found their dad waiting for them, a bandage on his head, wondering what had kept them so long?

Even for Hazel, what had happened yesterday was too much. Though she hadn't been as hysterical as Lottie, seeing their mom unable to answer, or even to open her eyes to look at them when they'd cried for her, had scared Hazel so badly, the sobs had nearly choked her, and tears had kept coming, on and off as strangers had bundled them aboard the noisy helicopter, taking them into a hospital room, where the nurses wouldn't let them see their mother while they worked to make her better.

This morning, a pretty, green-eyed social worker named Sara had come to explain that their mother wouldn't be able to take care of them for a while, so they were going to a really nice house with a grandmother type named Miss Rita who helped kids when they needed somewhere to stay a little while. Lottie had pitched a fit about it, wailing about how she wanted to stay there with their mom. That was when Hazel realized it was up to her to set a good example.

She'd concentrated on being brave, so brave their parents would have been proud, telling Lottie it would be okay even though inside she was screaming. But now, as she heard Miss Rita talking to the two other grown-ups on the front porch, Hazel's stomach started doing flips and her lips shook as she understood her mother was much worse than the nurses at the hospital had tried to make out. Hazel let herself worry, for the first time, that she and Lottie might end up being actual orphans, something she'd thought only happened to children in storybooks and on TV and not to regular kids. But that was what they called it, wasn't it, when your dad and mom both got killed?

At the thought, her eyes burned and her nose got stuffy, especially when she heard the man talking about asking her and Lottie questions. Questions about who might have done this to their family. And who might come back and to try to hurt them, too.

When she imagined the bad man coming back with his gun, Hazel forgot all about trying to be brave as she slid down against the wall, bowing her wet face to her knees and wrapping her shaking arms around her legs. Though the sky outside the door and window had been bright blue, the world around her seemed to darken—and to her horror, those squirming worms inside her stomach could no longer be kept down.

"I'm not saying you need to invite him for dinner," Kate told her mother on the front porch once Hayden left for home with Ryan, after asking her to call Deputy Yarborough about her statement as soon as she was feeling up to it. "Just work with him the way you would've worked with old Sheriff Turner, if he'd been investigating a case involving any of your other fosters."

Her mother sniffed, straightening her spine. "As if the likes of Hayden Hale-Walker could ever hold a candle to Arlo Turner, rest his soul."

Kate resisted the urge to roll her eyes, knowing her parents had loved the former sheriff for the same reason she'd found him so frustrating to work for. The man had done everything he could to prevent their "baby," as they'd continued to think of her long after she'd earned her degree in criminal justice, from endangering herself by doing anything remotely risky.

"I'm sure Hayden's a qualified and conscientious sheriff," she said. "We both know that's not your problem with him. And those girls deserve better than being held hostage to some ancient, personal grudge."

Anger flashed in her mother's brown eyes at the accusation. "I'd never do anything to compromise their well-being. Honestly, Kate, if you don't know me better than that by now, after everything we've been through together— Of course, I'll do what's best for the children, *if* the social worker believes it's appropriate."

Conscience burning, Kate shook her head, a wave of fatigue rolling over her. "I'm sorry, Mom. I think—I'd better get inside. I'd like to lie down for a bit, after I take my medication."

Her mother's expression softened. "Of course, you should, you poor thing. Let me help you with your bag there."

"There's no need to fuss. I've got one good hand."

But her mother would not be dissuaded, taking Kate's things and opening the front door to usher her inside, where Kate nearly went sprawling over a pale and shaking brown-haired girl on her hands and knees only steps from the front door.

As she was hop-stepping and grabbing for the wall with her good arm, the girl looked up sharply. "I'm sorry! I threw up—I didn't mean to."

Narrowly avoiding the mess, Kate heard her mother tell Thunder to stay on the porch before saying, "Oh, Hazel, honey. You don't have to be sorry. I'm sure it isn't your fault. Just let me help you to the kitchen—unless you need the bathroom instead?"

"I'm okay now, I think," the girl said, though her face remained pale and dotted with perspiration as Kate's mother helped her to her feet.

"I'll grab some paper towels for this," Kate said, eyeing the floor.

"Don't you dare think of cleaning that, in your condition. You need to sit down, both of you." Her mother's tone made it an order as she hustled them into the spacious country kitchen. After directing Kate, along with Hazel, toward the counter stools, her mother hurried to grab a ginger ale for Hazel's stomach and cold water for Kate after she passed on the soda.

Kate quietly fished out the prescription bottle from the bag her mother had set down on the island beside her. Her mom excused herself and disappeared with cleaning supplies she'd grabbed from underneath the sink.

As Kate popped the bottle top and shook out a pain pill, Hazel studied her with worried blue eyes. "Does it hurt a lot? Where the bullet went in?"

"Not as much as it did." Kate realized that the girl, who clearly remembered her from the canyon, must be thinking of her mother. "But to tell you the truth, when it first happened, I was so worried about your family and Sheriff Hayden that I could hardly feel it."

It wasn't until after her coworkers arrived and took charge of the scene and Hayden had regained consciousness that the sickening waves of pain had hit Kate. Even then, she suspected, she'd been spared the worst by the adrenaline roaring through her body from the exchange of bullets—and the shock of knowing she'd just killed a man.

Hazel nodded. "I thought you were really brave out there." Her blue eyes shone with admiration. "When you saw those men hurt my mom, you—you just picked up your gun and, *bam, bam-bam!*"

Kate flinched at the way the girl perfectly mimicked

the cadence of the shots she'd fired. "I'm trained to do that," she explained, "to stop people from hurting others."

"And then you tried to—to help my mom—even though you were— There was blood all over your hand—"

As her voice broke, the girl's head drooped forward, and Kate saw the first fat tears splash down on the island.

"Hey, I know. It's pretty hard to talk about for me, too," Kate admitted, quickly downing her pill before reaching over to touch the top of Hazel's head. Someone at the hospital must have washed and brushed her long hair, for it felt smooth and silky. "It was pretty scary out there, wasn't it?"

Hazel nodded as she looked up, her eyes shimmering. "I heard you talking outside just now. Lottie doesn't understand, but I know our mom could end up— That she might…"

Kate met her gaze and held it, remembering all those times when she'd been a kid and wanted nothing more than for one adult—a school counselor or her caseworker or one of her foster parents—to just go ahead and tell her the way things really were for once instead of always dancing around the truth.

From an adult vantage, she supposed they'd imagined they were sparing her, allowing her to hang on to whatever hope she could scrape together. But how long could any kid go on believing that the next time she was sent back to the run-down trailer that had so long haunted her nightmares, things would really be the paradise her biological mother always promised? Or what about believing the next foster home would be better than the last, where Kate had gotten lice so many times that none of the kids at school would sit near her?

With a sigh, she nodded at the girl. "It's true about your mom. I won't lie. I'll never do that to you, Hazel, so if you need to know, you can come and ask me anything, and I promise you, I'll always tell you what I can. My name's Kate, by the way." Yesterday, neither of them had been in any state for introductions.

"I know." Hazel nodded. "Miss Rita says she's your mom."

"She is now," Kate explained matter-of-factly, "but it wasn't always that way. You see, she was my foster mom once, too. I was a kid like you once. A kid she took care of when my real mom couldn't."

Hazel studied her intently before blurting, "Did—did your real mom get hurt, too? D-did somebody kill her, and that's why you had to stay here forever?"

Seeing the terror in her eyes, Kate shook her head, realizing that she'd just put her foot in it trying to establish a bond with the frightened little girl. She should have known to leave the child psychology to the experts and stick to mules, horses and the volunteers she managed.

Now that she'd started, there was nothing for it than to try to muddle her way through this conversation. Praying she wasn't about to muck things up worse, she explained, "No, um, she didn't die." At least she hadn't until Kate was twenty-four, when the woman she hadn't seen or spoken to in sixteen years had finally succumbed to an overdose in Houston. "She just had too many problems to take care of me, and I never had a real dad, until Miss Rita's husband. He's dead now, but he was really nice, too, like her—"

Apparently, all this was too much for Hazel, for she leaped up off the stool, her small hands knotting into white-knuckled fists. "But Lottie and me, we already *have* our own mom—a good mom, and a dad, too. Or we *had* a dad…before he—before those men got him, too—"

"I *know* you did," Kate said, guilt cascading through

her as she rose to lay her uninjured right hand on the girl's stiff shoulder. "I'm sorry. I'm so sorry for what happened."

"We aren't going to end up like you! We aren't going to be stuck here forever! And we won't ever call Miss Rita or you or any other lady but our mom our mom!" Hazel erupted.

"You won't have to, baby," Kate tried to tell the sobbing girl. "In your case, this is only for a little while."

As she spoke the words, she prayed she wasn't already going back on her word, doing to Hazel what so many well-intentioned adults had done to her in the past, what she'd sworn she never would…

Attempting to comfort a heartbroken child with an assurance that might turn out to be a lie.

Chapter 8

Headache or no headache, rest wasn't possible for Hayden until he'd closed the blinds in every room of the remodeled and expanded one-time vacation rental cabin he called home, turning down the wattage on his pain with every room he darkened.

But even then, his encounter with Kate and her mother had left him too restless to settle, so he found himself going from his living room—which Ryan had pronounced "pathetic" after surveying his single recliner in front of the big-screen TV and the chipped, blue coffee table that, aside from a ramshackle and badly overstuffed assortment of bookcases, were the only furnishings—to sit on the mattress in his equally sparse bedroom. There, he noticed that his sole nod to decor, the potted cactus on the windowsill, had gone brown and shrunken in on itself so badly, its internal ribbing stood out like a starved dog's bones. He winced, recalling how he'd scoffed when his secretary, Mrs. Hobbs, had remarked on presenting him with the housewarming gift that she'd figured was the one plant he might be able to keep alive. Even then, his predecessor's longtime secretary had gotten that look, the one that told him she didn't quite believe he'd manage, any more than she figured he could possibly fill Sheriff Turner's boots without her assistance.

To Hayden's profound irritation, he'd quickly discovered she was right about the latter, preventing him from putting the rigidly inflexible and occasionally terrifying woman out to pasture and hiring someone less inclined to raise his blood pressure on a daily basis. More annoyed than he should be to find the infernal woman right on this count, too, he walked over to the window and glared down at the dead husk. "What kind of self-respecting cactus are you, anyway?" He picked it up, surprised by the pang of remorse that hit him when he felt the featherlight pot and spotted the fuzzy layer of dust and a small dead fly caught among its needles.

Not wanting to look at the evidence of his neglect, he walked to the bathroom and stepped on the foot pedal of the trash can and dropped the cactus in, where it landed with a crack. He walked away but turned back on impulse and rescued it. Then, for some reason he couldn't explain, he partly filled the sink before setting the clay pot, barely holding together with its new set of fault lines in the bottom—as if his belated action might somehow resurrect the dead.

Feeling ridiculous, he was grateful for the distraction of his vibrating cell phone.

Pulling it from his pocket, he saw Deputy Yarborough's name flash on the screen. "Clayton, how's it going? I was meaning to call you and let you know, Kate had surgery on the hand this morning."

"How's she doing?" Sounding as if he were on the road, his voice betrayed concern. Though Kate may not have fit in well with her fellow deputies during her time in the department, she'd still been one of their own, making her injury in the line of duty nearly as upsetting to the employees of the small, tightly knit department as Hayden's.

"Well enough to be released around the same time I was, but she's staying here at her mother's place while she recovers."

"Just down the road from you…" his deputy said drolly, a sure sign of his relief. "Should I warn the dispatchers to be expecting fireworks calls from your neighbors?"

"I think it's safe to say that both of us are going to be focused on recovery from the shoot-out—and making sure the Kessler girls are kept safe."

"I did hear that Rita McClafferty would be fostering them," Clayton said.

Hayden didn't bother asking how, since his department worked so closely with the county's foster care and social services director. "I'm sure the kids'll be in good hands there," he said, "but I asked Kate to call you as soon as she's feeling up to it. I thought maybe it'd be more appropriate if you were the one to take her statement on the shooting."

"You aren't thinking she did anything wrong, are you? Way I've heard it, she most likely saved some lives."

"I agree, but you know how it works. We still need the interview for the record."

"I'll get it handled," Clayton said, "but I was wondering if you're feelin' up for a quick visit? Mrs. Hobbs's been tellin' everybody we're not to bother you at home, but I figured you have to be half dead not to want to hear the latest on the Kessler investigation."

"So something's up?" Hayden asked, his interest piqued. With a couple of decades of experience and a good head on his shoulders, his chief deputy wouldn't bother him over trifles.

"A couple things, yeah. And I'm actually just rolling up to your place. Brought you by some chicken and rice for your dinner later from my missus. Dorie said to tell you she was thinkin' of you and remembered how you liked it. She's worried about you here alone, after hearing you were injured."

"I hope you'll tell her that I'll be just fine and thank her for her kindness," he said, meaning it. "Come right on in the back door. It's already unlocked."

Hayden met him in the kitchen. Wearing his khaki-colored deputy's uniform, Clayton was a welcome sight with his prematurely pure white hair, a somewhat darker, neatly trimmed mustache and a ruddy, earnest face. Well regarded in the community, he would've been tough to beat had he chosen to throw his hat in the ring and run for sheriff. But he always had claimed he'd "quit in a New York minute" if he had to put up with the politics or mounds of paperwork the job entailed.

After Hayden had stashed the food in the refrigerator for later, he offered the deputy something to drink.

Clayton declined the offer. "I won't stay long, but thanks just the same. I've gotta get back out on patrol again before the good citizens run amok on us."

Nodding in approval, Hayden leaned up against the counter. "So you have more information on our dead John Doe?" he asked, thinking of the shooter Kate had taken down.

"No match on the prints yet, but I do have news on the ATVs those guys were riding."

"Did you find the one our missing gunman got away on?" Hayden asked.

Clayton shook his head. "No, sir. We did get a report, though, from a fellow named Earl Judkins over near the Camp Wood city limits, that somebody had busted the locks off an out-of-town owner's storage shed and made off with a matched set of ATVs. Description matches the Kawasaki we've got in custody with our dead shooter's prints all over it, and I'm pretty sure when the owner comes up with the serial numbers, it's going to be the right one."

"Outstanding." Hayden smiled, thanking his lucky stars for owners who kept records. "So where's this property?"

"About six miles down the road from where the Kesslers drove their car off the highway. But the really good news is—we've got pictures of the crime."

"What? When did this take place?"

"Three nights ago, according to the security camera date and time stamp. Owner says two men showed up right around two a.m.," Clayton explained. "He'd only installed those cameras just the week before that because one of the neighbors right around there had had some lawn equipment ripped off."

"I seriously doubt these will be the same guys," Hayden commented.

"Agreed," Clayton said, "but I do think the thieves knew exactly what they were after. You see, the ATVs were up for sale. The owner had put up ads and photos around town and on some online bulletin board, along with his contact information. A few people had contacted him, asking him where the ATVs were located."

"I'd love to see those messages or phone numbers, if he still has them. Maybe we'll get lucky and end up with one we can trace back to our missing killer." Hayden wasn't betting on these guys proving to be so stupid, but in his experience all it took was one careless or distracted moment for criminals to give themselves away.

"I'd like to make that bust myself," Clayton said with surprising heat, his face going a shade darker. "Those two could've killed you all—and those innocent little girls, too."

"They've done more than enough damage as it is," Hayden told him.

Clayton nodded, saying, "I've asked the ATV owner to forward me all the messages and phone numbers as soon as possible. He's already sent the attached still photos and video files via e-mail. I went ahead and copied them to your account as well."

Anticipation bumped Hayden's heart rate faster. "Any usable images?"

"I couldn't rightly tell from my phone, and I haven't gotten to a computer to look them over yet myself. Had to deal with a loose heifer on the highway and a report of tourists parking too close to a river crossing."

Ignoring the routine calls, Hayden said, "I'll take a look myself as soon as you leave."

"I thought you were supposed to be resting your eyes and keeping your mind off work. At least that's what Mrs. Hobbs keeps telling everyone while she's issuing threats about what she'll do to us if she finds out you've been bothered. *Dire* threats, Sheriff."

Hayden chuckled. "Those threats don't apply to me. Most likely, anyway."

Clayton gave him a skeptical look. "I'll keep my mouth shut, just in case."

"See that you do, or I'll be sure she knows who turned me onto the information." Hayden lightened the threat with a half smile.

Taking it in stride, Clayton told him, "Once I have that serial number on the missing ATV, I'll be sure to get out that information along with a photo of the one we recovered, to all the departments in the surrounding area. I'll be sure to warn them, too, that the person who has the other one is likely armed and dangerous."

"Sounds good, but I can't imagine our suspect hasn't already long since ditched the thing at this point." Hayden figured they'd probably find it burned out in some ravine, if the ATV was ever found at all.

"I imagine so, especially since the Kesslers are out of the back country."

"What we could really use is a picture of the vehicle they were driving when they stole those ATVs. Or better yet, the plate number so we can run it down." The vehicle might be stolen as well, but if the culprit was still using it, it could be the break they needed.

"I've got Gonzalez on that," Clayton reported, referring to the deputy assigned to the department's Camp Wood annex. "He'll try dusting for prints, too, around that lock they broke off, just in case either of our guys wasn't wearing gloves."

"Excellent," Hayden said, glad Gonzalez was crosstrained in evidence collection, since the department was too small for a dedicated tech. "Keep me posted on that. You have anything else for me?"

"One more thing. That Memphis PD investigator called the office earlier, when I was still there. Robinson, I think his name was?"

"That's right. When's he getting here?" Lamar Robinson had indicated to Hayden on the phone when they'd last spoken that he was planning to make the trip to Texas, now that his missing persons case had become a full-fledged murder investigation. A multiple, if Ada Kessler didn't pull through.

"He's not, I'm afraid. Apparently, he couldn't get departmental approval on the travel."

"Seriously? You'd think this would be a priority, with a supposedly upstanding family being involved."

"Budget constraints," Clayton explained. "He didn't sound happy about it, either."

"I can imagine." Robinson, who'd mentioned that his own kids were about the same ages as the Kessler girls, had seemed hell-bent on bringing home the missing family... one way or the other.

"He did tell me we should expect to see Nicolas Kessler's boss, Tim Spaulding, sometime later today," Clayton said.

"His *boss* is coming down, not a family member?" While Hayden would appreciate the opportunity to interview the children before some relative could spirit them away, he knew it would undoubtedly be best for them if a grandparent or some kindly aunt stepped forward to comfort them while they awaited news about their mother.

"Robinson said Spaulding and his family were pretty close friends of the Kesslers. Apparently, they did a lot of holidays together since Nicolas's dad remarried and moved to Costa Rica, and Mrs. Kessler's only family is a brother on the West Coast."

"This brother—has he been contacted about his sister's injury?" Hayden asked, thinking of Ada, lying alone in the hospital. Since he didn't have the manpower to keep a deputy guarding the room, he was counting on the hospital's limited security—but a watchful family member would be a hell of a deterrent in the unlikely case that the suspect had the brass to show up to attempt to finish what he'd started.

"Robinson's left multiple messages and is waiting for a call back, but according to Spaulding, the two of them had fallen out around the time their father died and hadn't spoken in years."

"I haven't always been close with my brothers, either, but it's tough to imagine not responding to a message asking me to call back law enforcement regarding a medical emergency." Hayden's stomach twisted to imagine the horror of learning that his family might lose whatever chance they had of fixing what had been broken for all too long among them.

"After this many years in law enforcement, it still surprises you that some people aren't decent human beings?" Clayton asked him.

"Point taken," Hayden said. "But I'll follow up with Robinson anyway and get this brother's name to make sure there isn't more to this than your usual family grudge."

"Sounds like a plan. Is there anything else you need me to get on?"

Recalling something he'd forgotten earlier, Hayden nodded. "I'm gonna need you to coordinate with the rescue people, because I want a nice, safe operation, but I definitely want someone to go down and take a closer look at the Kesslers' car. Photograph it in place before we have it winched up."

"Anything in particular we should be looking for?"

"Unless I miss my guess," said Hayden, "there's a GPS locator somewhere on the vehicle. It could be hidden almost anywhere, but check the wheel wells and beneath the undercarriage first because I'm betting the person who stuck it there didn't have access to the interior."

"If it's still there, I'll do my best to find it."

"I appreciate that. And I'll need you to make it a priority, because it could lead us to a killer."

Late that afternoon, once Kate had finished giving her statement to Deputy Yarborough in the quiet of her mother's craft room, her mother said, "You look a little tired, dear. Why don't you lie down for a bit while I take the girls out to go meet Moonlight and the chickens?"

"That sounds like a good idea," Kate agreed. "But do me a favor and take your cell phone with you, just in case you see anything concerning out there."

Her mother looked at her intently. "Surely, you're not thinking there could be a problem *here*?" Lowering her voice, she added, "If you believe there's any sort of danger—"

"I don't really," Kate said, unable to imagine how the shooter would learn where his targets' daughters had been taken, since their whereabouts were strictly confidential. "I'm probably just being paranoid."

"Considering what you've been through, I don't know who could blame you." Sympathy softened her mother's expression. "But don't worry about us. I'll keep my phone with me, and you know Thunder, always on guard. Now try to relax, Kate, and remember, you're here to rest so you can heal."

But it wasn't the soreness of her hand that had left Kate so exhausted. It had been reliving the harrowing details of the ambush and its aftermath for her statement. And recalling that she'd killed a man, even though she'd had no choice in the matter.

Left alone in the house, she didn't even make it upstairs, kicking off her shoes and stretching out on the sofa. She must have dozed off, because knocking at the front door awakened her what felt like only minutes later.

Realizing her mother and the girls weren't yet back, Kate rose, smoothing her disordered hair before checking the door's peephole. She didn't recognize the neatly dressed woman standing out there, but nothing about her set off any alarm bells, so she opened up to get a better look at a female in her early thirties with blond-streaked, sandy-brown hair, held back in a clip behind her shoulders.

"May I help you?" Kate wondered if the stranger might be selling something, though solicitors were a rarity this far out in the country.

"Hi, I'm Sara Walker." A warm smile accompanied the greeting. "The social worker assigned to Hazel and Lottie Kessler."

"Oh, yes. My mother mentioned you. Come in," Kate invited. "Mom and the girls—they're still out with the animals, I guess." Looking past her visitor, she saw no sign of them, but they could easily still be in either the barn or the henhouse.

Just how long was I sleeping?

Sara's big green eyes turned sympathetic as her gaze dropped to Kate's sling and lingered on the bruising that had edged out from beneath the bandages to stain her fingers. "So you're obviously Kate, then. I was sorry to hear about your injury, but I'm so grateful, for the girls' sake, that you happened to be there during their moment of need."

"I only wish I'd been a little quicker to recognize the threat. It all played out in a split second—or at least that's what it seemed like," Kate said, wondering how long it would take people to quit bringing up the shooting. Probably a decade, given how little excitement there was around here to compete for their attention. Though she knew that foster placements were supposed to be confidential, she worried that, inevitably, it would also get out that the children involved in the incident were staying with her family.

With a shake of her head, she pulled herself back to more immediate concerns. "You didn't happen to spot my mother and the girls out there as you drove up, did you?"

Sara canted her head, looking at her oddly. "Is everything okay, Kate?"

"I'm sorry. I was napping when you knocked, so I'm afraid I'm still a little— I'd just like to check in with my mother and the girls," she said, returning to the sofa to find her phone, which had slipped between the cushions.

"Of course," Sara said as Kate hit the button to call her mother's number.

Her mother answered on the first ring. "I thought you were napping?"

"Where are you, Mom? I looked outside, but I didn't see you."

"For heaven's sake, Kate. We're right in the turnout behind the barn. The girls were especially excited about the idea of brushing Moonlight. But if you need us to come back inside now—"

In the background, Thunder gave what sounded like a playful woof before her mother said, "That's enough now, Thunder. Now, the next time you throw the stick for him, Hazel, be sure to toss it well away from Moonlight."

Kate felt her tension ease at the reminder of the big dog's reassuring presence. "Please don't rush back inside on my account," she said before abruptly remembering Sara. "But the social worker's come by to—"

Sara held up a hand, interrupting, "Please tell your

mom to take her time. The *last* thing I'm here to do is interrupt their bonding."

Once she'd ended the call with her mother, Kate apologized for her behavior. "I guess I'm still a little on edge about what happened, so when I couldn't see where everybody was—"

"Of course, you're worried," Sara said. "Hypervigilance is a perfectly normal reaction to your experience."

Kate didn't imagine there was anything *hyper* about worrying about an unknown shooter who remained at large. But she needed to find some way, she told herself, to put things into perspective, or she was going to end up driving herself and her mother crazy. "I'm sure you're right," she told Sara. "Could I get you something while you're waiting? Some coffee, maybe, or what about some tea?"

"Tea sounds nice," Sara said. "But I'm trying to cut back on caffeine, especially this late in the day."

Once they'd settled on some herbal mint tea, Kate filled the kettle.

Sara offered, "Please let me help you with that. I was in a cast last summer and remember what it's like trying work with a hand immobilized…"

"Thanks, but this is nothing," Kate insisted as she turned on the electric kettle. Still, she let Sara assist her with putting the bags into a pair of mugs and getting out spoons, honey and sugar while the water heated.

"So does your mother often use animals as a bridge to forge a connection with her charges?"

"They were always my parents' icebreaker. What with my dad being a vet, there were always plenty around."

Grief twisted hard, the way it sometimes still did as Kate recalled the man who would later adopt her gently settling her aboard Moonlight's predecessor, an equally sweet-natured pinto gelding during her own first days here. She remembered her nostrils filling with the scents of horse and hay, her heart swelling with pride when he'd said, "You're a real natural at this, aren't you? We'll have to get you signed up for a few riding lessons if you think you'd like that."

It had been the first time she could remember anyone suggesting she might be actually *good* at something— or that she be provided with anything beyond what the bare-bones foster stipend allowed. And the fact that he'd *asked* if it would be something she might like, while his kind-eyed wife had looked at her expectantly, as if her opinion on it really mattered, had been a revelation. This was the first inkling that life held possibilities Kate had never guessed might be meant for her.

"You were in their shoes once, too," Sara said, her voice gentle.

Kate shook her head. "My situation was a whole lot different. I certainly wasn't missing loving and attentive parents, just hoping I hadn't jumped out of the frying pan and into the fire once again."

Sara studied her briefly before asking, "But that wasn't the case, was it?"

"Definitely not," Kate confirmed. "I thought I'd won the lottery, ending up here." She remembered running and hiding underneath beds, in the chicken coop or in the hayloft whenever she'd spotted her caseworker's car coming, seized with the sheer terror that an indifferent— or actively hostile—system's mistake was about to be corrected.

"That's funny." Sara smiled. "Your mother said *exactly* the same words when she told me the story of finding the one child meant to be her and her husband's forever family."

Sighing at the reminder of how, after years of failure to carry a pregnancy to term and a crushing disappointment over an adoption that had fallen through, the McClaffertys had given up on the idea that they were meant to be anyone's permanent parents, Kate pleaded, "Don't do this to me, will you? I'm always telling people how I'm not a crier, and I've got a serious tough-girl reputation to maintain."

"Sorry." Sara turned up a palm. "It's an occupational hazard, I'm afraid, talking so openly about feelings. My husband keeps reminding me that not everybody loves that."

"That's right. Hayden tells me you're married to his brother Mac."

Sara beamed. "Five months now."

"I'm so happy for you both," Kate said, finding that she meant it, for it was impossible not to see how perfect someone as caring as Sara clearly was for a man who'd dealt with the struggles Mac had. "I hope you'll say hi to your husband from me. His brothers and I hung out a lot as kids."

Sara nodded. "He's mentioned you a few times. He'll be glad to hear we've finally met."

Kate tensed slightly, studying her for any sign of how much Mac might have said regarding her and Hayden. But Sara's pleasant expression never wavered, so Kate instead turned her attention to pouring the steaming water into their mugs before plating some of the oatmeal cookies her mother had baked earlier.

"They *do* have raisins in them," she warned, "so don't set your hopes too high."

Sara laughed and snagged one. "Thanks. That means I get to delude myself into counting them as healthy."

"So that's the rationale for raisins. I've always wondered what it could possibly be," Kate said.

Smiling, Sara lowered the cookie she'd just claimed, with one bite missing. "I'm actually glad we have a few minutes to talk, Kate. I'd hoped for the chance to tell you, Mac's not the only person I've met in the area who remembers you."

"Who'd you meet?" Kate asked, her interest piqued.

"Her name is Greenville now," Sara said, "but you might remember her as Amanda Hackett. From when you both were—"

Kate flinched at an unwelcome memory. "When we were with the same fosters for a while. The Ryders— my last placement before my biological mother regained custody one final time…" *And turned a blind eye whenever her boyfriend of the moment decided to take out his frustrations on me.*

As an icy shudder rippled through her, Sara's hand covered hers.

"I'm sorry, Kate. I realize the memories from that time may still be painful."

Kate snatched her hand away, jerking her chin upward to look Sara in the eye. "I'm over it. You just took me by surprise, that's all. And the Ryders weren't the worst of the lot, not by a long shot. They just had a few too many kids to care for. Things fell between the cracks at times. Especially tiny, quiet slips of things like little Mandy Hackett."

"You looked out for her, Amanda says. Made sure she wasn't overlooked, that the bigger boys didn't snatch the food off her plate."

Kate shrugged. "It was every kid for herself there, but at five, she was barely bigger than a toddler—and so pretty with those sad, gray eyes. I used to secretly pretend she was my little sister." She'd loved playing the protector, dealing out swift justice when one of those jerk boys dared to push Amanda out of the way. Casting herself, Kate now realized, as the kind of mother she'd so desperately wanted but had never known for herself at that time.

"She said that even after you left the Ryder home, you'd find her on the playground and slip her a note sometimes or a treat out of your own lunch when you could." Sara smiled warmly. "You'd be surprised what that meant to her."

"Actually, I wouldn't," Kate said, saddened to think of how the tenuous connection between the two of them had gradually faded—a consequence of the difference in their ages and living arrangements. "But may I ask, how is it you know Amanda? Last I heard, she'd gotten into real estate and was doing well for herself."

"She helped me with a rental when I first arrived here, and since then we've gotten friendly," Sara told her. "But I'm afraid she's having a very hard time at the moment."

"What's wrong?" Kate frowned, recalling something else she'd heard about Amanda Hackett. "It's that husband of hers, isn't it?"

She'd known she should have warned Amanda the day she'd heard she was marrying Pete Greenville. But by then, it would have been too awkward, since Kate hadn't spoken with her for years, not for anything more consequential than a murmured hello when they'd passed one another walking into a café or waved on the street. It was hard enough imagining speaking to her now, reminding them of a time when they'd been small, helpless and unwanted. But Kate couldn't picture the conversation would go well if she started with, I understand you're planning on marrying into one of the county's richest families in a few weeks. I know we haven't really talked since you were five, but here's why I think you should bail on that idea right this minute.

"In a manner of speaking, yes," Sara said. "Or I should say, he *was* the problem—at least until he turned up dead."

Then her head turned toward the sound of voices from the porch, accompanied by the clatter of footsteps that preceded Kate's mother's return with the girls and the end of their opportunity to discuss her one-time friend in private.

As Lottie and Hazel, looking better after their walk outdoors, excitedly showed off the eggs they'd collected from the henhouse and told Sara how Miss Rita had promised they could make them into a breakfast casserole in the morning, Kate made a mental note to find out what had happened to the husband she'd always feared might someday harm Amanda...

And she could think of no better source than the sheriff of this county for the information she desired.

Chapter 9

Though it wasn't quite eight thirty in the morning, Hayden was already sweating and cursing, frustration mounting as he faced the fact that another night's sleep hadn't solved his issue. While resting in his recliner or navigating his darkened house, he felt relatively decent, but every time he attempted to read a message on his cell phone or the larger, glowing screen of his laptop, the words squiggled and spun away from him, the images doubling as his skull throbbed.

Last night, he'd kept going back to it, intent on at the very least getting through the images the property owner had sent related to the theft of the ATVs used by Ada Kessler's two attackers. But all he'd gotten for his trouble was a headache that had forced him to retreat to his bed with an ice pack.

He'd tried again this morning, but this time the repercussions slammed down with the speed and ferocity of a steel trap. With a shaking hand, he closed the laptop, wondering how much more of this he was really in for—and how on earth he was supposed to run an investigation, much less a department, when his eyes and brain refused to work together.

As he downed a couple of over-the-counter pain tablets with his coffee, he pondered whether he might be able to manage better at the office. But he didn't need a doctor to tell him that driving was a terrible idea. While he knew he could assign a deputy to act as his chauffeur and to assist him in reading his e-mails and other correspondence, the idea of appearing before his people in such a sorry state filled him with self-loathing. He couldn't stomach, either, the thought of leaving a case of this complexity and seriousness in the hands of Clayton.

He trusted his second-in-command to do his best, but Hayden's gut told him this investigation would involve a degree of subtlety his plainspoken and straightforward chief deputy might not have in him—especially interviewing a pair of terrified children.

While Hayden racked his brain for some way to hasten the healing process, he heard tires on the gravel driveway outside. Figuring it was Clayton coming by to fill him in, he went to the blinds, carefully parting two slats to peer out, and was surprised to see Rita McClafferty's pollen-filmed Grand Cherokee. Before he could wonder if she was about to drop more food on his porch, or perhaps a note warning him to stay away from her new fosters, Kate emerged from the driver's seat. She looked especially pretty this morning in formfitting jeans and a V-necked forest green top that set off her glossy red hair to its best advantage.

Irritated at the strong tug of attraction that caught him off guard, he grabbed a pair of sunglasses from a small shelf by the front door. Donning them, he headed out to stalk toward her. "What're you doing on the road with that injured hand of yours when you're supposed to be home resting?"

"Oh, come on, Hayden. It's not like it's illegal."

"It is if you're half-looped on prescription pain meds."

Brown eyes sparkling, she shrugged off the objection. "Then you'll be happy to know that this morning, I felt well enough to go with over-the-counter ibuprofen."

"Glad to hear you're doing better."

"Besides," she said, evidently not yet finished arguing her point, "I come bearing gifts from my mom. Breakfast. You still like to eat, don't you? And I didn't figure you'd feel much like cooking."

As she lifted a zip-top insulated bag out from behind the seat, he tried—and failed—not to notice the curve of her rear end in those jeans. Was the woman looking sexier than ever just to spite him?

"Of course, I still like to eat," he said irritably, "but given the reception I had from your mother yesterday, I've gotta ask, are you sure it isn't poisoned?"

She snorted. "Positive, since I just saw her serve the girls and herself a big helping, but if you don't believe me, I'll eat with you...if you're up for sharing a meal, that is."

Suspicious of her motives, he looked her over. "Why would you want to do that?"

"Maybe I just wanted to check on you this morning, see how that head's doing."

"Still on my shoulders, so try again."

Her lips tightened for a moment before she shook off what appeared to be annoyance. "Why can't you just accept that I'd do something nice? Do you really imagine I'm so hateful—or indifferent to your health, after what we both went through together?"

The accusation stung enough that he softened his tone. "I don't think that about you. It's just, after everything—"

"Well, putting *everything* aside," she said, the word infused with a drop of acid, "I did want to check in on you."

"Thank you," he said, feeling chastened. "Let me help you with that bag, why don't you?"

"There's no need but thanks." She nodded, allowing him to take it from her.

Once they'd gone inside, he returned his sunglasses to the shelf as she looked around the place.

When he headed toward the kitchen, she said, "Um, mind if I turn on a light? After coming in from outside, it's like a cave in here."

"Sorry, yeah," he said. "It's my—"

When she switched on an overhead light, he jerked his head toward the darker kitchen. Too quickly, causing a waving of dizziness to make him groan.

"Of course," Kate said, hitting the switch again to shut the light off. "Sorry, Hayden. I didn't think about your eyes being sensitive from the concussion."

He braced his hand against the counter for a moment until the world steadied before saying, "It's proving a helluva learning curve for me, too."

She gave him a sympathetic look. "Is the pain bad?"

"Not half as annoying as not being able to look at the screen on my cell phone or computer without wanting to be sick. Can't get a damned thing done."

"Maybe you're not meant to," she said. "Aren't you supposed to be resting until you do feel better?"

"Could *you*, if you were me and worried about those girls and their mother? That's not the kind of thing a sheriff can just *delegate* and walk away from. Well, not this sheriff, anyway."

With a sigh, she admitted, "I can respect that. Is there

something I can do to help? Maybe read some e-mails to you or help you look up things on your computer?"

He scowled at the suggestion. "You can't do that. For one thing, you're hurt yourself. You're here because you've been shot, I'll remind you, and you're recovering from surgery."

"I'm capable of multitasking."

"Plus, you're no longer law enforcement," he said, "so it wouldn't be appropriate to allow you access to department communications—especially where there's a conflict of interest involving a family member."

"A family member?"

"I shouldn't have to explain this," he said, "but with your mother fostering the Kessler girls and you living in the same household—"

"I don't *reside* there—I'm just staying for a short time," she reasoned, "and as for the law enforcement consideration, that's easy enough to get around. Just swear me in."

"Swear you in?" he erupted. "As *what*?"

"A reserve deputy, while I'm here," she said. "That way, you don't even have to pay me for my services, yet you're getting a fully trained, experienced volunteer to help out. I'm still even licensed by the state."

"And what's in it for you?" he asked, wondering if she might somehow be out to score some payback by taking advantage of his weakness.

"Breakfast, while it's still warm, I hope," she said, going to his kitchen counter, where he'd set the insulated bag, and unzipping the top. "Let's have some of this casserole—and my mom threw in some of those cranberry-orange muffins you used to love so much, too. I have to tell you, they smelled amazing baking."

He couldn't help but smile, his mouth watering at the

memory of the flavor…and a time when things between him, Kate and their families had been far less complicated.

"Let me set the table," he said, heading to a cupboard. "We can talk more while we eat."

Once they'd washed up and sat down with coffee from the pot he'd brewed earlier, he insisted on allowing him to serve her from the still-warm dish containing the baked egg-and-cheese-and-sausage mixture. "Tell me when," he said as he spooned some onto her plate.

"That's good." She scooted her chair closer to the round, wooden dinette table.

"How about some butter on your muffin, too?" he offered as he sliced one open on a plate. "Probably easier than you having to wrestle it one-handed."

"I *hate* asking for help," she admitted. "And even worse, I loathe how everything's so awkward. I realize lots of people get along perfectly with one functioning hand, but this morning, even putting on a bra felt like wrestling with a giant python."

"For what it's worth, you *didn't* ask. I offered." He buttered the muffin and wished she'd kept the bra-and-python observation to herself, since he now struggled not to picture her in the midst of dressing. "Here you go."

"Thanks. Oh, how I've missed these," she said, making happy noises as she bit into half the pastry. "I could be in real trouble if my mom keeps baking for the girls while I'm not able to get out and move as much."

"If I know you, you won't be able to sit still long enough for a few extra treats to make a lick of difference," he said after swallowing a forkful of the casserole. "It's probably why you were so quick to offer to help me out—because the very thought of being forced to rest too long makes you want to climb the walls."

"Guilty as charged," she admitted. "But it's not only that. You see, yesterday, right after you left, I discovered an eavesdropper on our conversation. You remember, when we were talking with my mom on the porch about questioning the girls about what they might know?"

"Oh, no." His heart sank as he recalled the conversation. "Did one of them—"

"Hazel, I'm afraid," she said. "Poor kid was so upset over what she'd overheard, she made herself sick over it."

"I'm so damned sorry. I shouldn't have just assumed."

"It wasn't your fault. And what she heard—it wasn't actually new information. She's already figured out about her father, and she's aware her mother's in pretty rough shape."

"I can't imagine." He hated to think of the girl's suffering. "Did she give any indication that she knew either of the men who were responsible for her parents' shootings?"

"We didn't really get that far, but I don't think so. Right now, she's mostly overwhelmed, bewildered—and trying hard to protect her little sister."

"Lottie," he said, recalling the nickname Kate's mom had told them the younger, freckled Kessler girl preferred. "What about her? Does she know about her dad yet?"

Sadness washed over Kate's expression. "She does *now*. Yesterday afternoon, Sara came and talked with them. She did her best, I know, and my mom's doing all she can, but there's no easy way to deal with such hard news."

"And I'm sure they're scared to death that they might lose their mother."

"Absolutely terrified and of course, worried over what might happen to them." Sighing, she pushed away the food. "I thought I was so hungry, but I—"

"Hey," he urged. "You need to eat to heal."

"I know, but—talking to Hazel, being around the girls last night—" She looked up at him, a raw vulnerability in her face that she seldom revealed to anyone.

A vulnerability that brought to mind a background she rarely mentioned, but one that he suspected she could never truly put behind her.

"They remind you, don't they?" he asked gently, reaching across the table to touch her arm. "They remind you of back when you were in foster care, too."

"Quite a bit," she admitted. "Though by the time I was Lottie's age, I'd been in and out of more foster homes than I care to remember. So it definitely wasn't the same shock they're experiencing."

"Maybe you could help them with the adjustment, at least a little."

"They have my mom and Sara. They're better off sticking with the pros." She frowned. "I really upset Hazel yesterday, and—I feel so out of my depth around them. Maybe it's a good thing after all I never had…"

He shook his head to stop her from putting a brave spin on a loss that still cut to the bone. "I'm sure you're better with them than you imagine. But if you'd like a bit of time out from the house, I will take you up on that help you offered and borrow your eyes for the computer."

"Glad to do it," she said, looking grateful for the change in subject.

"But let's say we both try to do a little more credit to our breakfast before we get down to work."

She nodded mutely, and for the next few minutes, they ate, the only conversation centered around Hayden's compliments on the food and request that she be sure to thank her mother for him.

"I'll definitely do that," she said.

As Hayden rose from the table, he held up a hand when she started to do the same. "Don't get up, please. I'll just put this stuff away and get these plates in the dishwasher while you finish your coffee."

After thanking him, she said, "Before we get down to work, I was wondering if I could get your take on an unrelated matter."

He looked up from snapping a silicone top back over the casserole dish. "Fire away."

"Yesterday, Sara mentioned something about a mutual acquaintance, Amanda Greenville."

"I didn't know you two were friends."

With a shake of her head, Kate flipped her hair over her shoulder. "I wouldn't say 'friends' is the right word, precisely, but maybe we were, in a sense, a long way back."

Puzzled, he frowned. "I don't follow."

"We were in a foster home together for a short time. She was younger, only about five then, and tiny for her age. That particular place was barely controlled chaos—they had like six kids there, all ages, so I sort of tried to keep my eye on her as much as I could."

"Who kept their eye on *you*, Kate?" he couldn't keep himself from asking.

She sniffed and straightened her spine. "Don't you worry. I took care of myself fine. I'd had plenty of practice already by then."

He looked down at her right forearm, and just as he remembered, the rounded edge of a red mark peeped out from the edge of her three-quarter sleeve. A puckered red mark that matched more than a dozen other burn scars he'd been so shocked and horrified to spot the first time he'd seen her remove one of the oversize T-shirts she'd so often worn over her swimsuit.

"You deserved a hell of a lot better," he said roughly,

angry all over again to imagine some monster putting out cigarettes against her tender flesh.

Seeing where he was looking, she tried to use the swollen fingers of her damaged hand to adjust the sleeve to cover the mark.

He touched the top of her wrist. "You never have to hide your past, not from me."

"Let's get back to Amanda, shall we?" she asked, her eyes pleading for him to let the subject drop. "Sara mentioned things haven't gone so well for her since her husband was found dead. I read online that his body was discovered last summer in a remote area, actually not all that far from where we were searching for the Kesslers the other day."

"If you're thinking his death's related somehow, I'm going to stop you right there," he said, understanding her reluctance to discuss a time when she had been so small and helpless. "Pete Greenville's death was ruled accidental, likely resulting from a fall while he was poaching on an absentee landowner's property. The horrible thing is, he broke a femur, so he might've lain out there for hours before internal bleeding or exposure got him. We had a nasty cold front blow through a day or two after he was finally reported missing."

"Finally?"

"He wasn't exactly husband-of-the-year material. Used to come and go quite often. Apparently, he didn't like looking at her until whatever bruises he'd most recently inflicted faded because it made him feel bad."

"So he *did* abuse her." Grimacing, Kate brought up her good hand to span her forehead. "I knew I should've tried to warn her about what a huge creep he was back in school, always bullying anyone he thought would let him get away with it. With her being so much younger, she wouldn't have crossed paths—"

"I hope he didn't give *you* any trouble," Hayden said, though Pete, who'd been a few years ahead of them as well, wouldn't have often encountered Kate, either.

"Me? He wouldn't have dared since he knew I ran with you and your brothers," she said. "Besides, when was I ever the type to suffer in silence back in school?"

"As small as our community is, I can't imagine she wouldn't've heard some things about him," he said, "but I expect people were mostly focused on telling her how lucky she was that one of the almighty Greenvilles would even look at someone from her background. Because around here, as you know, money and family connections talk."

"She's beautiful, successful—if you ask me, he was the lucky one to get her," Kate said, sounding defensive.

"You'll get no argument from me about that," Hayden said as he slid the container into his fridge. "I know old Pete had supposedly reformed since the days his parents bought his way out of trouble for causing that tour van to run off the road back when he was still a teenager. At least to the point that he'd avoided further arrests—"

"I'll still never get over how he got away with injuring so many people," she complained. "But if he was hurting her before his death, what I don't understand is what's the issue now? Surely, she's not pining away over this loser?"

"Who knows how she really felt about him?" he said. "I suspect that was complicated. Certainly, she never said a word against the man while he was living, not even when I tried to have a conversation with her—carefully— after I heard whispering about the bruises."

He still remembered the denials, the excuses about a skin condition being the real reason she wore long sleeves during a hundred-degree heat wave when everyone else in town had on as little as they could get away with.

Kate set down her coffee. "We both know how long it can take battered women to get up the nerve, if they ever do. And for someone with no family of her own to help support her, I can imagine it'd be nearly impossible."

"The thing is, people around here couldn't imagine how she wouldn't hate him, especially when she started looking so much better after he disappeared and prospering with her real estate sales since she didn't have to worry about him turning up and causing trouble every time she showed a male client property. That's when the gossips got the bright idea that maybe she'd somehow figured a way to make her life easier by getting rid of him. His family, who was furious when they realized she now had control of all the prime grazing land they still considered theirs, did nothing but stoke the rumors that she'd probably done him in."

"I can hear it now," Kate said bitterly, "that filthy little foster kid, ungrateful for everything she was given…"

Hayden winced at the way she'd put it but couldn't deny that some in the area had probably felt that way. "Once he was finally found and the medical examiner's findings were made public, I hoped things would get better for her, especially when I went out of my way to say that no foul play was suspected. But you can't unring a bell, and the family's still plenty sore about her inheriting, especially since she hadn't given them grandkids."

"It's a wonder she doesn't just sell off to them, pack up and leave this town forever."

"Maybe she doesn't feel she can, for whatever reason," he said as he scraped a bit of cheesy goop from the plates before sticking them in the dishwasher, "or maybe she's found a spine. Whichever's the case, she doesn't seem to be backing down, no matter how uncomfortable the Greenvilles and their hangers-on make things for her. I have to say, she's earned respect in at least some quarters for the way she's toughing things out."

"Well, I'm glad she has a friend like Sara. And if there's anything I can do to help while I'm around, too, I'd be willing."

"Glad to hear it. She deserves a break, which is exactly what we need, too, if we're going to get past first base on this Kessler case this morning."

"I guess that's my cue that it's time to get to work then."

"Then why don't you raise your right hand so we can get started?"

Though being sworn in as a reserve deputy at Hayden's kitchen table was mostly a formality, it hit Kate harder than she'd imagined, knowing she was once again officially serving in a law enforcement role. A role she'd deeply missed, despite its frequent frustrations and the way she'd walked out on her position as a deputy in this county.

But there had been rewards, too, both in the job she'd done here and the position she'd taken afterward, as an officer at a small police department outside of San Antonio before her volunteer work with search and rescue had unexpectedly led her to her present dream position. She'd never forget the little zing of excitement she'd felt going out on patrol each shift, never knowing what the day might bring. Some days had brought the rush of pure adrenaline when she'd surprised a resisting suspect nearly twice her size by using his own weight and momentum against him before cuffing him neatly. On others, she'd felt the simple satisfaction of knowing she'd helped those who were powerless to help themselves—even those in-clined to curse her for her trouble.

"I hope that grin on your face is because you're eager to dive into this—" Hayden gestured toward the open laptop in front of him "—and not plotting to tell me you're see-ing chupacabra footprints on these security images I'm about to show you just to mess with me."

She smiled at the reference to a goatlike legendary creature people occasionally claimed to see running in the local hills. Mainly intoxicated people, in her expe-rience. "Nope. Just remembering how excited I was the first time I was sworn in, going off to work in my own hometown's department."

"That came as quite a surprise to me," he said, his tone desert dry.

"Not a very pleasant one, I'll bet." She had a stab of unaccustomed sympathy as she tried to imagine how he must have felt. "I'm pretty sure my head would've ex-ploded if I'd had to deal with some ex-boyfriend show-ing up where I'd been working for years."

"It was…" Hayden's mouth twisted. "I guess you could call the experience *character building*."

"Ouch. Well, for what it's worth, I'm sorry if it was difficult. I'll admit, I'd thought of applying elsewhere, but after spending those two years after the accident getting me back on my feet before I headed off to college, my parents were really excited about having me back close to home again."

"I suppose that's only natural," Hayden said. "And most parents worry at least a little about their kid going into law enforcement in the first place."

"I think they figured I'd be safer right here, where they could sort of watch out for their baby." She felt a rush of heat at the embarrassing admission.

"Water under the bridge now," he said gruffly before changing the subject. "Just let me type in my password here, and we can open up those files I wanted to review first. I managed to squint my way through dragging the icons into a folder on my desktop earlier."

"There you go," he said after clicking to open the folder a moment later. "You can move forward through this series of still shots, and you'll see a couple of video files down in the—"

"Got it," she said, sliding her chair closer. "Why don't you let me turn the computer my way, maybe save myself a sore neck and you another headache?"

"Good idea." He raised his mug. "I need a refill on my coffee anyway. You?"

"No, thanks." She didn't need more caffeine, not with her pulse already speeding as she flipped through the images and got her first glimpse of the two ATV thieves, almost undoubtedly the same men she'd encountered during the ambush at the spot she'd mentally rechristened Heartbreak Ridge.

The first few images proved a major disappointment. Not surprisingly, the pair had chosen the cover of darkness to help obscure their crime, so the camera had taken the stills in black-and-white. Worse yet, the men's faces weren't visible since the shots captured them turned away from the camera. They were also hidden in shadow, because of the hood of the sweatshirt one wore, and the other had been standing in the dark lee of the storage container.

Impatiently clicking through the next shots, she finally got to one with better lighting. The hooded man's face was a pale blur of motion, but the other man's, when she enlarged it, struck her like a blow to the solar plexus.

"It's *him*," she told Hayden, who walked back from the kitchen, his coffee mug in hand.

"Him, who?"

"Our dead John Doe."

"You're certain?"

"Trust me," she insisted. "A woman doesn't forget the name of the first man she's ever killed."

He smiled at her. "You say that like somebody who's not sure she's finished racking up her body count."

"Just remember that," she warned, "the next time you're tempted to push your luck around me."

Unexpectedly, he laughed, a deep, rich sound that took her back to when their playful, if at times wickedly barbed, exchanges often had them cracking up. But she remembered, too, when their shared laughter had led to a look, a touch, that had flared hotter than the Texas sun—and how that had culminated in the kind of heartache that she'd never guessed existed in this world.

Throat tightening, she looked past one of his many bookshelves—packed with hardbacks covering topics from the opiate crisis to criminal justice reform along with a surprisingly large collection of tattered Old West paperbacks—before returning her attention to the screen. There, she flipped through a couple more images before enlarging one profile shot that included their surviving suspect wheeling one of the ATVs out of the storage container. The detail wasn't great, and neither his hair nor his ears—often especially helpful as identifying features—were visible since he had his hood up. Still, it was a decent enough shot, she decided.

"I'm cutting and pasting a detail from one of the photos of our missing suspect's face into a new image file," she said. "It's a side view, and not wonderful, but there's a distinctive bump on the bridge of his nose. Aquiline,

I think you'd call it, and it's definitely larger than your average beak."

"Any detail could be helpful," Hayden said. "With luck, when we send it out to other law enforcement agencies, someone will recognize that nose and the fella who goes with it from a previous arrest."

"Or in a perfect world, realize they have him locked up in a holding cell after nabbing him on a traffic violation."

"We should be so lucky," Hayden said. "But my money's on this suspect being a lot more careful."

She nodded. "Unfortunately, I'm inclined to agree, especially since you can see he's wearing dark gloves in this photo."

"What about the deceased suspect? Gloves on him as well?"

"His hands are out of the frame or hidden in all the shots," Kate said, "but you'd think if one suspect was being that careful, the other'd take the same precautions."

"More than likely, if they're pros," Hayden agreed. "What about the video footage? Have you watched it yet?"

"On it now," she said, clicking on the tiny icon in the folder and pressing the play button on the first of two video files.

"I've got eyes on the vehicle they used," she announced to Hayden, who stood watching her intently as she observed the thieves loading an ATV onto a trailer. "Definitely a pickup, darker in color, though this is in black-and-white, too."

"Got an idea of the make or model?" he asked. "Or—I know this is pie in the sky—but is there a license plate visible in any of the frames?"

"Let me run it back." She replayed the brief clip. "Sorry to say this video quality's garbage."

Apparently unable to restrain himself, he looked over her shoulder before almost immediately groaning and turning away. When she glanced up, she saw his eyes were closed, and one hand clutched the back of her chair.

"You need to take a break, maybe lie down with an ice pack?" She twisted in her seat to touch his upper arm beneath the edge of his T-shirt sleeve.

"I'll be fine," he said, waving his hand at her, so that she felt the ripple of thick muscle beneath her fingers before abruptly pulling away. "Just forgot myself for a second."

"I can't imagine how frustrating that must be." Turning back to the computer, she forced herself to return her attention to the video.

Peering at it, she said, "This truck's definitely a two-door model, not one of the double cabs."

"That narrows the search some. The single cabs aren't as popular these days, except in work trucks, and those mostly tend to be white," Hayden said.

He paced between her and a living room that she noticed contained no sofa but a lot more bookcases, along with a big-screen TV, as if he preferred to spend his time here alone. Years alone, just like her...

"Well, it's definitely dark in color, and he's towing a utility trailer that they used to haul away the ATVs."

She moved on to the next video, hoping to find something more helpful. It appeared to be another shot of the same truck and trailer backing down a driveway.

"Aha," she said, catching the light glinting off an emblem. "I can tell you it's a Chevy, most likely a late-model Silverado."

"Good work." Coming up behind her once again, he gave her shoulder a squeeze that she felt all the way down to her toes. "We'll send that information out with his photo, ask other departments to be on the lookout for us."

Instead of removing his hand, he left it sitting there as she kept looking.

Move it, right now, she meant to tell him. Except Kate didn't, couldn't for some reason, not with her body soaking in the warmth and weight of his touch like a parched field drinking in the summer rain.

"Sorry I couldn't see the plate number here, either," she said, trying to distract herself from the slight movement of his thumb—a nervous tic, maybe? Or, slow and rhythmic as it was, did he mean it as a caress? "But it's not—it's not in the frame at all, and even if it were…with the video this grainy and it so dark outside when this was taken… It looks like there was moonlight, at least, but…"

Abruptly aware that she was babbling, she felt her face burn as the words trailed off.

"What's the matter, Kate?" Hayden turned to look at her intently. "Your face is going all red."

Relief flowing through her at the broken contact, she said irritably, "You were— I wish you wouldn't touch me, all right? Because it isn't— We can't be—"

"I was *touching* you?" Gritting his teeth, he glanced down at his own hand, as if it had betrayed him. "Hell, Kate. I didn't even realize that I had. I swear, I'm not like that, not the type to make assumptions. It's just, with you, sometimes—"

"Sometimes, *what*?" she demanded after he'd cut himself off, still embarrassed that he'd called her out on her flushing—and ever more ashamed how she was behaving over what her rational mind told her had been a simple shoulder squeeze. Yet, once set in motion, her reaction only gathered in size and energy, mowing down every logical objection as it rolled downhill.

"Sometimes my brain skips back in time," he said, "and I forget—"

"I *never* will," she fired back, tears pricking at her eyes. "I don't have the luxury of forgetting what you did to me."

"What *I* did—to *you*?" he had the nerve to ask, looking so genuinely bewildered that it was all she could do not to ball up her fist and send it swinging at that infuriatingly handsome face of his.

Because she couldn't do that, she spun away from him, not wanting him to see the furious tears in her eyes. Why could she never stop herself around him? "I thought I could do this with you, could work with you like any other colleague, but I—"

"Please, Kate. I'm sorry I ever touched you," he said. "Believe me, it was the last thing on my mind, and I swear it won't happen again."

"How can I trust that, if you're just going to say you *forgot* again the next time?" Her mother's key ring jangled as she ripped it from her pocket, her feet already pointed toward the door. "The way you've forgotten lots of things, apparently."

"If you have something to say, just go ahead and say it," he challenged. "That is, if you have the guts to."

"Oh, I have guts to spare. That's never been my problem, and you know it," she said. "What I don't have is the will to waste my breath—or another minute or another tear—on you."

Chapter 10

Later that afternoon, Hayden was duct-taping the fractured pot of his dead cactus and trying to ignore the ever-present headache when he heard the death march theme playing from his favorite classic science fiction movie.

Grimacing at the sound of his secretary's ringtone, he cast one final look at the only gift she'd ever given him before making an effort to banish all traces of dread from his voice. "Good afternoon, Mrs. Hobbs," he said, mindful that after more than four years in office, she still hadn't invited him to call her Eva, the way the former sheriff had.

As usual, Mrs. Hobbs didn't bother wasting time with anything as inconsequential as a greeting. "That Clayton was expressly *told* I didn't want you to be troubled at all today. And yet, what do you imagine the first thing is he suggested to the gentleman who'd just traveled here all the way from Tennessee regarding the Kessler investigation?"

"Deputy Yarborough probably asked if he'd mind accompanying him out to my place to be interviewed," Hayden answered, eager to meet Nicolas Kessler's boss and friend as soon as possible, "because that's precisely what I asked him to do."

"But you're just home from the hospital yesterday—you're resting." Mrs. Hobbs's tone made it an order rather than an observation.

Reminding himself he was the one who gave the orders—at least in theory—Hayden said, "I've been resting all day, in the dark, practically *drowning* in all the nothing that I'm doing." He'd had little to distract him from the throbbing in his head and his frustration over the way his visit with Kate had ended.

"Except that you've called me at least three times to read your e-mails to you," she reminded him, her voice bringing to mind her unnaturally stiff posture and disapproving pucker, "very much at the expense of my own work."

"But who else would I trust to do it?" It was true, but Hayden had never realized how pathetically hollow it made his life seem. Especially since, during that brief span when he and Kate had actually been cooperating, he'd gotten a taste of how things might work between them—if they could ever forget how much they hated each other.

A thought pulsed with his pounding head: *You damned well don't hate her, you idiot... That's half your trouble and you know it.*

Pushing it down, he said to Mrs. Hobbs's harrumph: "As I told you before, I very much appreciate your help."

"I hope you don't believe I called to hear your gushing, Hayden. I simply want my department in good order. Which begins with you getting the rest you need, not attempting to conduct an investigation from your sickbed. So I ask you, please, tell Clayton you have every confidence that he can handle witness interviews while you're recuperating—"

"Thanks for the concern, *Eva*," Hayden said, deciding that if she felt free to call every younger department employee by his or her first name, she could darned well expect the same form of address. "I know it comes from a good place. But there's one thing we need to get straight. For all the respect I have for your know-how and for everything you've done for me and Sheriff Turner, this isn't *your* department to run. It's mine, at least until the voters of this county decide otherwise, which means the staff is mine to supervise, not yours—so please quit terrorizing my chief deputy and let him follow orders from his actual boss in peace."

"If that's what you prefer," she said, in the subarctic tones of a woman contemplating rigging his office chair with explosives.

Wondering if there would be enough left of him to bury, he nonetheless committed. "I absolutely do."

"Then I'll get back to compiling my monthly report," she added crisply, "since I presume you'll be too occupied to keep me from finishing my own tasks in a timely manner any longer."

Once she'd disconnected—not bothering with a goodbye—he downed a couple more headache tablets before briefly inspecting the cactus to see if it looked any better after last night's soaking. Still sad and brown, he noticed, and it remained furred with dust, the dead fly still stuck among its spines like a monument to poor housekeeping.

Disgusted with himself for caring, he grabbed his sunglasses and marched outside with it and headed for the trash bin on the side of the house. Before he left the porch, however, he spotted Clayton's patrol unit, a creaky gray Explorer that Hayden was praying wouldn't literally fall apart before he scraped together the budget to replace it. It was followed by a full-size sedan, a black Lincoln rental car that had already picked up a film from the roads and pollen out here.

Hayden set the duct-taped pot under the porch railing and headed over as Tim Spaulding emerged from the driver's side. A deeply tanned white male with a slim, streamlined build that reminded Hayden of a competitive bicyclist, he had short, thinning, dark hair and serious blue eyes. He looked sharp but out of place here, in an eye-catching royal-blue-and-white golf shirt, black pants and a belt and shoes that Hayden imagined cost more than he'd spent on clothing in the last five years.

Approaching, Hayden introduced himself, offering him a hand and thanking the man for coming. "Normally, I'd be meeting you at my office, but—"

"Your deputy explained, something about doctor's orders. It's fine. Tim Spaulding, Spaulding and Associates." He followed up the declaration with a solid handshake.

"I wanted to personally tell you how sorry I am to hear about your employee—and I understand he was a personal friend as well."

"For almost twenty years, yes." Spaulding shifted his gaze, but not quickly enough to hide the fact that his eyes were watering. "I can't believe— It's unimaginable, that this is happening to Nic and Ada and their family. So whatever I can do, however I can help you bring whoever did this to justice—"

"I appreciate that," Hayden said as the breeze rippled over the meadow adjacent to his house.

Clayton belatedly emerged from his Explorer. "Sorry, Sheriff. I've got a call from the rescue people that they can meet me at the accident site, about that matter you wanted me to prioritize."

As thunder murmured in the distance, Hayden said, "You'd better head on out there, then, before the weather turns. I've got this."

Clayton started to turn away before stopping himself and pulling a folded note from his shirt pocket. "Oh. Almost forgot this. Investigator Robinson called back from Memphis and left some information you'd requested."

Though he was surprised Robinson had called the office instead of using his cell to return his own earlier call, Hayden thanked Clayton and pocketed the paper to read when he had a private moment.

As Clayton returned to his unit, Hayden invited Spaulding into his kitchen, where he offered him coffee, water or one of the sodas he had on hand.

"Water would be great, thanks," Spaulding told him as he claimed one of the chairs at the kitchen table Hayden had just indicated.

Hayden brought them each a bottle before grabbing a yellow legal pad and fine-line marker and took the seat across from Spaulding. He didn't expect to be able to take detailed notes, but he hoped to at least jot a few key phrases to remind him of important points.

"Please, can you tell me anything about Ada's condition?" The skin around Spaulding's eyes crinkled with emotion. "I tried to get someone at the hospital to talk to me, but I'm sure you know how they are about patient privacy, and they're saying she can't have visitors at all."

"She wouldn't be able to speak with you," Hayden said gently as he pulled out his cell phone. "They're hoping she'll be well enough for surgery soon."

"My wife wanted to come, too, to sit with her and see what she could do to help the children. But our son has special needs. There's no way we could both leave him, and pulling him out of his own routine is…" Spaulding raised his palms, a look of helpless frustration crossing his thin face.

"I'm sure your friends would understand," Hayden said before asking permission to record their talk to help him refer back to any details he might need for his investigation.

Once Spaulding agreed, Hayden started the app and officially identified their names, the date and time and the participants, since he planned to have Mrs. Hobbs transcribe the recording later. He then asked Spaulding about his business and the work Nicolas Kessler had done for him.

"In the fifteen years we've been in business, we've established ourselves as one of the highest-rated CPA firms in Memphis, specializing in corporate solutions and tax planning."

"But not only corporations, right? I understand Mr. Kessler had recently been auditing nonprofits?" Hayden asked.

"They're not as lucrative from our standpoint." A frown flitted across Spaulding's face. "But Nic convinced me that working with charitable organizations, offering them a reduced rate, would offer us some real benefits in terms of community goodwill and getting our name in front of the type of people who tend to sit on those groups' boards."

"Makes sense," Hayden said, jotting the word *charities* in large, block letters on his notepad.

"I thought so at first, too, and then he started doing outreach, offering educational programs to help these groups navigate regulations so they don't get themselves into hot water, and sure enough, many of these nonprofits came to us for audits and other work, which they tended to want Nic to handle since they knew him. My assistant's putting together a list of his clients over the past six months for you."

"I'd appreciate that," Hayden said. "But I don't understand. What was the problem? It sounds as if he accomplished exactly what he set out to do."

"It would've been fine if it had led to business or corporate referrals." Spaulding turned up a palm. "Instead, I found out that Nic was offering ridiculously lowball rates to shoestring local animal rescue groups, just because he knew they'd had a ton of vet bills lately and a flat-out *free* audit to another outfit because he was all gung ho over their spay-and-neuter efforts." He snorted and shook his head, reminding Hayden of Mac when he was exasperated with one of his twins.

"I take it that was it for you."

"Listen, I've always loved Nic's big heart, but I told him, you can't start donating all your time like this, or before you turn around, it'll spread like wildfire that we're the place to come with hard-luck stories." Spaulding sighed. "Sure enough, pretty soon we were swamped with requests from charities left and right, practically down to the Advocates for Left-handed Armadillos, asking about our firm's pro bono program. *Pro bono*, can you imagine, for a firm our size? I had to have Nic set them all straight, forward everyone an explanation of our corporate rates and business-oriented mission until they finally quit asking."

Hayden circled the word *charities* on his notepad before drawing a slash through it. "So how did this go over with Mr. Kessler?"

"Nic was furious, said I'd taken all his community reputation-building efforts and set fire to them with that money-grubbing document I'd made him send out. But the two of us go way back, all the way to when we were fraternity brothers in college." Spaulding's eyes gleamed. "He blew up at me, and I blew up at him back, and then we went out for a couple of beers later, the way we always have."

"And he was all right after that?"

"I thought so, especially after I reminded him we were both working toward the same goal, opening up the Nashville branch, which I sincerely hoped he'd head up for me—if we could meet the earnings goals we'd established for the remaining quarters of this year."

"And this was what he wanted? A chance to call the shots in Nashville?"

"He sure seemed motivated. He spent the next few weeks wrapping up his charity stuff so he'd be able to focus strictly on our bottom line. He even mentioned how excited Ada and the girls were about the coming move— And then..."

Spaulding sighed and muttered, his gaze glued to the table. "Why the hell'd I let him go? Why didn't I demand more of an explanation? He was my *friend* first, not just some employee..."

"What happened?"

Spaulding drank from his water, making an obvious effort to pull himself together.

Hayden jotted *Nashville* on his legal pad.

"Everything seemed fine. Fine enough that Nic and Ada and the girls had come to a backyard get-together at our place afterward to celebrate our little guy's birthday."

"At this party, did either of the Kesslers mention any issues?" Hayden asked him. "A falling-out with an old friend or neighbor, say, or someone else they might be having trouble with."

Spaulding shook his head. "We didn't get too much of a chance to talk, since we had other guests that day, too, but they seemed perfectly fine. And as far as I could tell, they normally got along with just about everyone."

His use of the qualifier "just about" got Hayden's attention. Reminded of one of the questions he'd asked PD Investigator Robinson, he pulled Clayton's message from his pocket and unfolded it. After blinking a couple of times and squinting, he was able to make out an answer to his request for the name of Ada Kessler's only blood relation.

It prompted him to ask, "What about Cal Thorley, Ada's brother?"

With a sound of disgust, Spaulding asked, "That guy? I can't imagine anyone not clashing with him, from what Nic's told me. All the years she was helping their father through his cancer treatments, Cal kept railing about how every medical treatment was some scheme for the medical community to siphon off the estate to rob them of their inheritance."

"So did Nic figure he was a conspiracy theorist or just a greedy jackass?"

"A little of both, but the father definitely didn't take kindly to it. When he did finally die a couple of years back, the family found out that he'd left everything to Ada. But that's really no surprise, since she was always there for him, while Cal and his father couldn't stand to be in the same room together."

"Is that when Ada's brother quit speaking to her?"

"After a lot of name-calling and threats of lawsuits," Spaulding explained. "He accused her of manipulating their father for her own financial gain."

"Just how much gain?" Hayden asked, running a thumb along his jawline.

"Hardly enough to sneeze at, after the medical and funeral costs were settled. Certainly not the kind of money anyone would bother killing over, if that's what you're thinking."

"Anyone like you and I, you mean," said Hayden, since he'd personally known of several sad instances where lives had been taken over amounts that would seem trivial to many. In this particular situation, however, wounded pride might prove enough of a motivation. Well, that and extreme hatred for and jealousy of the sibling who'd come out ahead.

But could this Cal Thorley hate his sister enough to try to wipe out her entire family? Maybe he'd thought there could be a financial windfall in that as well for some reason.

Looking to his list again, Hayden wrote the word *Beneficiaries*, thinking it would be smart to figure out who would gain financially from the Kesslers' deaths…other than any surviving children of the union.

If Cal had intended for Hazel and Lottie to survive at all…

Thinking of another question, Hayden asked, "Did Nicolas ever mention either of them being worried that Cal might do them physical harm at any time—or did he say anything to you about possibly buying a handgun for protection?"

"A gun? Nic? I'd be surprised. He once mentioned to me that Ada was dead set against having them around the house because of the children. But as far as I could tell, her brother was more of a thorn in their sides than a threat, especially with him living out of state."

"You haven't had any contact with him, have you,

since the family's disappearance?" Hayden asked. "Just to let him know what happened, I mean."

Spaulding shook his head in answer. "I didn't even know his last name until just now when you told me, and I wouldn't have had any idea how to reach him."

"So you didn't enter the home after the family disappeared, looking for phone numbers of anywhere they might be staying?"

His color deepening, Spaulding said, "I called the police. I thought I'd better, under the circumstances."

"Why?" Hayden asked him, simply and directly.

Spaulding looked away, only for a moment, before drawing an audible breath and meeting Hayden's eye again. "Because suddenly, last week, at the end of an ordinary-seeming Tuesday, everything between us shifted."

"How so?"

Huffing out a breath, Spaulding said, "Nic waltzes into my office and announces that he's taking some personal time—all of his accrued vacation. We're talking about six weeks, just as tax season is really starting to heat up."

"And you allowed him to?" Maybe it was guilt that was eating at him now.

"I couldn't." Spaulding threw up his hands. "And what's more, he had to know it would create a huge burden on everyone in the office. If he could've just waited until we were past our major deadlines, I told him I'd be glad to give him the time."

"That doesn't seem so unreasonable."

"Tax season's sacred in our line of work. He should've known exactly how I'd answer."

"So how did he take it?"

"He was frantic, claimed I didn't understand. So I told him, 'I want to, Nic. What's happening? Is something going on with you and Ada?'"

"What was his answer?"

"He told me if I really gave a damn about him, I would quit badgering him about why and just let him go, right then."

"So what did you do?"

"Realized that I'd allowed friendship to blind me and chosen the wrong man to head the Nashville branch, for starters. I couldn't possibly trust someone so erratic with the future of our business."

Hayden ringed and drew a slash through the second word written on his list. "I see. Did you tell him that?"

Spaulding shook his head. "He was way too worked up right then. I decided it could wait until he worked out whatever the hell was bugging him. So I told him to go ahead, to take a short vacation, but to be back bright and early by this past Monday morning…"

Spaulding looked particularly haunted as he looked up and added in a strangled voice, "Or not to bother coming back at all."

The following morning, as Hayden rolled into the Mc-Clafferty driveway in his sheriff's department Tahoe, which one of his deputies had dropped by his house the preceding afternoon, he realized that driving even this short distance had been a terrible mistake. Though he'd worn his sunglasses despite the low cloud layer and donned his backup Western hat to shade his eyes as well, the act of focusing on the road while the SUV was in motion had his head throbbing already and his stomach threatening a rebellion.

But he was here now, parked in front of the house, sweating through the button-front Western shirt he'd donned with jeans in an attempt to look respectable while returning Rita McClafferty's clean dishes in her insulated container. At least that had been the excuse that he'd come armed with for heading over when he'd woken up this morning feeling better than he had since he had been injured. Well enough, he'd decided, to personally see to the interviews he couldn't afford to put off any longer—not after the dialogue with Tim Spaulding the previous afternoon and his call back to follow up with Lamar Robinson from the Memphis PD afterward.

And then there had been the news he'd gotten just this morning, news he wanted to share with Kate personally.

When Rita McClafferty stepped out onto the front porch, her arms crossed over her chest, Hayden inwardly braced himself, wondering what, if anything, Kate had told her mother after she'd come home from his place yesterday. Nothing good, he suspected, since he could all but feel the daggers bouncing off him from her glare.

Or maybe Kate hadn't said anything, and Rita was still holding on to the same grudge she'd been nursing for years. Blaming him for compounding one of the worst days of her and her husband's life with the shocking news that their daughter had been pregnant—and somehow hiding the fact from them for more than five months.

"Please, you have to let me see her." He heard his younger voice, cracking with desperation, echoing across the years. "Your daughter's carrying my baby. We're going to get married—"

"The hell you are," her father had told him, his redeyed wife at his side. "There is no child, not anymore, and there's damned well not going to be any wedding. Now get out. We don't ever want to see your face again—and neither does our daughter."

For a moment, Hayden had to close his eyes as pain pulsed through his center, through a part of him still as raw and bloody as the day he'd held on to the simple band of gold he still kept hidden in his wallet. He'd been telling himself he was only carrying it to get rid of the thing the next time he happened to be in a town that had a pawnshop for years. Slowing his breathing, he reminded himself that day was long over and that Kate's parents must have been as devastated as he'd been after they'd all watched a metal gate meant to be left open suddenly swing shut directly in front of her horse as Cloverleaf had been rocketing down the alley. Too close to stop, the mare had—in the midst of a full gallop—desperately attempted a jump at the last possible moment. Caught at the wrong part of her stride, she had instead twisted her body, flinging Kate into the gate like a rag doll before crashing down on top of her.

Shoving down the most horrific memory of his life, Hayden blinked hard as he turned to grab the insulated bag out of his vehicle. He then pasted on what he hoped would pass for a polite smile—since he absolutely needed Kate's mother's cooperation—and left the Tahoe to meet her as she came stalking toward him.

"If you're here to upset my daughter again, you can darned well turn around and—" she started before cutting herself off to study his face. "Are you...unwell? You look—you look almost green underneath that hat."

"I, um, may have gotten a little ahead of myself, figuring I might be okay to make the short drive to bring back your containers. And to thank you for the delicious breakfast. There was plenty left to feed me this morning, too."

"Oh, for goodness' sake," she said, waving off his gratitude. "It would've just ended up going to the chickens otherwise. I always make too much. And there was no need for you to make yourself sicker trying to drive over. One of us could've picked up the containers. But you knew that, didn't you?"

"I suppose I did," he admitted. "But then I wouldn't get a chance to chat with you in person."

"Because that's always so pleasant for both of us," she said, a wry quirk of her lips drawing a smile from him, too, as he offered her the pack by its handles.

She accepted it, telling him bluntly, "I won't have you upsetting her, stirring things up. She's better off forgetting, moving on with her life."

He stood there for a moment, while a mockingbird's sweet song floated across the nearby pasture. "The thing is, though, none of us really *can* forget, can we? Maybe that's the whole trouble with trying to board up an old house with the bodies moldering inside."

"I don't know how hard you banged that head of yours, to talk that sort of nonsense. What matters now is my Kate's *happy* with her new job. Her new life, away from here, from you."

"I can't imagine why you think I'd want to do anything to jeopardize that. I only mean to get this case solved, not try to—"

"Is there some kind of problem out here?" Kate asked, her eyes narrowed as she stepped out on the porch, with Thunder trailing just behind her.

"I was just returning your containers, and thanking your mother for the food, I promise," Hayden told her as Rita's dog went to stand guard in front of his mistress.

"So why do you look like you're about to keel over. Did you— You *drove* yourself here, didn't you?"

"It's, what? A quarter mile?" he defended. "As I believe you pointed out yesterday while you were tooling around one-handed."

"At least I had a functional, unscrambled brain to do it with."

"Maybe we ought to take you back to the hospital and get a second opinion on that, considering how touchy you've been acting."

"Oh, good grief," her mother grumbled, her free hand resting on Thunder's neck. "Sometimes, I think you two actually *enjoy* fussing at each other. I'm going back to the dining room to check if the girls are finished making those get-well cards for their mother. Then I'll see if I can interest them in letting me lead them around on Moonlight."

"Lottie, especially, will be so excited," Kate said. "I was talking it up with them earlier and promising we'd take pictures to show their mom when she feels better."

Looking at Hayden, her mother asked, "Have you had any further word on her condition?"

He nodded before glancing at the front door.

Apparently remembering how Hazel had listened in before, Kate took the hint and stepped back to carefully close it.

"Thanks," he said, lowering his voice. "She's breathing on her own, which I'm told is a good sign, but she's still not strong enough for them to go in and remove the bullet. If they can get that out and infection doesn't get her, she could have a full recovery."

"Those sounds like a couple of pretty big ifs," Kate said.

"It could be a long road back, according to the doctor."

"But we can't underestimate the motivation to get well she has, living right inside our walls." Rita nodded back in the direction of the house. "So let's not forget for a single moment how precious these children are to her."

Deciding it was now or never, Hayden asked her,

"Would you mind if Kate and I were the ones who took the girls out riding?"

"What?" Rita shook her head, obviously confused. "But you're not well at all—and Kate can't possibly, with her hand."

"I'm feeling better now that the truck's quit moving, and I'll do all the saddling and lifting, promise," he said. "I'd just like the chance to get to know them, and this could be a perfect distraction—"

"So you can interrogate them," she finished, her voice as cold as dry ice.

"If it makes you feel any better, I left all my bright lights and rubber hoses back at the house," he said.

"There's no need to be flip," Kate scolded.

"Just trying to lighten the mood a little," he said, deciding his timing needed work. "But I'm afraid this is serious business. You see, just before coming over, I received word that we've gotten a hit on the dead shooter's prints from the FBI's database. I wanted to let you know personally, Kate."

"Who was he?" she asked, all signs of annoyance evaporating at this news about the man she'd shot.

"His name was Henry Bonner—though he was better known among his criminal associates as H-Bomb. Back in Tennessee, he's got a rap sheet a mile long—grand larceny, auto theft, conspiracy to commit fraud."

"What would a man like that want with the Kesslers?" Kate asked.

"That's what I'm hoping to find out here," he admitted, "if I can convince the girls to talk a little about the things they've seen and heard."

Rita shook her head. "You can't honestly think those innocent children would have actually known a man like you're describing? Or that their parents were involved in criminal activities? Didn't they both have respectable jobs?"

"Outward appearances can hide a lot. And kids can't help what they've been exposed to," Hayden said.

"I can definitely attest to that," Kate said, a look passing over her face that made him ache for the things she must have witnessed in her early years.

"Of course," Kate's mother said. "It's just difficult to imagine that even if their parents were wrapped up in something illegal, the children would've known anything about it."

"You might be surprised," Kate said. "When you're growing up in tough situations, you tend to notice even tiny details that might give you an edge."

Her mother reached up, briefly touching a lock of Kate's red hair. "I wish you'd never known that."

"It's okay now, because of you and Dad," Kate assured her. "And we did talk about why it was so important for Hayden to question the girls. I've seen him handle delicate situations before and know he's the right person to do it. And this way, I can be there, too, to end the conversation if I see they're getting upset."

"I *will* be as gentle and patient as I possibly can, I promise," Hayden assured Rita.

Ignoring him, she kept her focus on her daughter, saying, "You promise me, then, Kate, you'll act as their advocate, and don't forget that you're not still in law enforcement?"

Kate's gaze flicked to Hayden's, her brown eyes pleading with him not to bring up yesterday's swearing in.

He nodded in agreement.

"I give you my word," Kate told her mother.

"Good. Then I'll give you a chance to groom and saddle Moonlight while I get them changed into jeans for riding and send them out in about ten minutes," Rita told them before fixing her sternest look on Hayden. "But I'm telling you right now, if *any* of my girls come back with tearstains, I'll be holding *you* accountable."

As Hayden led Moonlight to a hitching post just outside the tack room, Kate noticed how troubled he looked. With the sun burning through the cloud layer, she wondered if the afternoon's brightness would be more than he could manage.

"Are you doing okay, Hayde? If your head's bothering you too much, I can drive you home, and we can do this later."

"It's not that," he said, patting the mare's neck before tying her to the post and adjusting his hat to better shade his face. "I was just thinking. There's nothing I'll ever be able to say or do to change your mother's mind about me, is there?"

"I don't know what to tell you." Reaching up to brush the gray back, Kate said, "Mom's generous and loving with everybody else, but there's this association in her mind, between you and everything that happened that day."

"It was a terrible time for all of us," he said, pain shading his voice. Pain she would have thought he'd put behind him years before. "Especially you, I'm sure. I only wish I'd done things differently back then. Fought harder to—"

"To be honest, I don't really remember any of it." She spoke quickly, her words clipped as she focused on brushing the dust from the mare's hide. "They had me on so many painkillers— The doctors told me later it can play havoc with a person's memory."

"So you don't recall the accident itself?"

"The last thing I remember is you kissing me for luck just before I mounted Cloverleaf for my run," she said, heart twisting at the memory of the sweetness of that final kiss—and last time she had climbed aboard her beloved palomino, whose own injuries that day had been beyond Kate's father's—or any vet's—capacity to heal. "I don't remember anything about that ride. I've heard, of course, what happened—how that new greenhorn had misunderstood the instructions he'd been given about keeping that gate open."

"I wanted to kill the idiot," Hayden admitted, his words roughened by long-steeped anger. "If my brothers hadn't held me back…"

"It wouldn't have changed anything, and the guy was practically a kid himself. He was devastated over his mistake, I understand, nearly suicidal. I've long since forgiven him. I had to."

"But never me," Hayden said bitterly. "No more than your mother has. Isn't that right?"

At the challenge, her heart skipped a beat, and Moonlight shifted, stamping a rear hoof. Stepping back to avoid a bruised toe, Kate said, "I *do* remember you tried to talk me out of riding that day."

"Not hard enough. I damned well should have forced the issue. If I had, you'd have never—never lost—"

He stopped himself there, apparently unable to finish. She realized she'd been wrong all these years, believing that day had cost him nothing. But he *had* walked away from the wreckage of her life. There was no forgetting that part.

Still, she took a deep breath, shaking her head. "Let's not talk about it anymore, okay? The girls will be out soon."

Hayden pulled a hoof pick from the tack box. "Let me clean her hooves, and then I'll get her saddled."

As they finished grooming the mare, Hayden told her he'd been disappointed to hear that no GPS tracker had been found anywhere on the Kessler car. "I suspect if one was even there, it was probably knocked off and plunged down through all those trees into the canyon. The odds of finding it now are too low to justify the manpower for a search, especially when tracing the thing's origin was such a long shot in the first place."

"It's too bad it didn't pan out, but I think you're right about it being unrealistic to imagine you'd ever find a tracker in that canyon—and that's if it wasn't taken off the vehicle by whoever shot the Kesslers in the first place."

"I did get a possible lead, though," Hayden said, "on someone with a grudge against the family." He filled her in on Ada Kessler's brother, Cal Thorley, and his threats.

"Interesting," Kate said. "But how long ago did this inheritance issue come up?"

"A couple of years back."

"Seems like a long span to let something like this brew before acting," she said.

"Unless the wound's festered over time, or the brother's suddenly having money troubles that have turned up the heat on his resentment," Hayden told her as he settled the saddle pad on the horse's back. "And when I finally got to talk with Investigator Robinson in Memphis again late yesterday, he told me he's still been unable to reach Thorley, even after leaving repeated messages."

"Maybe he hates his sister so much, he's beyond caring what's happened to her and her family."

Hayden lifted the saddle onto Moonlight's back. "It's certainly possible. But at Robinson's request, local law enforcement, out in Oregon where Thorley lives, went by his address to see if they could personally make contact. The house was locked up tight. Neighbors say they haven't seen him in days, at least. Weeks, maybe. He wasn't the friendly type, by all accounts. And he was living on disability, so he didn't have a job to go to or anyone to miss him if he didn't show."

She frowned. "What kind of disability? Do you know?" Maybe it was something that would exclude him as a suspect.

"Psychiatric, according to the local authorities. Whatever his exact problem, it made him extremely paranoid at times, so they were aware of his tendency to call and report his neighbors for spying on him or plotting against the government."

"One of those, eh?" she said, having encountered similar citizens during her career in law enforcement. "But he wasn't violent, was he?" Most people with mental illnesses weren't, she knew, in spite of the stigma surrounding their condition.

"He doesn't have a record of assault, although he's had a handful of misdemeanor charges for menacing and harassment," said Hayden as he tightened the cinch.

"Sounds like a guy with serious anger issues," she said. "But one who's prone to verbal abuse instead of physical acts against his target."

"It's altogether possible that with enough time to fixate on his rage and jealousy toward his sister, whatever self-restraint he had broke down."

"Good theory, but can you really imagine a paranoid loner like Cal Thorley being involved in any way with a Tennessee thug like Henry 'H-Bomb' Bonner?" she said, naming the man she'd shot near Heartbreak Ridge.

"It does seem unlikely," Hayden agreed. "But crime can make for odd bedfellows, so I'm not ruling anything out. Including Nicolas Kessler's boss, Tim Spaulding. Clayton brought him by my place yesterday to offer any help he could give. It was an interesting conversation."

Hayden gave her a brief rundown on what had been discussed.

"So what was your personal take on the man?" Kate asked once he had finished. "You don't think this conflict between him and his friend about the charity work could've blown up into something bigger, do you?"

"Spaulding's definitely focused on the bottom line," Hayden said, "but he seemed genuinely upset by what had happened to his friend—and sick with regret that he didn't stop Nic from leaving when he had the chance to."

"He had no idea why the Kesslers had to leave in such a hurry?"

"None at all. Apparently, he decided that the way Kessler was acting, it'd be safer to press him on the issue after he came back. Only now he has to live with the knowledge that his friend never will."

Kate felt for the man, having to deal with that regret. "So will he be sticking around or heading back to Memphis?"

"He's staying the night in Kerrville, he said. He'd hoped to see Ada, to see what he might be able to do for her before he has to fly back home tomorrow, but I've let him know that won't be possible at this point."

"Did he ask to see the children? You said the families socialized together, so they'd know him pretty well, I guess."

"He didn't mention it. Maybe he imagines that seeing a familiar face might just upset them."

"He could be right about that," Kate said, supposing it was probably better to allow the girls to become more secure in their new situation than reminding them of a past they couldn't return to. After Hayden made an adjustment to Moonlight's cinch strap, she noticed that he came up frowning when he straightened.

"What's the matter?" she asked. "Did bending over like that make your head worse?"

"It's not that." He readjusted his silver hat. "I was just thinking that you know who else might want to avoid facing a pair of newly bereaved children?"

"Who?"

"A man who's got some reason to feel responsible for that family's grief."

Chapter 11

Though Lottie begged for one more ride on Moonlight, Hazel saw Kate glance at Sheriff Hayden—who acted really nice even though it kind of bugged Hazel that his eyes were hidden behind his dark glasses. But at least he hadn't gotten mad, the way that some adults would, when she and Lottie hadn't wanted to talk about the scary things that had happened with their family, or even much of anything at all that had taken place before they came here.

Kate, who was holding the horse's reins, shook her head and told Lottie, "Sorry, but it's getting pretty hot and I think we've all had enough sun for one afternoon. Moonlight's probably tired, too. She's not as young as she once was, so we'll let her rest up for the next time."

"Can I ride again tomorrow? Please!" Lottie asked, sounding like such a baby that Hazel rolled her eyes.

But Kate only smiled at Lottie. "We'll have to see. I promise you, though, I'll do my best to make it happen as soon as possible, especially if Sheriff Hayden would be willing to help out with the saddling again."

One side of his mouth curved up. "I'm pretty sure I'll be able to fit that into my busy schedule…as long as your big sister wants to come, too."

"Of course, she'll come," Lottie insisted, before sending a pleading look in her direction. "Won't you, Hazel?"

Hazel shoved her hands into her pants pockets and said, "I'll think about it," her stomach squirming again when she thought about the sheriff's questions. She knew things Lottie didn't. Things she'd never say in front of her little sister, who'd kept her up half the night crying for their mom and dad.

"That's great," Kate said. "Why don't you girls run inside, wash up a bit and get something cold to drink? Tell Miss Rita we'll be putting up Moonlight here, and then I'm going to drive Sheriff Hayden back home in the Jeep."

"I appreciate the thought, but you don't need to do that," he told her.

She was already shaking her head. "Oh, just let me take you. I can see you're hot and tired, too, and your truck will be just fine here. We'll get it over to you later."

As the two of them led Moonlight toward the barn, Hazel and Lottie headed back inside the house, where they found Miss Rita in the kitchen, cutting up some peeled potatoes. Taking one look at the girls, she stopped what she was doing and said, "You look hot. How about some nice, cold water?"

"Yes, please," Hazel and Lottie told her.

Once she had pushed a glass of cold water into each girl's hands, Miss Rita asked if they'd had fun.

Hazel quickly gulped down half her water.

"I never wanted to come back inside." Her sister's

eyes were sparkling with excitement. "We were having so much fun. Miss Kate said I'm a natural!"

"A natural? Oh, my, that sounds very special." Miss Rita was smiling in that way that Hazel knew adults did when they wanted to make a kid feel good, the way Hazel ached to remember her mom or dad doing when they'd looked at her.

"Sheriff Hayden said we looked just like real cowgirls," Lottie boasted. "But I think he mostly meant me because Hazel kept slouching and not paying attention whenever Kate was telling us how to hold our feet and stuff."

Lottie cast a superior look in her direction, which Hazel answered with her fiercest glare before noticing Miss Rita studying her.

"And what about you, Hazel? Did you have a good time out there?"

She shrugged. "It was okay, I guess. Kinda sweaty, though. And stinky." She crinkled her nose, just like one of those prissy girls she'd always laughed at.

"Who cares about some dumb smell?" Lottie challenged. "Since when did you ever worry about a little dirt anyway? Moonlight's as *beautiful* as a unicorn! I would ride her every day if I could! And sleep right next to her in her stall!"

"That's because you already love it here," Hazel accused, abruptly furious with her sister for being a dumb little kid with no idea what was going on. "If you had your way, you'd forget all about home and live here with the stupid horse and the stinky chickens. You're probably already half hoping that Mom will hurry up and die just so you can!"

Lottie's blue eyes filled, her face going flame red, which made her freckles seem to disappear. Instead of bursting into the tears Hazel was already dreading, she did the very last thing her sister was expecting, balling up her fists and shrieking before flying at her in a fury.

"The older one knows something," Hayden said as Kate started her mom's Jeep. Though his head had gotten worse from being out in the heat and sunlight, he was doing his best to keep his mind focused on his still-unanswered questions.

"Hazel?" Kate asked. "I'm not so sure about that. I think she may just be conflicted, that's all. Feeling as if liking anything about this place is a betrayal of her parents. I remember giving my early fosters grief, pretending to hate everything in the hope that if I were difficult enough, my bio-mom would be forced to get her act together and come get me back."

Hayden snapped his seat belt into place. "I'm sorry you had to go through that."

She switched on the AC before putting the car in gear. "I'm not looking for any kind of pity, just trying to explain that it can take a long time—sometimes years, or even forever, for a kid to come around."

"Not Lottie." He smiled, thinking of the younger girl. "You've got that one eating out of your hand already—or you and Moonlight, I should say."

Kate smiled, too. "I'm so glad I was able to make her happy. To help her forget what's going on in her life, at least for the moment."

"She definitely looked transported."

"Seeing her light up like that made me remember what it felt like, the first time Mom and Dad opened my eyes to a world I'd never imagined existed. A horse, and a little attention, can save a girl's life, Hayden."

"You're great with them, you know," he said, pained

to realize it was true, and what an excellent mother this fierce—and fiercely loving—woman could have been. And still might be, if she'd ever risk opening up her heart again. It was not too late for her yet.

But in all the time he'd been able to observe Kate since the accident, he'd rarely known her to date any other man for more than a few weeks at a time before coming up with some excuse to drop him. *Just like me with other women*, he thought, for the first time wondering if his independent streak hadn't just been a result of watching Mac go through hell after his first wife's drowning. Maybe instead, Hayden realized, he and Kate had broken something in each other years before…

Did that mean they might be capable of fixing each other, too—if they could manage to stop themselves from repeating the same mistakes of the past?

"All these years, I've been afraid," Kate admitted as she backed the Jeep to turn it around, "that I'd be like my birth mom or her creepy relations, that being lousy with kids was encoded in my DNA—imprinted on me when I was little."

"All I see in you is the same loving support you were surrounded with right here, Kate," he said, fighting to ignore the way the world seemed to swirl around him with the Jeep's movement. "And an eagerness to share the kindness Doc and Rita showed to you."

Her eyes glistened when she glanced his way. "Thanks, Hayde. It's really nice of you to say that, especially after the way I acted toward you."

"What do you mean?" he asked as she drove past the field of bluebonnets, where Moonlight was rolling in a sandy patch of dirt.

"*She* certainly looks happy," Kate remarked, smiling before answering his question. "I meant, the way

I stormed out on you yesterday instead of just talking things through like a reasonable adult. I left you high and dry when I knew you needed more help looking over files on your computer. I swear, I'm not like that with anybody else. It's just, when it comes to you—"

"We lost a child, and we've never talked about it," he said, nausea rising with the motion of her making the turn toward his place.

"A little girl…" Kate said, speaking just above a whisper. "We lost a daughter."

He shook his head, voice cracking as he confessed, "Damn it, Kate, your parents never—they never told me, and I've never dared to ask. They only wanted me out of there, as fast as possible. I've never seen your dad so furious."

"Wasn't that what *you* wanted, too?" she asked. "To get as far away from it, from me, as you could? They said you all but ran out after telling them that you were off the hook—"

"Only after they told *me* I was *never* going to marry you, that you never wanted to see my face again."

He jerked his gaze toward the passenger window, unable to look at her. But he heard her pained gasp, and it combined with a renewed throbbing in his head to hit him like a gut punch.

When she pulled into his driveway, he was opening the Jeep's door before she'd even come to a stop, his bile rising hot and acid.

"Hey!" she warned. "Careful there."

But he was already getting out—too fast—as the SUV jerked to a hard stop. Head spinning with the awkward movement, he stumbled and then fell onto his hands and knees.

Skull pounding, he focused on not vomiting. Before

he understood what was happening, Kate was crouching down beside him, her hand on his arm.

"What on earth were you thinking, jumping out like that?" she demanded, sounding half scared and half angry. "Here, let me help you up."

Rolling away from her, he tried to push himself up. "I can damned well stand myself."

Except it turned out that he couldn't.

Chapter 12

Kate had been on the verge of doing it again, of driving off—on Hayden—when talking about, or even thinking about, their past overwhelmed her. But seeing him go down again pulled her out of her own head, and back into the present, with ruthless efficiency. However complicated her feelings for him were, she wasn't about to leave him lying out in front of his house.

Getting him to his feet wasn't easy, especially without the ability to use her left hand for leverage. Eventually, Kate managed, by having him drape one arm over her shoulders and pushing upward with her legs at the same time he did. Still, he nearly sent them toppling, he was so unstable when they tried to walk.

"I'm going to end up hurting you." He groaned, sweating and shaking with the effort of remaining upright. "Just go ahead and let me fall."

"Not a chance," she told him, though it was all she

could do to keep him on his feet. "I need you to just trust me. Close your eyes, and take small steps. That's right, move with me."

"If I get sick on you—"

"Don't worry about me right now. Just focus on taking another step toward the porch. Like that—and now another. We'll get you inside, and you'll feel so much better."

He blew out an audible breath but complied with her directives, and slowly, they made progress, until they were at the front door.

When he stopped to dig out his keys, he didn't resist when she said, "Let me catch this door," taking them from him and unlocking the dead bolt.

After helping him inside, she nodded toward the living room recliner. "You want the chair, or would the bed be better?"

"As grimy as I am, let's try my chair for right now," he said. "But I think—I think I've got this."

He started to remove his arm from her shoulder, but she said, "We've got a good thing going working together, don't we? So let's not mess this up now."

Once she'd finally gotten him in the recliner and switched on the ceiling fan, Kate breathed a sigh of relief.

Hayden took off his hat and sunglasses, his face flushed as he raked back damp hair. "Sorry about all the sweat. I could use a shower."

"You're not the only one," she admitted, smelling the horse and perspiration on her own clothing, too. "First, let's get some nice, cold water in you. You're probably dehydrated from too much time in the sun."

"Thanks," he said. "If you give me just a minute, I can get it."

"Don't even *think* about getting up from that chair,"

she ordered before heading for the kitchen and opening his fridge. After snagging a couple of bottled waters, she returned to hand him one and then tucked hers under her upper left arm to crack open the top one-handed.

After they'd had a drink, he said, "I hope you didn't strain yourself doing it, but I really appreciate the assist getting inside."

"I'm afraid *you* strained yourself helping *me* with the girls, Hayden. It was clearly too soon for you to be outside like that."

"Maybe so," he admitted. "But I wasn't about to pass up a chance to get some answers about what happened with their parents—for all the good it did me."

"You've laid the groundwork, establishing trust with them. It's about the best you can expect at the moment, considering the trauma they've experienced," she told him. "Now, how about I get you something for your head. Is there an over-the-counter pain med you have on hand? Or maybe something for your stomach?"

Grimacing, he appeared to think it over for a moment. "I think I just need to sit here for a few minutes and make sure this water's going to stay down before I go adding meds to the mix."

Nodding, she said, "I'm going to hang out for a bit, then. Just until I'm sure you're okay."

"You don't have to do that, Kate. I'm sure I'm going to be—"

"Humor me," she said.

His mouth flattened as if he meant to argue, but instead he countered, "All right. If you wouldn't mind checking out a couple of things on the computer for me while I have you here."

"Are you serious?" she asked. "You're not fit right now to do anything but try to feel better."

"You'll be handling all the work. I'll just be giving orders."

She rolled her eyes at that. "I'll tell you what. Rest here for a few minutes while I grab a couple of paper towels from your kitchen. I need to go wash my face and hands in your bathroom."

"Why don't you use a fresh towel and washcloth out of the closet in there? Or, heck, if you want to, take a shower if it'll make you more comfortable."

"Tempting as that offer is, a shower will have to wait," she said, unable to wrap her head around the thought of getting naked in Hayden's private space. She did take the time to wash up as best she could, though. Afterward, she felt a great deal fresher for her efforts, though there was nothing she could do about her clothing at the moment.

When she came back out, she found Hayden missing from his recliner. As she looked for him in his kitchen, he emerged barefoot from a small half bath off the utility room that she hadn't noticed before, pulling a clean T-shirt over his bare torso. For a moment, she was speechless, glimpsing the abs he'd been hiding beneath his uniform shirts all these years. Abs that proved his bachelor lifestyle had to include more workouts and healthy eating than she'd given him credit for.

When she thought about what he could do to her with that hard body, her toes curled inside her shoes before the scent of his soap—and the amused twinkle in his blue eyes—brought her back to her senses. Recovering, she stammered, "Y-you look a whole lot better."

"Feel better, too, for now," he said, raking his fingers through his dark hair to straighten it. "Or better than I did, at least. I was thinking maybe a sandwich would help settle my stomach. You want one? I make a mean PB&J."

"So you're still into those, after all these years?" She

smiled, somehow loving that even as the thirty-six-year-old sheriff of this county, he was in some ways still the boy that she remembered… The boy that she'd first loved and still couldn't help but care for, in spite of all the heartbreak he had brought her.

"Some loves are meant to last forever."

Ignoring the comment, she said, "I'd better pass, this close to dinner. But why don't you park yourself at the table and let me make that sandwich for you? Or I'm betting I could find something more substantial to make you in there."

Complying, he pulled out a chair next to his laptop. "Thanks, but the sandwich sounds just right. Honestly, though, I never figured I'd live to see the day you'd be offering to make me food. Without ground glass in it, anyway."

She snorted. "You never have to ever worry about me doing you in." Opening the pantry, she reached for the peanut butter. "I'd be at the top of everybody's suspect list, so the idea's a nonstarter."

"Actually," Hayden said, a teasing glint in his eyes, "I'm more worried about your mother. You McClafferty women are not to be crossed."

"Mom's way too worried about Hazel and Lottie right now to mess with the man trying to keep them and their mom safe." A growl from Kate's stomach prompted her to pull out an extra slice of bread to make herself a half sandwich after all.

"Thanks for this," Hayden said when she set their plates and napkins on the table a couple of minutes later. "And I see you changed your mind about spoiling your dinner."

"Just don't rat me out to Mom," Kate said, thinking of the chicken she'd seen marinating in her mother's fridge.

"Why would I do that, when we both know she'd only blame me for leading you astray?"

Kate couldn't help but grin at that. "You always were a bad influence."

"That's funny," Hayden said, giving her a sidelong glance as his voice took on a husky rumble. "That's not the way that *I* remember things…"

Though she sensed the danger in it, the faraway look in his eyes still had her asking, "Exactly what is it you're thinking of—or do I even want to know?"

"That day it was just you and me, out near the old dam just down the way from Clearwater Crossing. When you finally untied that little bikini top you'd been tormenting me with all summer."

"Sorry I asked," she said, suddenly transported back to that same heady moment when she'd been intoxicated on stolen kisses and untested feminine power when she'd caught him studying her so longingly on more than one occasion. She'd finally pulled the loose string and let her top float downstream to snag among some tall weeds. She still remembered the warmth of the July sun, shining on her bare breasts, and the sensation when they'd flattened against his strong chest as they'd kissed and touched, standing right there in that cool, clear, waist-deep water. Before they'd moved their explorations to the shoreline a short time later.

"All these years, we've tried pretending that none of it ever happened," he said, the regret in his voice mirroring the pain in his eyes. "I don't know about you, Katie, but that hasn't gone so great for me. And being around you these past few days, cutting up a little, heck, even going toe-to-toe with you has been reminding me that there were good times, too, between us. Times so good that nothing since has ever held a candle to 'em."

* * *

His heart pounding with the risk he'd taken, Hayden left the words hanging. The words he knew might scare her off again. But holding them inside him hadn't been an option, not with the past—and his resurfacing emotions—hanging so thick in the air between them that he could barely draw breath.

"Do you—do you want some milk with yours?" Kate said, her brown eyes damp and her voice nearly breaking. "With your sandwich, I mean. So we can get back to the case and I can make it back home in time for dinner."

Grimacing, he stared at her, tasting disappointment. *Let it go,* he told himself, thinking that just maybe, now that he had opened the door a little wider, she might eventually step through.

And then what? What is it you really want?

One look at her gorgeous face, at the long, red waves he remembered sliding, soft as satin, between his fingers, had arousal stirring—giving him the answer to his questions. Heaven help him, but he wanted *her* again. Maybe he had all along, since her fire, her intelligence and her spirit had imprinted themselves on his heart all those years before.

He wondered if in all the years he'd spent denying it, he'd only been spinning his wheels, wasting his time and the time of basically decent and well-meaning women like Stacey.

Clearly, Kate wasn't on the same page. Most likely it was self-preservation making her shy away from the same heartbreak that he himself had so strenuously avoided repeating up until now.

As if to drive home the point, she asked—more pointedly, this time, "Or would you rather stick with water, Hayden?"

"The water's fine, thanks." He swallowed back his disappointment, telling himself that she was probably doing him a big favor, ignoring the awkward reminiscing of a head-injured man. Even if he knew it hadn't been his concussion talking but his heart, which he damned well ought to keep muzzled. "And I suppose you're right. I wouldn't want to take up too much of your day."

They finished their snack quickly, though every bite threatened to stick in Hayden's throat and he barely tasted any of it. At least he was feeling better, however, as he wiped his hands on his napkin and reached across the table for the laptop.

"Why don't you let me do all that?" Kate asked, setting down her water bottle. "You don't want to do anything to make your headache flare again."

"Believe me, there's no need to remind me," he said grimly. "I'm just unlocking it."

As the screen flashed to life, he turned his face away, wincing at the brightness and the fuzzy text that wavered whenever he tried to focus on it.

"What did I tell you?" she couldn't resist scolding as she stacked their plates out of the way and spun the screen around to face her. "Now what is it I'm looking for?"

"Can you double-click to open up the e-mail program?" he asked.

"I'm in," she said and glanced down. "Before we look at anything else, you have what look to be a handful of work-related e-mails. Would you like me to go through those first?"

"Anything to save me from having to ask Mrs. Hobbs to read those over the phone to me, too."

Kate, whom he knew had faced Mrs. Hobbs's barbs as often as any of the department's deputies, snorted. "I'll bet she makes that loads of fun."

"You know Mrs. Hobbs. Every day is a party."

Kate's smile faded as her fingers danced over the keyboard, far more swiftly than Hayden's usual hunt-and-peck style. "I don't see anything pressing here. Gonzalez wants to switch his shift with Deputy Alvarez two weeks from now so he can take his wife to some out-of-town doctor's appointment."

"Approve that for me, will you?" Hayden said.

Following some rapid-fire tapping, she said, "Done. And you have several notes here from constituents wishing you well after hearing you got banged up." She named various supporters, from a local café owner to a rancher to Amanda Greenville, who'd taken time to write in spite of her own recent troubles.

"I'll ask Mrs. Hobbs to thank them and let them know that I'll be back in my office in a few days."

Kate looked up, her expression sympathetic. "From what I've seen, I'm not sure that's a realistic promise."

"I can't just sit around here. It's like my dad always used to say when my brothers and I were little. You get knocked down, you brush yourself off and shake it off— and don't roll your eyes at me again."

"I'm sure that's generally sage advice whenever one of your brothers knocked you on your butt or a steer stepped on your foot," she said. "But you can't just shake off a head injury because you're some big, tough, macho sheriff."

He puffed up at that. "So you really think I'm a big, tough, macho sheriff?"

She laughed. "A blockheaded one, I *should've* said. It's nice that Amanda would reach out to you, especially considering all she's been through lately. Do you know her well?"

He grimaced. "I'm not sure anybody can really say

they *know* that woman. Seems like she's always been the type to play her cards close to her vest."

"Growing up in foster care will do that to a person…"

Noticing the sadness in Kate's eyes, he shook his head. "You shouldn't feel guilty that you were adopted and she wasn't. None of it was any more your doing than the abuse was that came before the McClaffertys took you in."

"I appreciate the reminder. I just wish I could think of something I could do to help her."

"I know. I've felt the same way. But only Amanda can decide who she wants to let into her life at this point or how much it's worth to her to hold on to her inheritance."

The chiming tone of a new e-mail hitting his inbox caught his attention.

"Hmm," Kate said a few moments later. "This one's from a Sheela Singh at Spaulding and Associates."

"That'll be Nicolas Kessler's office. He promised they would send a list of clients he'd been working with."

"From the looks of it, there are a bunch of files attached, too. Since I know you can't look at these, do you mind if I go ahead and forward this to my e-mail so I can review it in my capacity as a reserve deputy from my mom's? I'm no forensic accountant, of course, but I'll let you know if anything jumps out at me as suspicious."

He nodded gratefully, trusting her eye for detail and discretion. "I'd really appreciate that."

A few moments later, he heard the whooshing tone of the outgoing e-mail. "So what else is it you wanted me to look at for you?"

"Do you see where Deputy Yarborough's forwarded a handful of e-mails from the owner of the stolen ATVs? I believe his last name's Jenkins—"

"Could it be Judkins, maybe?"

"That's it, yes. These were messages from people

expressing an interest in potentially coming to look at them."

"Okay," she said before asking, "So do you want me to read each message to you?"

He shook his head. "I've already had Mrs. Hobbs do that. But she got all flustered when I tried to get her to expand the e-mail header and trace a sender's IP address to try to figure out the location a message was sent from."

Kate laughed. "I can only imagine. Is there any specific message you're particularly interested in tracing?"

"There were a couple, both unsigned, asking for specifics on where the ATVs were located."

"Okay, let me see if I can find— Here's one," she said before looking up at him. "But this is no good. I'm not getting any info beyond Deputy Yarborough's on this… Hmm. On either of them, actually. Anything that might've been there was stripped away by multiple forwardings—or maybe it was never there at all. I recognize the e-mail domain name as one of the more popular ones. I read that they quit sending any of that information because of privacy concerns."

Hayden cursed under his breath. "Just my luck."

"Or maybe the sender disguised it in the first place by sending the message through a virtual private network, if he's savvy that way," she said. "Even if he didn't, he's likely on the move, right? So we're very likely chasing useless information."

"If I had something better to chase right now, don't you think I would be on it? But with the girls all bottled up, Ada Kessler still unconscious, her brother missing and no way to track the second shooter from the canyon—" Hayden said, rising from the table and walking away in pure frustration. "Hell, you might as well head home. I don't want your mother sending a search party."

Looking up sharply, Kate said, "There's no need to bite my head off."

He grimaced. "Sorry for snapping at you, Kate. It's just—being forced to lay low, ask for help with every little thing—it's galling as hell to feel so helpless."

She stood, too. "Believe me, I remember," she said as she carried their plates to the kitchen counter. "After the accident, I was far from a pleasant patient. Anyone I couldn't outright push away, I treated horribly. I could spend a lifetime trying to make it up to my poor mother."

"I should've been there." He followed her into the kitchen, regret welling up like blood from a wound that should have long since healed over. "I should've fought harder for you..."

"I only wish—" She turned around to face him, looking startled to see how close he stood behind her.

When she splayed her hand across the center of his chest, he thought she meant to push him back, to give herself some breathing space. Instead, she gave him a look that seem to bore straight through him. "But why waste one more second regretting what either of us might've said or done half a lifetime ago?"

He grasped her upper arm, his gaze dropping to her lips before returning to a pair of beautiful brown eyes in what felt like a homecoming. "Maybe I'm not thinking at all about the past right this second—not when the present's standing right in front of me, looking a hell of a lot better than anything I've seen in years."

Chapter 13

I could do this. Just once, Kate found herself thinking as she stepped forward into his arms, her body remembering the steps to a dance without music. *Prove to him—to both of us—that he's dead wrong, that there's absolutely nothing left between us but hard feelings.*

Though the pure anticipation pulsing through her body as he lowered his head, angling his mouth over hers, suggested otherwise, as did the moan of pleasure she couldn't hold back when their lips came together. Taken by surprise by the jolt of desire—of what her traitorous body registered as pure, unadulterated *relief*—surging through her, she reached higher, instinctively pulling him closer, unable to get enough of a kiss that deepened by the moment as he pushed her back against the counter.

There was a loud crash as something—it took her a moment to realize it had been the plates—slid to the tile floor and shattered. She didn't care. Neither of them did, not with his kisses moving from the corner of her mouth to the column of her neck and his strong hands stroking, kneading—and then undoing the front of her top.

Though she knew she ought to stop him—that if she had a single lick of sense, she would stop this while she still could—and quit adding fuel to the fire by nibbling at his earlobe, whispering, "Like that, please. Yes, more..." But she couldn't remember the last time she'd felt so young, so carefree, so deliciously tuned in to every sensation.

Leaning back, she closed her eyes, feeling the river cool against her legs, the sun warm on her shoulders and Hayden's kisses so hot as they fell on her breasts. Arching back her neck, she moaned, every inhibition—and all her good sense—washed downstream...

When he took her hand, looked her in the eye and said, "How about we take this to the bedroom—before somebody ends up bleeding?" she could think only of the shards lying on the floor, Hayden's bare feet—and how damned long it had been since she'd felt anything like the connection arcing so bright and hot between them now.

"I won't lie," he said. "I want you, Kate. I want you like I've never wanted anyone since— I've been such a fool, not seeing that you've always been the only woman. Or maybe just too damned stubborn to admit it to myself and do whatever it would take to try to convince you—"

"No, Hayden." She shook her head as inside her, something molten was plunged into ice water. She practically heard the hiss of steam that rose, a cleansing cloud that cleared away enough lust to let her see the pain behind his plea.

He hadn't lied before. He *had* had been hurt, and terribly, by the accident and the sudden loss of their unborn child and the future they had planned together. A future that remained impossibly out of reach, no matter how they attempted to delude themselves half a lifetime later.

But she couldn't live that pain again—or inflict it on him, either.

He shook his head, looking bewildered as he asked, "What's wrong? I'm coming on too strong, aren't I? I know, this must seem crazy, coming out of the blue like this after all these years, but—don't you think, Kate, maybe we were brought back together this way for a *reason*? A chance to get things right this time?"

"We *are* here for a reason," she reminded him. "Finding out who's trying to wipe out the Kessler family so those little girls can have a future. We've *had* our chance, Hayden—and we messed things up royally—"

"I'm sorry for that. I'll never *finish* being sorry for the way I let you down."

"It wasn't only you. I'm sorry for pushing you away, too."

"Then, or now?" he challenged, looking longingly at her still-open top.

Feeling her face heat, she fumbled in an attempt to re-button it one-handed.

His smile was pained. "Are you sure you really want to do that?"

"Of course, I'm sure," she lied, though what she really wanted was to feel his hands, his mouth on her again... and more.

But there was no way she could open herself up like that again. Or put herself in a position where she'd feel the need to explain the real reason she had refused to see him all those years before.

He can never know the rest of it, why I wouldn't see him...

Shaking her head, she told Hayden, "We can't—I can't

do this. Whatever's been happening between us—this was a mistake."

"Funny," he said. "I was thinking it's the beginning of a course correction."

"You're not thinking straight. It's just nostalgia, the two of us living like teenagers again, so close together—except we're all grown up now with adult responsibilities."

As if on cue, the cell phone in her back pocket chimed and vibrated, and she knew, even before she pulled it out to check it, that it would be her mother wondering what was keeping her, or reminding her that they had plans for dinner shortly.

"What's wrong?" Hayden asked, suddenly all business when he saw her frowning down at her screen.

She shook her head in confusion. "The girls have been fighting. *Physically* fighting. Mom says she could really use my help to get things sorted out."

"That's odd. They seemed to be getting along well enough when we were all together," he said before reaching between her breasts.

"No more of that," she warned.

He made a face. "Give me just a little credit, will you? I'm only trying to help you redo this, considering your hand."

"Sorry. Thanks," she said, as he finished with the buttons, "and you're right about the girls—though I seriously doubt we've seen their true personalities at this point. But what struck me as strange is my mother wanting my help to iron out a squabble between fosters. I don't know if you've ever seen her in action with kids—"

Hayden laughed and squatted down to pick up some larger pieces of the broken plate mess. "I can remember her pulling Mac and me apart when she caught the two of us hammering on each other over who knows what one day. Scared the liver out of us when the nice neighbor lady who baked such good apple bread barked at us to straighten up and fly right."

"She definitely has a gift for it—and watch your feet there with those shards."

"I am. But your mom *has* been out of the kid-wrangling business for quite a few years up until now," he reminded her.

"She's not getting any younger, either," Kate agreed, passing the trash can closer to him. "Let me grab a broom or something. After all, I'm the one who stacked the plates so near the edge of the counter."

He grinned. "At least I got the enjoyment out of helping to break them. Plus I have two good hands for the cleanup. So you go help your mother. See if you can figure out what's got those girls so stirred up."

"Other than their whole world being shattered, you mean?"

"I agree with you on that point," he said, "but I keep going back to the way Hazel was acting earlier, which makes me wonder if whatever that girl is hiding might be coming out in misbehavior."

"Down, Thunder," Kate said when her mother's dog forgot himself for a moment and tried to jump up as she was coming inside. As much as she adored the fluffy bear of a white dog, she didn't need to be bowled over by one of his enthusiastic greetings.

When Kate found both the living room and kitchen empty, she called out for her mother, thinking she might be somewhere upstairs. But the voice that answered came from a seldom-used room on the ground floor.

"We're in your father's study," her mother called out.

Drawing in a deep breath, Kate steeled herself to enter a spacious room she'd rarely ventured into since her father's passing. She still couldn't look at his vacant desk and chair and the collection of antique veterinary tools without missing the man fiercely. But her mother wasn't showing the girls any of that. Instead, she and the girls were admiring the many ribbons and trophies Kate had removed from her own room, along with the photos of herself riding Cloverleaf, because they were too painful to look at following the accident.

Looking toward her, her mother said, "I hope you don't mind," her brown eyes asking forgiveness. "It seems we needed a bit of a distraction."

Kate, who'd been unaware she'd been biting her lip, looked at the two girls, whose faces were still red and blotchy.

But Lottie's blue eyes shone with wonder as she pointed to the larger trophies and asked, "Did you really win all these?"

"Of course, she did," insisted Hazel. "Can't you see, that's her in the picture? Look at that red ponytail."

"You look like you're flying," Lottie said admiringly.

For the first time in more than eighteen years, Kate allowed herself to really see herself aboard Cloverleaf, the two of them captured as they'd raced down the alley after successfully rounding a third barrel at a race that had ended far differently than their last. The mare's legs were extended, and Kate's own expression was fiercely focused, but she could still feel the excitement, the pure joy thrumming through her veins.

"We *did* fly," Kate told the girls, "both of us, or at least that's what it felt like."

"I want to learn to fly, too," Hazel surprised her by

saying, her eyes blazing as she added, "to fly far away from here."

Feeling the girl's emotions washing over her, Kate was reminded sharply of her own sadness and anger long ago. Looking over at her mother, she asked, "Would you mind if Hazel and I talked in here for a little bit, in private?"

"But she's not the natural. I am. You said it," Lottie reminded Kate, looking worried. "So if you're going to teach anybody to win one of those big trophies, it should be me. Okay?"

"We won't be talking about horses, Lottie. Promise," Kate said. "I'll save my supersecret riding tips for you."

"And I could really use your help with getting dinner ready. Have you ever learned to set a table?" Kate's mother put in as Kate winked at Hazel.

"I'm the best at that," the younger girl boasted as Kate's mother shepherded her out of the room, quietly closing the door behind them.

Hazel looked at Kate with frightened eyes. "I don't want to get in trouble."

Kate sat down on the deep red leather, nail-head sofa, where her father had sat with her so many times, sipping his coffee while encouraging her to celebrate her triumphs or, more importantly, share her frustrations and her sorrows. Unlike her, he'd always seemed to know exactly how to make things better, so she tried to imagine what he might say to put this clearly struggling ten-year-old at ease.

"Here's the thing, Hazel. There's literally nothing you could say to me right now that's going to get you in trouble. Nothing, no matter how bad."

"Even if I said I hate you?" the girl threw back, her tone a challenge.

"Even if you said that, or that you think my mom's a mean witch whose cooking tastes like garbage."

Blue eyes flaring, Hazel shook her head. "She's real nice, just like you. And her food's good, too."

"I'm not sure how you'd know that, since I keep seeing you slipping yours to Thunder whenever you think no one's looking."

The girl shrugged. "I'm eating *some.* I try to anyway, but it's hard when I keep—keep hearing all the shooting and seeing that blood on my mom."

When she starting crying, Kate obeyed her instinct, pulling the child into her arms and letting her sob against her chest. It lasted longer than she might have expected as all the emotion Hazel had been bottling up racked her small but sturdy body. Kate stroked her hair and made soothing noises, waiting out the storm.

When it finally ended, she leaned over to a drawer in the lampstand next to the sofa and pulled two tissues from a box her father had long kept there to dry her tears when needed.

Once the girl wiped her blotched face with them, she asked, "You won't tell anyone I cried, will you?"

"I won't tell anyone anything you don't want me to. And I guess it must be hard, trying to stay strong for Lottie."

Hazel nodded. "She's only little, and she doesn't understand as much."

"Like about your father?" Kate asked.

"That and...other things."

"Like what?"

When Hazel only sniffled, Kate tried another tack. "That gun your mother had out there, was it your daddy's? Or did it belong to her?"

Pulling away from her, Hazel receded to the most distant corner of the sofa and cast her gaze from the window to the door, as if looking for an escape route.

"It's okay for you to tell me," Kate said. "I'm sure your mom and dad aren't going to be mad at you, either."

"You don't know that!" Hazel blurted, her cheeks flamed. "She told me not to say anything! Not even to Daddy. He didn't even know about it."

"Do you know when your mother got it? When was the first time that you saw it?"

"I saw when the lady gave it to her. It was after school, the day before we left on our surprise vacation..."

Chapter 14

Awakened from a deep sleep, Hayden groped in the half light of early morning for his cell phone, his heartbeat accelerating. Instead of grabbing the phone off the stand where he'd left it charging, he only succeeded in knocking it to the floor. Grunting fully awake, he swung his feet over the side of the bed before reaching toward the lit screen. But by the time he'd finally wrangled the cell, the damned thing had quit ringing.

With his eyes refusing to focus, he held the button to activate the phone's virtual assistant feature and asked it for the time.

"Four twenty-two a.m.," the female voice dutifully replied, making him wonder if it was dispatch calling— reporting in on some incident serious enough that someone had felt the sheriff needed to be alerted, despite the early hour and his injury.

The thought sent adrenaline sluicing through him.

Praying he wasn't about to hear about an injury to any of his people, he played a new voice mail the moment it came through.

"This is Sergeant Linda Darnell from the Kerr County Sheriff's Department," began a confident-sounding woman. "Sorry to bother you so early at home, Sheriff, but I have some information regarding a case of yours, so you can call me back at this number."

Rising, Hayden pulled on a shirt and headed to the kitchen with the phone to return her call. She picked up right away.

"This is Hayden Hale-Walker. What's going on?" he asked.

"We had a report from the hospital regarding a disturbance in the lobby. A man identifying himself as Ada Kessler's brother, Cal Thorley, showed up at two thirty this morning, demanding to see his sister."

"Thorley showed up *there*?" Hayden asked. "Last I heard, the authorities were still trying to make contact with him back in Oregon about his sister's medical condition. He hadn't returned any phone calls, most likely because the siblings weren't on speaking terms."

"Well, apparently he'd gotten the message about her somehow and decided to let bygones be bygones," Sergeant Darnell said, "because Thorley told them he didn't give a damn about their visiting hours. He'd driven all the way there to see his sister and wasn't taking no for an answer."

"But I specifically requested the hospital restrict all visitor access to her room, unless it had been cleared through me first," Hayden told her.

"Even if you hadn't, there was no way they were letting this guy in at this time of night, especially not the way he was behaving."

"How was that?" Hayden asked, as he opened the cupboard and pulled out a coffee filter.

"Loud, disruptive—accusing the clerk and the hospital of scheming to keep his sister a vegetable so they could jack her bills up."

Removing the top from the coffee can, he said, "That sounds extremely on-brand for this guy. He has a history of psych issues and hostility when it comes to the medical establishment. So please tell me he made just enough of a stink that you have him in custody—because I'd love to ask him a few questions…" Hayden was dying to know when Thorley had learned about his sister—or whether he'd really been in the area for some time and had only now decided to play at being the concerned brother. Certainly, he could have been checking his voice mail from his home remotely.

"Sorry to disappoint you, Sheriff," said the sergeant, "but the moment hospital security told him they were calling law enforcement, Thorley bolted. Took off driving a late-model Corolla—looked to be a light-color vehicle, possibly a rental."

"Plate number?"

"Unfortunately, the security guard didn't get it, but I can have a deputy head back to the hospital and look over their parking lot camera footage to see if we get any decent angles. This guy's important?"

"I'm not sure yet," Hayden answered honestly. "Maybe. I don't like him simply turning up here, out of the blue, after being in the wind for who knows how long around the same time his estranged sister and her husband both end up shot."

"So what was this beef of theirs about?" Darnell asked.

Hayden recounted the story about their father's death

and Ada's receiving a small inheritance after he'd been cut out of the will. "It was barely even any money."

The sergeant gave a mirthless laugh. "My mother and her sisters haven't spoken for *twenty-three* years over Grandpa's pocket watch and some moth-eaten quilt that would probably fall to pieces if you sneezed on it."

"I've seen that kind of thing, too," Hayden admitted, thinking of several domestic disturbances he'd been called to deal with. "Which is why I need to get a bead on Thorley, quickly. Did he ask about his nieces?"

"As far as I was told, he seemed fixated on the sister. He insisted he'd come through hell to see her."

Hayden wondered if Thorley had been referring to the length of his drive, his change of heart or something else entirely. "What's this guy look like, anyway? You have a description?"

"Balding, brown-eyed white male, midforties, dressed in wrinkled khaki pants and a food-stained flannel shirt. Average height and a slight beer belly. What hair he does have is dark, with a fair amount of silver threaded through it and a raggedy goatee."

"Sounds like he could've been living on the road for a while," Hayden said. "Did he indicate that he intended to come back to the hospital, maybe to try again to see his sister during daylight hours?"

"I'm not sure what exactly was said, but if you'd like, I can put a plainclothes deputy in the lobby area, ready to bring this guy in for questioning the moment that we spot him."

"I'd appreciate that very much if you can make it happen, along with putting out a BOLO with his description and the car's as well. Cal Thorley's too much of a wild card to have floating around loose in your city—or possibly deciding to go looking for his two nieces instead..."

* * *

Despite a late night, Kate was still the first up that morning, too restless to sleep when she was awakened well before dawn by a dream where she'd been sinking deep in quicksand, a hazard she'd previously come across only in old movies. When she'd gasped to consciousness, she'd been up to her neck and reaching out a desperate hand to someone—she couldn't make out the face—she couldn't be certain was inclined to help her, or perhaps shove her deeper under.

Though she might be cutting short her sleep, she counted herself fortunate that she hadn't come to screaming bloody murder, as poor little Lottie had following last night's night terror. When the girl's cries rang out, Kate had been standing downstairs in the kitchen, about to call Hayden with Hazel's revelation before the hour grew too late. Instead, she'd put the phone down and gone running to help her mother comfort both girls, who'd been deeply shaken as Lottie cried, "The bad men! They're coming back to shoot us, too!" her blue eyes wide with terror.

It had taken a long time afterward to get both the girls settled, with her mother taking Lottie downstairs to warm some milk with cinnamon and honey—her traditional remedy for bogeymen—for all of them while Kate talked with Hazel in the bedroom until the girl finally fell asleep curled up against her. By that point, it was too late to think of calling Hayden. And now, she thought, spotting her cell in the kitchen where she'd left it, it was far too early. Tabling the idea for the time being, she made a pot of coffee, moving quietly so as not to disturb the sleepers upstairs—or get Thunder barking where she'd left him, still shut in her mother's room, keeping her safe from whatever might trouble her dreams.

Once the coffee was finished brewing, Kate reached

into the fridge to use a little of her mother's hazelnut creamer. She noticed they were almost completely out of milk, something the two girls seemed to drink a lot of.

Deciding to buy more before her mother woke up to nag her about driving around in her current condition, she slipped back upstairs to change into a comfortable pair of jeans and a long-sleeved T-shirt before slipping her feet into a pair of flats. Back in the kitchen, she transferred her coffee to a travel mug and then left a note—on the off chance anyone missed her at this hour—and grabbed her mom's keys before heading out beneath a sky still the color of a dusty plum. Breathing in the night's lingering coolness, she paused for just a moment, catching the soft tones of an owl's cry, and savored the simple freedom of an early-morning drive to the area's sole convenience store, which was located a few miles down the road.

But as she reached the end of the long driveway, the thought hit her. *I might just as easily turn left instead, and go by Hayden's, surprising him in his bed with the message that I've reconsidered his invitation.*

She sat there several minutes, the Jeep idling as she ticked through the annoying qualities she'd taken such peevish pleasure in listing during the years they'd worked together. But the funny thing was, those petty gripes now paled against the enormity of the courage he'd shown. The courage of confessing his feelings—not only his lust—to a woman who'd for years given him every reason to believe she despised him.

"Except that I don't," she admitted, before reflexively looking around to assure herself that no one was in the back seat listening. That bit of foolishness at least made her laugh—and come to her senses to resume her intended errand.

Happy to find the store's parking lot empty, other than

one driver fueling his pickup, along with a dented, older sedan she figured was the clerk's, she quickly ran inside and made her purchase from an older man who never looked up from his phone while checking out her purchase. Happy to have escaped another conversation about the shooting, which Kate was certain would still be a hot topic around town, she hurried for the exit with her gallon of milk. Leaving the doorway, she nearly barreled into none other than Amanda Greenville, though Kate barely recognized her at first, since the normally well-dressed real estate agent was not only without her perfect makeup but wearing an oversize gray sweatshirt with the hood pulled up to hide her long, black hair.

Allowing the door to swing closed behind her, Kate offered up a smile. "Looks like I'm not the only one trying to avoid the early-morning rush. Hi, Amanda."

"Hey, Kate," Amanda said, her large, gray eyes looking haunted—or maybe *hunted* was the right word for it.

She looked pale as well, Kate thought, and even thinner than she'd been the last time Kate had seen her, when she remembered envying Amanda's long, lean dancer's build. At the moment, though, she looked unhealthy—or badly stressed by the issues she'd been having.

"I was sorry to hear about your loss," Kate said, not knowing quite what else to start with. "Sara told me you've had a difficult year."

Amanda's expression warmed a degree. "Sara's been a good friend. She tries…"

"Well, how about if I tried, too?" Kate offered. "I'd like to be your friend as well, maybe take you out for coffee—or dinner, if you'd like."

Stiffening, Amanda said, "I'm not looking for treats out of your lunch box anymore, Kate."

Kate smiled. "Let's not figure it for pity. I could use

some friends myself here. I'm afraid I burned a few bridges during my last stay here."

"Burned a few—are you kidding? You're all anyone is talking about right now, you and Hayden. People are calling you a hero, shooting that criminal out in the canyon and—and taking a bullet yourself saving everybody out there." Giving Kate's bandaged hand a look of sympathy, Amanda shook her head. "How *are* you after all that?"

"Honestly, a little rattled," Kate admitted. "Like I said, I could use someone to talk to. Someone who's not my mom, a kid—" *or someone I'm trying very hard to keep myself from losing my heart to,* she admitted to herself "—and isn't likely to endlessly rehash the worst moments of my life for the chance to bask in my so-called *glory*."

Amanda smiled. "I always used to admire the way you rolled your eyes like that. It made you seem so *worldly*-wise, back when I was five."

"I was faking it then," Kate confided, "and half the time I'm still faking it now. The trick is never letting anybody guess which half the time you actually *might* know what you're doing."

"Let's discuss that sometime, over coffee…" Amanda said, pulling out her cell phone, presumably to exchange numbers. "If you're really sure you want to be seen with me in this town?"

"Let's just say I'm willing to cash in a little of whatever good grace my supposed 'heroism' has bought me for the privilege," Kate told her. "And if you'd like, we can invite Sara along, too, add a touch of respectability to this whole gathering."

Amanda smiled wryly. "Is that what we're going for here? Restoring my so-called *respectability*, when the Greenvilles still have half the town thinking I might've—"

"Let them," Kate said. "Sara and I—and Sheriff Walker—we all know it's not the truth. And that's all that really matters."

"I used to think the same thing," Amanda told her, looking away as an older woman in a silver Escalade pulled up to the gas pump, only to stiffen and peel out, wheels squealing, the moment she caught sight of the two of them standing there and chatting. "But life teaches us such different lessons than the ones we learned in school."

Chapter 15

As she parked the Jeep in its usual spot back at her mother's, Kate hoped she wasn't making a mistake, making promises to someone as vulnerable as Amanda. As eager as she was to help, she reminded herself she would be gone soon, taking whatever dubious protective qualities any friendship might offer. Was it really fair to Amanda to allow her to count on her?

Or was she more worried about herself, since reaching out left her vulnerable as well—to the possibility of forming real relationships with both Amanda and Sara? Friendships that might, along with her mother's loneliness since her dad's death, her inability to properly maintain the property and the man Kate hoped might try again to kiss her, risk making her forget all the excellent reasons she'd put this place and its painful memories behind her.

Grabbing her purchase, she looked out toward the barn and henhouse, both buildings now easily visible in the pinkish dawn's light. From the pasture, movement caught her eye: a trio of deer grazing. As she watched, the animals' ears flicked toward a noise at the barn: a loud neigh, followed by what sounded like hammer blows against wood. Or a horse kicking at the side of its stall.

As the deer fled, flashing their white tails in alarm, Kate frowned before calling, "Hold on, you old hay-belly. Just let me put this milk up."

Once she'd placed the gallon in the fridge, she had barely reached the porch when her cell phone started ringing. Answering it, she asked, "What are you doing up so early?"

"Hope I'm not waking you," Hayden began, belatedly looking at his kitchen clock and realizing it wasn't even six yet. "I've had a couple of calls already, so I lost track of the time."

"I'm up," Kate said, sounding more distracted than annoyed. "Is everything okay?"

"As far as I'm concerned, yes," Hayden said. "But I've had some news about—"

"It's not Ada Kessler, is it?" Her apprehension came through loud and clear, a deep-seated dread he knew because he shared the same fear of having to tell little Lottie and Hazel that the mother whose recovery they'd been hoping and praying for was dead.

Eager to set her mind at ease, he rushed to say, "Actually, I just spoke with the nurse on duty a few minutes ago and got an update on her condition. I'm happy to tell you her vitals have improved to the point that her medical team may be doing the surgery she needs to remove the bullet today."

"That's *fantastic* news."

"Don't get too excited yet," he warned. "The nurse

said it's still possible that infection could cause a relapse or that she won't survive the surgery."

"Oh. In that case...couldn't they bring her out of the medically induced coma *before* the surgery?" she asked. "I'm just wondering if there might be a window in there where she might be questioned about what happened, in case, heaven forbid, things don't go so well."

"I'm sure her doctors will decide on what's best for her medically, without stopping to think about my needs or wants." Hayden put down a mug of the coffee he'd already had far too much of. "And honestly, that's for the best. Questioning a person who's been heavily sedated isn't likely to yield any useful information. It could take her days to fully wake up, and the doctor I spoke to initially told me that very often in these cases, people don't recall what actually happened to them or any of the events that happened just beforehand."

"Retrograde amnesia—I know about that, too..." she said.

"Everything all right there?" he asked, hearing something in her voice.

"Oh, yes. I was just about to go feed Moonlight—she heard me up and about earlier and was fussing for her breakfast early. Now she's really carrying on out there. Mom's got that mare so spoiled..."

"Horses'll come roust you out of bed if you let 'em get into that habit," Hayden commented before returning to the subject that concerned him. "Anyway, I can't imagine anything that Ada might actually say would hold up in court, even if she did miraculously sit up and point a finger at somebody. Not with a half-conscious defense attorney on the accused's case."

"I'm not worried about court so much as I am keeping those girls safe," Kate said, a slight quaver in her voice giving away what she'd gone through in the canyon during that brief span he'd lain unconscious.

"I understand you do," he said gently. "It's my top priority as well. But I didn't only call to tell you about Ada."

"If this is about what happened yesterday between us, Hayden, I told you I can't go back, like the past eighteen years never happened—"

"Cal Thorley's turned up in Kerrville," he said, unable to bear speaking of a conversation he'd tormented himself with half the night, wondering how he could have been such a fool to suddenly blindside her with the complete one-eighty in his feelings. No wonder he'd scared her off—but he'd be damned if he would make the same mistake twice.

"Ada's brother? Why?" she asked, clearly distracted from all thoughts of how things stood between them. "Where is he?"

"At around two thirty this morning, he showed up at the hospital where his sister's staying, demanding to see her."

"But I thought he hadn't even returned Investigator Robinson's calls."

"That was my understanding as well," he said. "But clearly, he got the message somehow. Anyway, he ended up causing a disturbance when he was refused admittance and then fleeing when law enforcement was called."

"Where is he now? Do they know?"

"They don't—but they're doing all they can to bring him in for questioning."

"You don't have reason to suspect he might be heading this way looking for his nieces, do you?" she asked, sounding alarmed.

"I thought of that, too, which is why I called you, but I do think it's a pretty remote concern. For one thing, he seemed really focused on his sister. And he'd have no way of knowing the children are an hour away, in another county."

"Kerrville may be a lot bigger than our hometown, but it's still small enough that people like to talk, especially when something halfway exciting's happened. Who knows what this guy could've wormed out of someone he met locally?"

"That might be a concern for someone with the social skills to work the locals for information. But Thorley's not a subtle man, by all accounts. My guess is, he'll end up being picked up returning to the hospital to make more trouble. And then I'm going to have a lot of questions for him."

"You might want to think about which of your deputies you'll delegate to do that interview," she suggested.

He gave a noncommittal grunt, not wanting to waste time arguing about it now, especially with Thorley still at large.

For once, she let the subject drop, instead saying, "You're probably right about Thorley being focused on his sister, but listen, I was going to call you this morning myself, about something Hazel told me last night..."

"You finally got her talking?" he asked.

"I did—and there's the rub, actually. To do it, I had to give her my word it would be between her and me. Yet here I am..." Her sigh sounded troubled.

"If there's one thing I know about you, it's that you have a good handle on your professional ethics. And if the information shared could leave anyone, especially a vulnerable ten-year-old child and her sister, in danger, we have an even greater obligation to break that confidence."

"I know," Kate said quietly. "But it doesn't make me

feel any better about turning on a kid as scared as I was a long time ago."

Hayden gave her a few moments to come to peace with the situation, which had clearly brought up painful memories, before prompting, "Did she finally talk about what happened with her family?"

"Not the shootings themselves," Kate said, hesitating for only a moment before apparently resolving herself to what she needed, "but she mentioned her mom meeting a woman at her school after-hours—a woman who secretly gave her a gun. And apparently, this was kept secret from her husband."

"Are you serious?" Hayden asked. "So it was *Ada* who was in some kind of trouble?"

"Either that, or she believed her husband was into something serious enough that she felt the need to protect him."

"Then why not tell him?"

"Maybe he'd been trying to downplay the situation," Kate guessed aloud. "Or maybe he didn't want his wife having a gun for some other reason. But it's also possible that Ada *did* tell him about the pistol later. Remember, we're hearing this from a kid, who might not have the whole story herself."

"What about this woman who provided the weapon?" Hayden asked.

"Hazel claimed she didn't know her, but she thought she might've been someone who works at the high school with her mom. A tall lady with light brown skin, wearing a tracksuit, she said. Really short, red-blond hair and bright white sneakers."

Encouraged by the detailed description, he asked, "Could she have been a coach there—someone working late with student athletics? Certainly, that would be the kind of person whose presence would be ignored by campus police."

"Could be."

"I'll call Memphis PD," he said, "see if Robinson can maybe track this woman down, find out what she might tell us…"

"Good plan," Kate said.

"Did Lottie happen to witness this exchange, too?" Hayden asked, hoping the younger girl might be able to provide even more information for them.

"Apparently, she'd had an upset stomach that day at school and fell asleep on the car ride over, so she missed the whole thing," Kate said.

"Well, that's unfortunate, but at least we have a solid place to start. I'd better go now and make that call to Memphis."

"Sure, Hayden," she said, "but please keep me posted, will you?"

"I'll definitely let you know as soon as Cal Thorley's in custody," he said, not wanting her to worry.

"Thanks, but I think you're probably right. I'm sure he's miles and miles from here."

Halfway to the barn, Kate paused, a sick feeling sliding through her stomach as it hit her that the restless sounds she was hearing sounded less like a hungry, spoiled horse than a seriously distressed one. As the daughter of a large-animal vet, she should have caught on far more quickly—

And would have, surely, had she not been so distracted by her conversation. Now worried that Moonlight, whose best years were behind her, might be hurt or ill, she broke into a jog, ignoring the way the jostling made her still-swollen hand ache.

Grabbing the right-side double door with her good hand, she pulled hard, pierced with guilt-spawned scenarios involving everything from muscle strains from yesterday's activity to deadly colic. "I'm so sorry, girl," she called. "I'm coming."

But the door stuck fast, refusing to yield more than an inch before something seemed to block it. Could it be another maintenance issue, perhaps a broken hinge—or had something fallen down to jam the track?

Frowning, Kate made a mental note to make convincing her mother to put aside her pride and accept the help needed to keep up the property a priority. Then, with a grunt of effort, she leaned her shoulder against the door and pushed as hard as she could. This time, she was rewarded with a bump as the door seemed to roll over whatever impediment had caused the issue. Afterward, it slid smoothly to the right.

Stepping inside to the sound of restless vocalizations, Kate reached to switch on the corridor lighting, assuring the mare, "It's okay, Moonlight. Whatever's going on, I promise you, we'll get you taken care of."

But the moment illumination filled the dark barn, a man-sized shape leaped from the shadows. Before she could scream, a pair of hard hands grabbed her by the collar, forcing her backward so quickly it was all she could do to keep on her feet.

Thorley?

Heart nearly bursting from her chest, she found herself slammed hard against an empty box stall to the left of the door, the back of her head cracking painfully against an upright post and her butt pressing—the cell phone useless in her rear pocket—into the wood.

At first, she didn't recognize the inhuman shriek assaulting her ears as her own, not until the man shook her, roaring, "Shut up, *shut up!*"

Something hard and cold—her instincts screamed it must be a gun barrel—pressed hard against her temple. "You don't stop that noise right this second, I will splatter your damned brains all across this barn. Do you understand me?"

The shrieking stopped—most likely because Kate had quit breathing to jerk a nod, her senses overloaded with the sight of his wild brown eyes and stringy dark hair, the stomach-turning reek of his body odor and—was that old blood or something even fouler?

Fighting to tamp down panic and nausea, she thought back to her law enforcement training, then forced herself to breathe because she had to think. To establish whatever control she might over this impossible situation. Because there would be no calling Hayden back for help, no doing anything else, unless she kept this assault from turning deadly within the next few seconds. "Y-you just startled me, that's all. I'm listening. Why don't you take a step back and tell me what it is you want? Are you—are you hurt?"

"Of course, I'm freaking hurt! You *shot* me, out in that godforsaken wilderness!" he screamed, pinning her even tighter up against the box stall. In the next stall over, unnerved by the noise—and probably the smell of blood—Moonlight squealed loudly, once more kicking at the wall.

Kate blinked, realized that, of course, this wasn't Ada's brother, Cal Thorley, but instead the same man who'd escaped the canyon—the man who'd shot down Ada Kessler and come back, it seemed, to finish what he'd started.

"Do you need medical assistance?" she asked, struggling to sound calm and reasonable, eager to help as she spotted the dark brownish spot on the upper right side of his shirt—a stain only partly hidden by the denim jacket that practically hung on his tall frame. "If you'll let me call help for you—"

"If that was all I wanted, do you think I'd have gone to the damned trouble to track you down after I heard those people goin' on about the hero lady who did the shooting in the canyon?" he yelled, sweat streaming down the side of a face gone sallow.

Though she'd barely glimpsed him during the canyon shoot-out—had been too far away to provide anything more helpful than "white male" by way of identifying features when initially giving Clayton Yarborough her statement—it was easy to see that his untreated injury had exacted a high toll since. A toll she needed to focus on if she hoped to get out of this alive.

"My father was the local vet," she said, recognizing the same aquiline nose she'd pointed out to Hayden from the security photo of the ATV thief. Definitely, this was the same man who'd been driving the dark Silverado. "And I swear to you, I can smell the rot in that wound from here. You'll die, you know, if you let it go much longer. And you have to be in agony."

Her honest statement was also an attempt to distract him from what she feared might be his mission to kill the remaining Kesslers—along with her, as a witness to his mayhem. Even if she could buy a little time, that time might turn into a chance. If not to call for help, then at least to shout a warning that would allow her mother to escape with the two girls before this desperate maniac left them all dead.

"You—you got anything for it?" He licked his lips, a dark hope burning in his eyes. "Oxy, maybe? Or any kind of pain pills? A vet would have stuff like that around here, wouldn't he?" He looked around the barn, as if her father would have kept controlled substances out in the unlocked outbuilding.

"We had to turn all the hard drugs in when he—when he retired," she said, thinking it might be better if her attacker imagined there was a living man inside the house. Especially since, in this area, most homeowners had firearms and a willingness to use them, even if it was normally on marauding coyotes or feral hogs instead of two-legged invaders. "But I can go get you my pain meds from the house, what they gave me at the hospital. I just had surgery, you know—bullet caught me, too, out there."

He glanced down, seeming to notice her sling and bandaged left hand for the first time before his face went red, and he erupted in a voice that made her blood run cold. "You shot my brother dead right there, so it serves you the hell right, bitch! Now let's go and get those drugs—you won't be needing them anyway when this is over."

"No!" she said, pure adrenaline pushing her pulse into overdrive as she thought of leading this nightmare into the same house where she'd left her mother and the two innocent girls sleeping. "Like I said, I'll go and get it for you. You're much too weak to—*unh!*"

His fist came out of nowhere, catching her jaw and sending her sprawling on the hard aisle floor.

"I'll show you how weak I am!" he bellowed. "Now *get* up! Get up now because I swear, I'd damned well rather shoot you dead than pick you up!"

Frozen with shock and pain, she lay there, half-certain she wouldn't live to see another moment. But, her heart hammering, she made out a tinny, distant-sounding voice— so unlikely that at first, she was sure she must be dreaming it—from her back pocket.

"Hold on, Kate! I'm coming!"

Hayden, she dimly realized, her heart leaping as it hit her that she must have accidentally pressed the redial button with her rear end when her assailant had slammed her against the box stall's outer wall.

Hope flaring back to life, she used her good right arm to try to push herself up but made a show of weakness as she stalled for precious seconds.

"Come on, come on," ordered her attacker, who evidently hadn't made out Hayden's voice over the sounds of the still-distraught Moonlight, pawing, snorting and shuffling around her stall.

"Hang on—just a minute," she said, moving stiffly. "I remember, we held back some of the really good stuff from my dad's meds—some injectables for this old mare's arthritis. I'm pretty sure we've got a—got a stash of bute right in the tack room."

Despite his earlier threat to shoot her rather than assisting, he grabbed her upper arm and hauled her to her feet. As she rubbed her throbbing jaw, he peered at her through eyes slitted with suspicion. "Really? Wait a minute—you tryin' to kill me, aren't you? I don't want some damned horse medicine—or poison, more than likely. Take me to the house—now."

"That bute won't hurt you, promise," she said, though her father had long ago warned her never to think of taking the veterinary painkiller herself, even in an emergency, because of the extreme danger of fatal liver damage in humans.

"They give it to racehorses all the time, and half the jockeys and the trainers use it," she continued, persisting in her lying, even as he dragged her out into the morning light.

Within a few steps, Kate's heart staggered at the sight of her mother stepping off the porch—without the girls, thank goodness, but right there, looking equal parts confused and horrified at the sight of her daughter being roughly hauled in her direction by an armed stranger. "Run back inside, Mom! Lock up tight, and get Dad's rifle!"

For a moment, Kate's mother froze, the anguish of indecision etched in every feature.

"Now!" Kate ordered as her attacker shoved her aside. Sprinting in the direction of the house, he stopped to fire wildly at Kate's mother, who ran howling up the steps, the door slamming in her wake.

She's not hit. She can't have been, Kate told herself, knowing the extreme unlikelihood of striking a moving target at such a distance. But now the shooter had a more pressing issue to deal with.

Thunder, who'd been right beside his mistress, came rocketing like a canine missile toward the gunman, barking as ferociously as Kate had ever seen him. Her father had long ago assured her the breed was rarely known for harming humans. However, the Great Pyrenees had evidently decided that this particular intruder was a predator out to harm the family he took it as his mission to protect.

"No!" Kate screamed, as she saw the gunman taking careful aim. Acting on pure instinct, she ran and leaped on him as he fired—taking them both down as the sound of a canine yelp told her she'd timed her flying tackle too late.

Tears pouring down her face, she channeled her rage and her sorrow into furious action, not allowing this soulless killer to desecrate the place she and so many other forgotten children had known as a safe harbor. She slammed her right fist again and again into his torso, raining blows directly toward the rotting source of his pain, intent on punishing him with every ounce of agony she could inflict before he could kill her, too.

With a wordless bellow, her attacker rolled away and came back up to his knees. His face an inhuman mask of rage and agony, he leveled the gun at her, his eyes burning with such hatred that she knew he was about to empty whatever was left of his magazine into her body.

Then, overwhelming as an avalanche, a snarling white wall of fur descended on him, slamming him facedown to the ground.

"Good boy! Very good dog!" Kate told him, her voice trembling as she jerked away the dropped weapon and then scooted backward to point it at her attacker from a safe distance—moments before Hayden's vehicle came tearing up the driveway, where it slammed to a stop.

"It's him!" she screamed as Hayden came running, his heart in his throat at the sight of Kate, looking so battered and disheveled. In spite of this, her brown eyes flamed with fury, and she looked about as far from helpless as it was possible to be, scrambling to her feet to aim a pistol at the man Thunder still stood over. "The shooter from the canyon! He claims the man I killed there was his brother."

Hayden pulled out a zip tie he'd somehow had the presence of mind to grab from his SUV. He was operating on pure instinct, adrenaline roaring through his system, the headache he'd had earlier temporarily forgotten.

"It's okay, boy. I'll take it from here," he said, moving in to grab the man's wrist as Thunder backed off a couple of steps, though his hackles remained up and his gaze watchful.

"Bonner?" Hayden called, guessing the shooter might share a name with the dead man already identified as his brother. "Are you with us?"

Still facedown, Kate's attacker failed to respond, even when Hayden shook him roughly. "Looks like he's out cold, but he's definitely breathing."

"Better call an ambulance," Kate told him. "He has a gunshot wound to the upper right quadrant—septic from the smell of him. I slugged him pretty hard there, so he might've passed out from the pain."

"You—you *punched* him?" Hayden asked, wondering how she wasn't dead.

"As hard as I could, as many times as I could. He was shooting at my mom and dog and planning to kill me, so asking him nicely to quit doing that didn't seem like the right option."

"Remind me *never* to mess with you," Hayden said as he restrained the downed man's wrists behind him on the off chance he was playing possum.

When the unconscious man offered no resistance, Hayden checked his pulse and breathing and rolled him onto his side so he wouldn't choke if he vomited—because he definitely wanted this suspect to survive long enough to answer the dozens of questions clamoring for attention.

"I would've thought you'd learned that lesson years ago," Kate said, though in spite of her bravado, Hayden noticed how hard she was shaking. And what looked like a reddened swelling on the left side of her jaw.

"You're hurt. Do you need help, Kate? And what about your mother?"

"I'm almost positive she's fine. As for me, the only treatment I need is a bag of frozen peas for my jaw where he clocked me and—I don't know. Is it too early for a glass of wine? Or maybe a whole bottle?"

"If that's what you want, I promise you, I'll buy out the liquor store." He could use a stiff drink himself about now, after she'd taken ten years off his life with that phone call. "Please, keep an eye on him while I call for help."

"Just keep in mind I'm feeling pretty jumpy. I can't promise you I won't twitch and shoot him if he breathes wrong."

"We really need to know who sent this guy and why he's here, Kate." Hayden laid a hand on her shoulder, a reminder to behave like the professional he knew she was. "So let's try and keep your twitches strictly nonlethal. You hear me, Deputy?"

She grumbled a complaint, but he trusted that she'd gotten the message.

Though Hayden had already made a quick call for backup during his panicked drive here, he walked a short distance away to phone dispatch to request emergency medical support and give a brief rundown of the situation.

After a quick look back at Kate to make sure she was holding steady, he tried his sister-in-law's number. To his surprise, however, his older brother was the one who answered.

"Hey, Hayden," Mac said, sounding a thousand times more laid-back than he had in all the years after his first wife's death, when he'd been denied the opportunity to see or speak to his twins. "I don't normally grab Sara's phone for her, but when I saw it was you calling, I thought I'd better check and see if there's anything I can do for you. The kids talked her into joining them for a little kayaking this morning since it's her day off, and she never takes her cell down near the water."

"I hate to bother her while she's relaxing," he said, knowing that as the county's sole full-time social worker, she was often interrupted outside of normal office hours.

"So why does it sound like you're about to, brother?" Mac asked, the teasing note in his voice a surprise to

Hayden, who was doing his best but still hadn't quite worked his way back to the easy relationship they'd had before the ranch—and the home they'd all grown up believing would remain in Hale-Walker hands forever—had been lost.

"Because I know she'd wring my neck if she found out there'd been an attack over at the McClaffertys' this morning and I didn't let her know about it," he said, his answer a little sharper than he meant it to come out.

"At Kate's mom's place? What the hell?" Mac asked, every trace of good humor stripped away in an instant. "Is everyone all right?"

Glancing back to make sure she wasn't listening, Hayden said, "She got roughed up a bit, but I promise you, she's in better shape than the sorry bastard who jumped her in the barn."

"*Jumped* her?" Mac asked. "You're sure she's not hurt?"

"She'll be sore, that's all, I think, because even with her left hand out of commission, she fought like a wildcat," Hayden boasted, feeling no small amount of pride as he admired how steady she looked at the moment, holding the weapon on her captive. "She basically beat the man *unconscious*."

"Damn," Mac said, suitably impressed. "I'm really sorry for what she went through, but I could've told that guy he'd picked the wrong woman, messing with our Kate. So I guess this means he's in custody now?"

"He is, though he'll need medical attention before I can bring him in for questioning," Hayden said. "But my gut tells me he's somebody's hired help, maybe here on a personal vendetta because Kate shot down his brother in the canyon."

"That woman's downright *lethal*…" Mac murmured.

"It's also possible that he knew the Kessler girls were

in the house and meant to finish off what's left of the family he was paid to kill as well," Hayden continued. "What I need to know right now is who sent him in the first place—and whether or not there could be other accomplices in the area that we don't know of."

"Do you imagine that's likely?"

"I haven't seen any evidence of it so far, but if he and his partner were really hired assassins, it stands to reason that whoever sent him might have backup on the way to finish the job."

"I can't imagine Sara or the foster care coordinator wanting to leave those kids in that house any longer. It's too big a risk, now that you know their location may be compromised."

"I hear you," Hayden said, "but I can't think they could find anyone better with those girls than Rita McClafferty— and Kate's incredible with them, too. Wrenching the girls away from them at this point, when they've just begun bonding— As a father yourself—"

"I remember how it hard it was after the twins were first brought back, when they were both traumatized over the way things went down—" Mac sounded haunted by the memory. "So I definitely want to help with this."

"I appreciate that, but if you'll just let Sara know, and have her call me back as soon as she can—" Hayden said, growing impatient to get back to Kate, who appeared to be checking over Thunder for injuries while still keeping an eye on her unmoving captive.

"Send them over here, Hayden—Kate's mother and the children," Mac offered. "We've just had a last-minute cancellation, and the guest cabin closest to the house is available. It's only a two bedroom, but there are bunks in one room for the kids. There's a pullout in the living area, too, so there's room for Kate as well. And you know how much I beefed up security here last year. They'll be safe. I promise, I'll see to it personally."

"Are you sure you want to—with your family so close?"

"Let me do this for you, man. I realize Kate's— I don't know exactly how things went so wrong between the two of you, but it's always been obvious to me that no matter what, she still matters to you."

Once, Hayden would have argued the point. Now, he only said, "Wish you would've clued me in a whole lot earlier. Could've maybe saved me years of wasted time."

Mac gave a scoffing laugh. "Would you have believed a word of it, coming from me?"

When Hayden didn't answer, his brother sounded smug as he said, "That's exactly what I figured. Please give Kate my best, and watch out for her, too, will you? Because as tough as she is, she's likely to come down pretty hard from this, once she's finally sure the danger's over."

"I think Sara's starting to rub off on you," Hayden told him. "But I have to say…it's a considerable improvement."

Chuckling, Mac said, "Speaking of Sara, I see her heading up to the deck with the kids now, so I'll fill her in. I'm sure she'll be right over as soon as she can get cleaned up."

"That'd be great. Thanks for everything," Hayden said before they ended the call.

Spotting movement from the direction of the house, he walked over to join Kate as her mother hurried their way. Still dressed in a bathrobe over her pajamas and slippers, Rita McClafferty looked shaken but determined, carrying a rifle in her arms.

"Whoa, Mom," Kate said as she spotted her. "Let's point that at the ground, *please*."

Bursting into tears, Rita instead passed the rifle over

to Hayden before running to her daughter and hugging her, sobbing. "I was scared out of my mind that you'd be dead before I made it out here! Turning my back on you like that was the hardest thing I've ever had to do in my life!"

"He was *shooting* at you, Mom! You had to run, if only to see to the girls' safety." Kate rubbed her back, trying to console her.

Pulling back, her mother looked her over. "But you're all right? He didn't hurt you?"

"I'm pretty much in one piece," Kate told her. "Are you—"

"I'm fine," her mother said. "And the little ones— they're still asleep upstairs. Can you believe it?"

Hayden shook his head, hearing the approach of the first sirens—one of his deputies, most likely. "They won't be for long, I'm afraid. This place is about to be crawling with emergency responders—starting with an ambulance for this guy—"

"He's not *dead*, is he?" Rita asked, staring down with her nose wrinkling.

"Not yet, but depending on what the medics say, we may have to call in an air ambulance."

"Infected gunshot," Kate elaborated, "from back at the canyon shoot-out. Apparently, I shot this guy that day, too, but later, he overheard some locals talking about me and was able to track me down."

"Did he mention knowing the girls were here as well?" asked Hayden.

"He didn't say, but there's no telling what's gotten around town by this time or what he meant to do after he had his revenge on me," Kate said.

"Thank God Hayden showed up to stop him," her mother said, surprising him with a grateful look.

"Your amazing daughter had him down already when I got here," Hayden explained, giving credit where it was due. "I wanted to tell you both, too, Sara's on her way over to help you with the children. After you've gotten them up and ready, I want you to take them over to the river resort. Mac told me he has a unit right by his house open for you and your family, and he's promised to see to your security himself."

"That's very generous of him," Kate said.

But her mother was shaking her head. "I can't leave my home. What about my animals, and all my—"

"You can ask Sara when she comes, but I'm sure that, under the circumstances, they'll let you bring Thunder with you," Hayden told her. "And this is only temporary, until we can be certain this man was acting alone."

Clutching at the two halves of the neckline of her robe, Rita stubbornly insisted, "I still don't like it, being driven from my own home."

"Would you like it better, giving up the girls to a different foster placement?" Kate asked. "Because I think you know, they're not going to let them stay here after this. Please…think about what's best for Hazel and Lottie, and leave Moonlight and the chickens to me. I promise, I'll take good care of them."

Her mother nodded. "All right, but—but you're not coming over to the resort, too?"

"I'll definitely plan to stay there tonight," she promised, "but I'll have things to do here first, including giving a statement on what happened after I get cleaned up."

Seeming satisfied, her mother said, "I—I'd better go inside then, get myself dressed and make sure the girls aren't frightened when the commotion wakes them."

"Why don't you take Thunder in with you, too?" Kate suggested. "I thought he might've been hit protecting me.

He yelped when the gun fired. But I can't find any blood on him anywhere—"

"He must've just been frightened by the noise. You know how scared he is of fireworks. But I'll be sure to look him over carefully," her mother promised.

"And give him some biscuits—lots of biscuits," Kate said, her brown eyes filling with tears. "He came running when I needed him—he and—and Hayden, b-both."

"You," Kate's mother said, her formidable gaze on Hayden, "you take care of my daughter. Promise me."

"That's why I'm here," he told her honestly, wondering why it had taken him so damned long to realize what he'd been put on this earth for all along.

Now, he needed to find some way to convince Kate that they were truly meant to be together...and to unravel the threat still hanging over the surviving Kesslers— and now the McClaffertys—before it could turn deadly once again.

Chapter 16

As deputies and emergency medical technicians swarmed the property, Kate forced herself to do what was needed, standing near the open rear hatch of Hayden's Tahoe to point people in the right direction and answer questions when she had to. Hiding beneath a thin veneer of normalcy, she managed, also, to dutifully kiss her mother goodbye when she came out to tell her she was leaving with the children for Sara and Mac's place.

"I'm so glad they're going," Hayden commented. "Mac's promised he'll make their security his business—and if anybody can help settle your mom's nerves after all this, Sara will know how to do it."

"I'm sure she will," said Kate. But as she watched her mother's Jeep follow Sara's car down the long driveway, Kate caught herself shuddering, thinking how horribly close she'd just come to never seeing the mother that she loved again…or the girls who'd stolen her heart.

Seeming to notice her distress, Hayden, who'd been hovering protectively, excused himself for a few moments before returning from the Tahoe's rear seat with one of the standard-issue emergency blankets members of the department routinely carried as part of their first aid kits. Ripping open the packaging it came in, he shook out the foil-like cloth before carefully draping it around her.

Blinking in surprise, she bristled. "I already told you, I'm not the injured party here. So don't even think of trying to bundle me off to the ambulance again."

She glanced to where two EMTs loaded her writhing, groaning assailant into the ambulance, while Deputy Alvarez stood guard as he'd been ordered, ready to record anything the man might say or stop further trouble.

"We'll hold off on the ambulance for you now," Hayden allowed, though his expression hinted he would have preferred that she had humored him and gotten checked out. "But you've had one hell of a shock to your system. I mean, look at you. You're shaking like a lapdog in the rain, cowgirl, so park it right here." He slapped the SUV's rear deck as an indication for her to sit.

When she tried—and failed—to hop up, using her good arm to push off, he caught her around the waist and gently lifted her up. Feeling like a child as he carefully tucked the blanket around her, she complained, "Please don't. I'm just a little clumsy, wrapped up like this. And besides, people will see—"

"See what? Me *caring* for a woman who was just nearly murdered?" he asked, adjusting the sunglasses he wore to block the morning light. "Or are you more worried they'll see what I've refused to see too damned long, that I've been living a half life all these years without you."

She stared at him, too overwhelmed to speak.

"I'm sorry if this is too much right now," he blurted. "But when I heard what was going on over my phone, I was scared out of my mind I'd get over here and find you dead, Kate. That you'd be gone, and I'd lose my last chance to tell you something I've been hiding from myself far too long. I'm in love with you."

"I can't do this," she said, her face wet before she understood that she was crying. "Not here and not now, Hayden. Please… I need to go inside."

Hayden's head was throbbing by the time he knocked at the door of the McClafferty house a couple of hours after the ambulance had left. He hadn't meant to stay out in the early-morning sun so long, but as soon as his people had shown up—including two off-duty deputies who'd heard the scanner call and taken it upon themselves to respond to the incident at their one-time colleague's address—he'd started directing them on where to search and what to do next. With the circumstances as they were, he was far too keyed up to stop himself from falling back into old habits.

For a while, adrenaline, determination and the momentum provided by the first of several discoveries kept him going. But now, with every sound crashing through his skull and nausea swirling in his gut, he knew it was long past time he headed home—once he checked in with Kate.

When she didn't answer his knock, he worried she might be avoiding him. Who could blame her, with him blurting out his feelings like a damned fool while she'd been reeling in the aftermath of an assault that could have easily turned deadly? While it was certainly possible that she might be resting upstairs, he couldn't help imagining her sitting in the next room, deliberately ignoring him.

Still, he knocked one more time, too concerned for her welfare to simply walk away. To his immense relief, she showed up and unlocked the door.

"Sorry." She stepped back to wave him inside. At some point, she'd changed into fresh clothing, and her hair was pulled back in a still-damp ponytail that smelled of the clean scent of shampoo. "I was just working on mom's laptop upstairs and got totally caught up in those financial records from Nicolas Kessler's accounts—"

"You were *working*, after what you went through? I figured you'd be uncorking your second bottle of wine by now—or figuring out how quickly you could put this place behind you."

Her gaze dropped to avoid his, her jaw tightening in a reflexive grimace.

"Nailed it, didn't I?" he asked, the question coming out more harshly than he meant. But he was disgusted with himself for coming on with all the subtlety of his former girlfriend Stacey—for whom he felt a sudden stab of sympathy—about his feelings. "Listen, I'm sorry about before. Sorry I couldn't keep quiet until a more appropriate time and place, at least, instead of just blurting—"

"Please don't be, Hayden," Kate said. "What happened was emotional for both of us. But I had to have some space right then—and for the last hour or so, I've needed a distraction to keep me from replaying the attack over and over again in my head and wondering who on earth that man was and if he really was here for the girls, too."

Seeing a plea for understanding in her eyes, he reached out, touching her hand. "I understand. And I do have some information for you. But first, could I bother you for some water—or maybe something with caffeine in it, if you've got it?" He frowned, gesturing vaguely toward his head. "And a couple of OTC painkillers would be great, too, if you could spare 'em."

"Your poor head, of course. Come, sit right here, in the kitchen." She waved him in behind her and then pointed in the direction of the island. "What on earth were you doing out there all that time, instead of handing command off to—"

"After what I heard and saw, you're not seriously expecting I was going to delegate this part of the investigation?" he asked.

Pulling a glass out of a cabinet, she used the refrigerator door dispenser to add ice and water before handing it over to him and then heading to another drawer and offering him some ibuprofen.

He shook out a pair of tablets and drank them down, though by now, the effort felt about as useless as trying to put out a forest fire with a tiny garden hose.

"Better leave on those sunglasses," she suggested, nodding in the direction of the large windows that made the room so bright, even though she'd left the light off. "Would you like an ice pack, too? If you think it would help, I can make one up for you."

"Sure, but I thought I was coming in here to take care of *you*," he complained.

"You've been out there, taking care of me," she said as she pulled out a plastic bag from another drawer in the kitchen island. "Now let me return the favor."

After she'd filled the bag with ice and wrapped it in a clean towel for him, he held it to the back of his head.

"Your attacker's name is Morris Bonner, from Tennessee. He had several false IDs, but that's the one Deputy Alvarez found stashed inside his shoe. After speaking to Investigator Robinson in Memphis, I'm convinced that's who we have here."

"So he *was* telling the truth about being the dead gunman's brother?" she asked.

"Seems likely. We found his transportation, too, a grungy, old panel van that was reported stolen out of Concan," he said, naming another small community just across the county line. "It was parked a couple of hundred yards down the road."

"Guess he was smart enough to ditch the Chevy truck he used to steal the ATVs," she said.

"It's definitely not his first rodeo in the criminal arena," Hayden confirmed. "Robinson says his record's longer than H-Bomb's—and heavier on the gun charges and violent crimes. He would've done hard time, but he had connections to some big-time bad actors that gave him access to bail money and the best lawyers."

"So you're talking organized crime?"

"Definitely. Which tells me the Bonner brothers were hired guns, *sent* here to eliminate the Kessler family. The question is, who's the paying party?"

"I may have found a lead on that," Kate told him. "Or I should say, Tim Spaulding's assistant, Sheela Singh, has. She flagged one of the files she sent us, with a note advising us to take a closer look at that one."

"So did you?"

Kate's shoulders heaved. "I honestly tried. But like I told you before, I'm no financial expert, so I really couldn't make a whole lot of sense out of the numbers. I did have her contact information, though, so I called her. She was busy at the moment, but she said she would make herself available to answer any questions via videoconferencing over the computer."

"How soon can I speak with her?"

Kate looked at the clock. "She should be available anytime now. But I was about to call her on my own, since I've already established contact."

Seeing that he'd stepped on her toes by trying to take over, he said, "That's a good point, but I'd like to be in on the interview, since I spoke with her boss, and I'd like to follow up on some of the questions that I asked him."

"You sure you're feeling up to it?" This time, she gave him a concerned look.

"I'll get through it," he said, removing the ice pack for the time being, "if you wouldn't mind covering the note-taking. Normally, I'd do it myself, but not with my head like this."

"I understand. It's not a problem," she said. "But why not use Mom's craft room? It'll be easier on your eyes, with only one small window, and there's a nice worktable for the laptop."

They moved down the hall, to a small room with walls lined with storage shelves filled with plastic bins and colorfully capped wide-mouth jars brimming with various supplies arranged around a long, white table with a pair of cushioned chairs on wheels.

"Nice setup," he said.

"Mom's gotten really into this stuff since Dad died. She's even started selling things at a couple of local gift shops." Kate smiled at a smaller table along one wall, where a half dozen hand-painted garden placards featuring friendly-looking dragonflies and ladybugs had been left, apparently to dry.

"Good for her. They're nice," he said politely, though his appreciation for arts and crafts items was right up there with his interior decorating skills.

"I'll be right back with the computer," Kate said, "and then we can get started."

Once she'd returned, it took her several minutes to set

up the videoconferencing software and initiate the call to the office of Spaulding and Associates. By that time, Hayden's pain medication started taking effect. With his headache somewhat better, he removed his sunglasses, since he already felt handicapped interviewing online rather than in person and felt eye contact would be especially important.

On the screen, a trim, well-dressed woman likely in her late forties or early fifties appeared. Her dark, professional hairstyle touched with silver, she introduced herself as Sheela Singh, the executive assistant for Tim Spaulding. To Hayden's practiced eye, she looked and sounded ill at ease, her hands flitting about her desktop and her dark gaze darting here and there as she sat behind a glossy, wooden desk in a neat, professional-looking private office.

He couldn't help but notice the healthy-looking houseplant among the items on the shelves behind her. The sight of its glossy, dark green leaves felt almost like an accusation, since he'd discovered this morning that his own brown cactus had finally toppled over and snapped off at its base, as if to mock his foolhardy attempts to coax it back from the dead.

Pushing it from his mind, he focused on establishing a pleasant rapport as they made their way through introductions and he and Kate expressed their condolences on the loss of the woman's colleague.

"Thank you." She nodded before admitting, "It's been a very difficult time for everyone here at Spaulding and Associates."

"Can you tell me, how long have you been with the firm?" Hayden asked her.

"About twelve years now." Her sigh was audible. "It was actually Nic who hired me. Tim had to take some time off because his little boy had broken his leg."

"Twelve years ago?" Hayden asked, confused, recalling what Spaulding had said about his wife and their childcare situation. "I'd been under the impression Spaulding's son was a lot younger—or does he have more than just the one boy?"

"Matthew's their older son," she clarified. "Fortunately, he recovered completely from that mishap, and he's a wonderful older brother to little Bryce, the five-year-old, despite his challenges."

Hayden recalled Tim Spaulding's comment about the child's special needs.

"It sounds like you know the family very well," Kate said.

"I've grown close with both men's families, especially since my husband's passing five years ago. Since I don't have any other relations in this country, Tim and Nic and their wives have been kind enough to welcome me to so many of their own occasions. And I'd like to think I've become almost an honorary grandmother to their—their children... Oh, dear. I'm so—sorry. When I think of that poor family—" Reaching behind her own desktop camera, Mrs. Singh's hand returned with a fluttering, white facial tissue, which she used to blot her damp eyes, smudging her mascara.

"Please don't apologize," Hayden said. "Take your time."

"I can't imagine someone doing this to such wonderful people. Nic lived for Ada and those sweet girls. Their photos are still all right there, displayed so proudly in his office, and I can scarcely—scarcely sleep for thinking about them all."

"I'm very sorry for your pain," Kate said. "But speaking of the office, have the police come by that you're aware of?"

Mrs. Singh shook her head. "After Tim made the initial missing persons report, I understand he answered a great many questions for a police investigator. But I don't believe that any officers have ever come by the office or gone through any of Nic's things here."

"Since he was killed out of state, that's not surprising," Hayden said, knowing that when multiple jurisdictions were involved in any one investigation, then more details normally checked were likely to end up slipping through the cracks.

"I'm almost positive I'm the first person to dig into Nic's work files since he left town. There's an electronic signature system that requires employees to sign in with a passcode."

Once she had settled, Kate said, "I appreciated the note on the one file you e-mailed, directing our attention to the charity known as the Hope for Homes Initiative."

"Actually, I'd meant to forward that to Tim first instead of you." Mrs. Singh's forehead crinkled. "But I was working through the night and realized now I left his e-mail in my drafts folder and sent out the wrong message. He could certainly explain the issue to you once he's had the chance to review the— When you next see him, you might ask him to explain—"

"*See* him?" Hayden interjected. "I was under the impression that he'd already flown home, that there are some pressing tax deadlines at the office."

"He certainly isn't back in town that I'm aware of," Mrs. Singh said. "In fact, I haven't heard from him at all in a couple of days. I thought he was still staying at a hotel in Kerrville, helping with Ada and the children."

"I let him know he wouldn't be able to see Ada, on account of her condition, and he informed me he'd be returning home," Hayden said.

Mrs. Singh said, "Then perhaps he has, and he's working out of his home office."

"Does he do that often?" Hayden pressed, concerned by the uncertainty he heard in her voice.

"On occasion, and I can certainly see why he might want to now. I'm sure Nic's death is hitting him harder than anyone, since they've known each other so long. He probably just needs some private time."

Hayden made a mental note to give Spaulding a call—and ask Lamar Robinson to personally reach out to him as well, just to confirm the CPA had really made it back to Memphis safely. Something felt off about Spaulding's silence.

"Since your note didn't get through to your boss, maybe you could explain to us what you discovered in that one file that you found troubling," Kate suggested. "I'd really like to hear from you about that. I tried myself to review the file, but I'm afraid I couldn't make much headway with the numbers."

"It wasn't the numbers so much as the Hope for Homes Initiative's mission statement." Mrs. Singh frowned. "Here, let me pull it up for you."

"What about the mission statement?" Hayden asked as, a few moments later, another box popped up on the screen, filled with text he couldn't read without making his vision blur and head hurt.

"As you can see," Mrs. Singh said, sounding righteously indignant, "they're boasting about how they're helping first-time home buyers from diverse and underprivileged backgrounds become the first in their families to own property."

Kate held up a palm. "Sounds like a worthy cause to me."

"It certainly *would* be, if this were what they were

actually doing." The older woman's dark brows slanted downward as the box changed to what appeared to be a list of names. "But anyone who knows who's who in this region would recognize that this list of *actual* recipients of their services is made up of nothing but younger members of the region's wealthiest families."

"So basically," Hayden summarized, "this supposed charity for the disadvantaged is nothing but some kind of real estate racket."

"Yes, to help the offspring of the area's most connected families push so-called *undesirables* out of what they've determined to be up-and-coming neighborhoods, undoubtedly using inside information," Mrs. Singh explained. "Then the investors turn around and sell the places they've bought using federal grants meant to aid the disadvantaged for huge profits once the prices shoot up."

"Sounds like the kind of fraud that ends up getting people sent to federal prison," Kate commented.

"With good reason," Mrs. Singh said, her words heated. "When I think of all the times people who look like me are told there are no listings in a certain neighborhood, or the property they would like to see is no longer available—this sort of thing makes my blood boil."

"I can imagine how that must feel," Hayden told her. "And you think Nicolas Kessler discovered this?"

"He would have *had* to have known about it," she assured them, "since these names included the children of a number of our firm's most profitable long-standing clients."

Hayden frowned. "Your clients? So this is why you wanted to give your boss a heads-up?"

Mrs. Singh nodded, looking conflicted. "I needed to advise Tim and give him an opportunity to recommend our clients secure proper legal representation before I pass this information on to the authorities."

"The authorities?" Kate said.

Mrs. Singh threw up her hands. "What else am I to do? If I say nothing, I could not only lose my professional licensures, I could go to prison myself as an accessory to serious financial crimes. Plus, I could never condone such actions."

But Hayden was shaking his head, warning her, "I appreciate your integrity, Mrs. Singh. Believe me when I say I wish we had far more people in this world like you. But you *absolutely* need to hold off on mentioning any of what you'd discovered to *anyone* else for now."

"I'll tell no one except for Tim, then."

"No one meaning *no one*," Hayden emphasized. "Not your boss or a single coworker—for their safety as well as your own until I give you the word."

"He's right." Kate nodded as she backed him up. "And that e-mail you were about to send Tim Spaulding—it's very important that you delete it. Delete it *right now* without sending it, and definitely say nothing to any of your clients."

Looking more nervous than ever, Mrs. Singh burst out, "You are frightening me!"

"I'm sorry we have to do that, ma'am," Hayden told her honestly. "But two people have been shot so far, and we don't yet know the motive. But a scheme like this one could very well be it."

Hands fluttering toward her throat, the older woman said, "I'm not—I'm not feeling very well. I may need to go home now and lie down…"

"Leaving doesn't sound like a half-bad idea," Hayden told her. "But is there someplace other than your own home where you might spend the next few days? Someplace where no one—even the people you work with—would ever think to look for you?"

Trembling visibly, she stared at them in wide-eyed horror before slowly nodding in response.

Chapter 17

Once they had ended the interview, Kate shook her head in Hayden's direction. "I'm afraid we scared that poor woman half to death."

"Better scaring her halfway there than finding out later she's been murdered. Speaking of which, I need to try Tim Spaulding right away." He pulled out his cell phone.

Alarm pulsed through Kate. "You aren't worried that he never left here like he claimed he was going to, are you?"

"Hell, yes, I am," he said as he looked up the CPA's phone number in his contacts. "For all I know, this guy's body's floating downriver somewhere, or in another remote canyon."

"You think Morris Bonner may've found him before he came looking for me?" The very thought sent a shudder through her with the memory of the thug pressing the gun to her head. "Or could there be others, too, perhaps sent as backup after the first team ran into trouble at the ambush?"

"Impossible to say who might've caught up with him. But whoever was desperate enough to want to wipe out the Kesslers to keep their scheme quiet won't stop with one set of thugs. Especially not if Spaulding's found his own way into Nic's files since his death and figured things out, too."

"You think he'd be as naive as his assistant, warning clients before tipping his hand to the Feds?" Kate asked.

"If he's an honest man, that may be."

"What if he's not?" she asked, wanting to consider every possibility.

Hayden rubbed a jaw more stubbled than his usual well-groomed look, a reminder of how he'd run out of the house to rush to her aid this morning. "I suppose it's possible he decided to try his hand at blackmail—especially if he had any suspicion that this fraud might be related to his friend's murder."

"That's a heck of a risk to take."

"Here's hoping, for his family's sake, he didn't find that out the hard way. Ah, here's Spaulding's number. Let's try him." After hitting Connect, Hayden turned the call on speaker so that she, too, could hear the ringing.

Kate felt her stomach drop only moments later when she heard a recording stating that the user's mailbox was full and he could not receive any more messages at this time.

Frowning, Hayden said, "I wish I had his wife's number to check in with her. Surely, she would've raised the alarm by now if she hadn't at least heard from him lately."

"You'd certainly think so," Kate agreed, "but without knowing the couple and how they operate, it's impossible to say for certain."

Hayden nodded. "I'm calling Investigator Robinson to see if he can send a patrol over to the Spauldings' home. I won't be satisfied until an officer's made certain he and his family are okay."

"You can't think they're in danger, too?"

Hayden said, "Who's to say these killers might not be willing to take out a second family to keep their secret safe—and cover up the shooting of Nicolas and Ada."

"There's another possibility as well," Kate suggested. "What if Tim Spaulding has known about this scheme all along?" She shrugged. "I mean, didn't you tell me this guy's top priority's his business and the bottom line? Wasn't Nicolas Kessler the one who was more focused on charitable endeavors?"

Lowering his phone, Hayden said, "I suppose it's *possible* Spaulding could've been in on some plot to get rid of a colleague whose conscience had grown inconvenient. But when I met with him, the man seemed genuinely broken up about his old friend. If you'd seen the way he was beating himself up about having let Nic Kessler leave town that Friday, I'm not sure you'd be floating that theory."

"Maybe not." She respected Hayden's instincts about those he interviewed, though they had worked long enough in law enforcement to know that on any given day, any individual could turn out to be far less harmless than he might pretend, whether they were sociopaths or simply gifted in the art of lying.

"Whether he's at risk or somehow complicit, I need this man tracked down quickly." Staring in frustration at the now-swimming list of contacts, Hayden muttered under his breath, "I know I have Investigator Robinson's number in here."

"Why don't you let me find it for you? You don't need to make your head worse."

"I've got this," Hayden said stubbornly before activating the cell's digital assistant feature. "Call Lamar Robinson."

"Calling Lamar Robinson," the smartphone dutifully replied.

When Robinson picked up, Hayden briefly filled him in on Kate's attack before explaining what they'd learned from Mrs. Singh. "Right now," he continued, "I'm extremely concerned for Tim Spaulding's safety since I can't reach him and it's been days since he's touched base with his office. Can I get you to send a unit to his family home, make sure everyone's all right there?"

Kate, who'd been searching online for social media accounts Tim Spaulding might have to see if she could find any recent activity, glanced up at Hayden's suggestion.

Robinson must have questioned the request because Hayden went on to say, "Yes, I did say *everyone*, and I hope to hell I *am* wrong, Lamar. But if these people were willing to try to go after Nic Kessler's entire family either to keep their secret safe or scare the hell out of anybody else who might think of talking, who's to say they won't be willing to wipe out all four Spauldings, too? So please… Great, thanks. I'll look forward to hearing back from you as soon as you know something."

After ending the call, he told Kate, "He's going to try Phoebe Spaulding's—that's Tim's wife's—phone first. Then he's going to personally stop by the house to see what other information he can shake loose."

"That sounds good, but here's what doesn't," she said. "Tim Spaulding's normally an active online poster. Apparently, he has this tax-tips-and-insights blog that's pretty popular—and probably excellent for business. But

over the last three days, he's gone silent, even when posters started getting concerned and checking in to make
sure he's all right."

"Could be a normal response to his friend and employee's murder," Hayden said.

"Or could be you were correct before, and he's not all
right at all."

Hayden's forehead creased as he considered, until he
abruptly blurted, "Damn it."

"What?" she asked as he again picked up his phone.

"I completely forget to fill in Robinson on Ada's
brother, Cal Thorley, showing up to try to see her at the
hospital. Sorry to interrupt what you were saying, but I
want to call him right back."

"Please, go ahead," she said, waving off his apology.
"And it's no wonder it slipped your mind, with everything
that's happened in the hours since."

Thinking back to the things he'd told her after the attack,
she realized just how badly her near miss with Morris Bonner had upset him. Otherwise, surely, a man like Hayden
Hale-Walker didn't come right out and admit he cared for
anything or anyone. As for *love*…had he ever used that
word with her, exactly, even back when the two of them
had been scheming to elope?

Would he be embarrassed, regretting later the words
spoken in such haste this morning? Or could it be, impossible as it might seem, that the pressure cooker of
emotion had only served to force the truth from his lips?

Moments later, she noticed he was scowling at his
phone. "He must've gotten busy because he's not picking up. I know that sometimes listening to voice mails in
the field can be an issue, so would you mind texting him
about Thorley from my cell here, please? I'd use voice

dictation to do it myself, but half the time, the stupid thing mishears me and garbles my messages."

She took a minute to type out the text but smiled at a memory triggered by his words. "There you go. It's sent. And I know what you mean about the garbled messages. I once tried to get Simon to order pizzas for everybody at some search and rescue training thing and my stupid phone mistook the 'extra pepperoni' for a confession that I was 'extra pregnant.' Talk about your awkward workplace conversations."

Hayden laughed at that—but their levity lasted only a moment before she saw the pain of awareness in the deep blue of his eyes. Because try as she might to normalize it, *pregnant* was a word that had forever lost its innocence for them.

Feeling her face fall at the sting of memory, she rose and started for the door. But in her rush to hide her own emotions from him, she missed noticing that the laptop's cord, still plugged into the central floor outlet, had wrapped around her ankle.

Stumbling, she pitched forward, but somehow, Hayden sprang to his feet in time to catch her before she fell.

"Of all the clumsy— Thanks," she said breathlessly, as he helped her regain her footing. "I can't believe how fast your reflexes are—but I'm all right now. You can let go of—"

"Then why are you still shaking so hard?" He drew her even closer, wrapping her in his arms.

Closing her eyes, she sighed, all the tension she'd been carrying between her shoulders since the attack melting away into the warmth, and safety, of an embrace that felt as right as the last eighteen years had felt wrong.

How she had missed the scent of him: simple, clean and masculine, and the rock-solid wall of chest and shoulder that she could lean into at her weakest moments. As she did now, tears clogging her nose and throat as they erupted. Tears of grief ran freely for something she knew in her bones she would never stop missing, no matter how hard she tried to lose herself in work or other relationships that always felt so flat and pointless, she was left wondering why she bothered trying.

"It's all right," he whispered to her, rubbing her back gently. "You're okay now."

"It's not—not what happened earlier," she admitted, pulling back to look up at him. "It's this. It's…us, the way we'll *never* be able to pretend we're just a couple of old friends, will we? Not even to ourselves…not when we're together like this."

"In some ways, it was a lot easier back when we were fighting," he said. "But I can't go back to hating you again, Kate, not now that I see it for exactly what it was."

"And what was that?"

"The only way to survive losing both you and our—our future."

"The baby, you mean."

"All of it," he told her, pain written in his face. "The entire future I'd imagined for us—you, me and the pack of kids I'd pictured us raising together on the ranch."

"A whole *pack* of 'em, huh?" she asked, a painful lump in her throat.

He shrugged. "I imagine my brothers would laugh at that, coming from a guy who's never committed to so much as a stray dog, let alone an actual relationship, but I haven't always been so—"

"Gun-shy?" she asked. Wasn't that what it was called when someone had been hurt so badly that they could never bear to risk the pain again? "I'm so sorry."

"Why would you be—"

"I'm sorry that I couldn't bring myself to see you, afterward," she said. "I was hurting so much, on every level—I just wanted them to let me die, too, with the baby and my Cloverleaf, when I finally came around enough to find out that they hadn't—hadn't made it."

"And I just wanted to be there for you," he said. "I did try again to come back. I want you to know that. I tried two more times after your parents told me you didn't want to see me. I kept thinking they must be lying for some reason, or that you might change your mind and need me."

He grimaced as the memory pained him. "But finally your dad came to the house, scared my mom half to pieces waving around a restraining order and ranting how he'd either see me thrown in jail or buried *under* the jail if he couldn't keep me away from his daughter."

"My father did *what*?" Horrified to imagine her normally mild-tempered father behaving in such a manner, Kate shook her head. "I had no idea, and I'm so sorry he did such an awful thing. It's no excuse, but all I can say is he must have been half out of his mind with grief over what had happened."

"He seemed mostly furious at me."

"He was, at both of us, for keeping the pregnancy a secret," she said.

"But with you hurt so badly, I'm sure at that moment it was a whole lot easier and safer for him to lash out at me than you, the guy who got their daughter pregnant and had been plotting to steal her away from them. Your mother even said, if you hadn't been so distracted by our plans to run off, there's no way you ever would've been hurt in the first place."

"You can't believe that because it's definitely not true," Kate insisted. "Every rider I know who was there that day said that with that gate coming out of nowhere, no horse and rider alive could've avoided a collision."

"It was a horrible time, everybody stressed to the max and no one sleeping," Hayden told her. "It's no wonder we all turned on each other."

"And all I knew," Kate said, "is that when I *did* ask for you, they said you'd told them that you guessed this left you off the hook, about having to marry me. I thought—I thought you meant because the baby was gone."

"I was so damned hurt and furious at that moment, I hardly understood what I was saying to them. All I knew when I saw that restraining order was that I'd just lost everything."

"I don't understand."

"I thought you truly didn't want to be with me any longer," he said. "That because of what had happened, you were bailing on the whole idea—on us. But with or without a baby to force my hand, I'd've still married you, Kate, that weekend like we'd planned or the next year when we didn't have to use the fake IDs or however long I had to wait. It would have been the honor of my lifetime."

Unable to meet his gaze, she turned away. "We were so young back then. Too young, and so foolish, thinking that secrets as huge as we were keeping weren't bound to blow up on us. But it doesn't have to ruin our lives. You still could marry, Hayden, could have that family you missed out on—"

"*We* could," he said. "Why the hell not? Don't you feel it, too? It's like we're *meant* to get this second chance—a chance to make each other happy instead of miserable for a change. And I swear that's all I want from my life, to know I've gotten this one thing right. Okay, well, that and caught my share of bad guys."

"Oh, Hayden…"

"Come on, Katie, please. Would you at least look at me? Because I've never proposed to anyone before, not even close—and I need to see your face to get some kind of idea just how badly I'm mucking this thing up."

Knowing he deserved at least that much—and so much more—she turned back around to face him, her eyes brimming as she shook her head. "You aren't mucking anything up. I'm the one who's honored, deeply, especially after all the misery I've rained down on you for so long."

"We're both well aware, I gave as good as I got…"

"I'm so flattered you still care about me," she continued before shaking her head. "And I care about you, too, deeply. But I can't do this, Hayde. I can't—because you deserve to have that family you dreamed of, and you won't—you *can't* have that with me."

He reached to feather a touch along her jawline. "Please, Kate. If you really care for me at all, do me this one favor. Lie to me if you have to, but stop now. And tell me you'll think about it. Because if all I get out of this is that much hope, then I damned well mean to have it."

When she looked up into his handsome face, she absolutely knew that no one else had ever or would ever again love her this way. She would always adore this man for that and so much more.

Her answer to his first question wouldn't change—the answer she'd have to give him to avoid a deeper pain. For now, though, it was enough that she raised herself onto her toes and softly kissed him. As his head dipped and his strong arms reached around her, she tried to pour the feelings she could never put into words into that moment. Her sadness over all they'd lost, her regret for the way she'd allowed her disappointments to at times turn her into someone she hadn't even liked…

But as his hand slid down along her flank, her worst moments fell away, and she remembered him telling her she was magnificent, saying it as if he'd truly meant it. And now, deep inside her grew a belief that, rather than a tiny girl whose screams had gone unheeded inside a rusting trailer, she might instead be the woman *he* saw, someone worthy to be loved and cherished.

When he dropped kisses to the curve of her neck, she gasped, arching her neck backward and allowing him to knead her breast as she ground her thigh against his hard length. But the more they kissed and touched and rubbed against each other, the more she wanted from him. Needed desperately and soon.

Finally, she panted, "Need to—go upstairs…because if I don't get out of these clothes right now, I swear I'm going to spontaneously combust."

Hayden grinned down at her, his eyes dilated with desire. "Would that be an invitation?"

"You still remember…" she asked breathlessly, "sneaking into my room?"

"There are some details that stick with a man forever. Although, if memory serves, I climbed in through your window last time."

"Well, I'm not willing to risk you slipping on the roof and knocking yourself silly again, so how about if we take the stairs this time?"

Hayden didn't delude himself into believing that her offer meant forever. But it was enough to know Kate wanted him, even if it was only just this one time—one chance to have what he'd been dreaming of since seeing her again.

Taking him by the hand, she led him up the staircase. He followed her into a bedroom that had been repainted and stripped of the posters and trophies he vaguely remembered from years past. But now, as then, he didn't waste much time admiring the decor as she softly closed the door against even the slightest chance of interruption. Especially not when the first thing she did, after giving him a look filled with such intent that it sent lust streaking straight to his groin, was pull the strap of her arm sling off over her head and remove it. After she kicked off her shoes, too, her top came off next, and then she reached behind herself, toward the center of her back.

Realizing what she meant to remove next, he whispered, "Stop right there, please. I need to—"

He could not stop staring at her. The bra was black, with just a bit of lace trim, molding and lifting her pale, perfectly formed breasts enticingly.

"So beautiful," he told her, planting the lightest of kisses in the divot between her collarbones, working his way downward as he traced a fingertip beneath one of the cups.

He heard her gasp. But when his kisses brushed one of her scars, she moved to cover it with her hand.

"I told you before," he whispered, "there's no need to hide them."

"But they're ugly," she said, emotion clouding her eyes. "And they make me feel so— I've always meant to get them fixed, have plastic surgery."

"The scars are the places where your skin's grown stronger, where you've grown tougher, wiser, more sensitive to the wounds of others. So they're just a part of what makes you so special to me—every gorgeous inch of you. Do you understand that, Kate?" he asked.

When she hesitated before nodding, he said, "But if they really bother you, and you want the reminder gone, why not look into what can be done?"

She shrugged. "I—I've tried to tell myself that they don't matter, and the truth is, most of the time, I hardly see them. But when it comes to the thought of being with anybody, letting them see me for the first time with the lights on… I can't stand the idea of being the object of anybody's pity. So I just— I'm stopped cold—"

"Is that why you've never…gotten close with anyone?"

"Maybe part of it," she said, her eyes avoiding his. "But—you've been the same way, Hayden, keeping every woman at arm's length. Emotionally, anyway."

"Guess something in me was just marking time, waiting for the only one I really wanted. And right now, Kate, I swear to you, I've never wanted anyone more in all my life."

"Then I believe it's time you stop talking and prove it," she said and reached behind herself and undid the bra's closure…

And after that he had no more words, but his body provided far better ways to show her everything he felt.

Chapter 18

Kate wanted to lie in Hayden's arms forever, nestling against a chest more muscular and somewhat hairier than she remembered. She reminded herself that he had been a boy when she had known him last. Now he was a man in his prime…a man who'd learned more than a few things in the time they'd been apart.

Things she quite approved of, she thought, a smile stretching her lips as she arched her neck to kiss the stubble along his jaw. But he was already pushing away from her, that talented mouth of his tight and his forehead creasing.

"That wasn't right, Kate. I should've stopped myself the moment I realized I didn't have protection on me, no matter how amazing it felt being with you." Rolling away from her, he sat on the side of the bed. "I don't know what the hell I was thinking, but once I got a taste of you, I couldn't seem to stop from—"

"It's all right, Hayden," she assured him, rolling onto her side. "I told you, I've been tested since I was last with anyone and—"

"Just like I was after my last breakup, but come on, Kate. We aren't a couple of horny teenagers anymore. Getting caught up in the moment's no excuse to risk an unplanned pregnancy. I'm so damned sorry that I wasn't in better control of myself. I swear, I've never been like this with anyone but—"

She shook her head. "Please listen— It's not— I'm not— That's...not going to be an issue."

She opened her mouth, meaning to tell him, *I'm on the pill. It's all right.* But she saw, in that moment, the way he looked at her body, apparently focused on the long, now-silvery scar where they had sliced open her abdomen so many years before, and the lie died on her lips.

Heat washing over her, she grasped the sheet to cover her shame. He touched her hand, his deep blue eyes reminding her of the boy she'd known and trusted forever with her most painful secrets. But never this one.

"Kate?" he asked. "Please tell me... You tried before, but I didn't listen. But whatever it is, I want to understand. I need to."

She tried to look away but couldn't, held captive by the intensity of his gaze. And the knowledge that she owed him this much. The truth of why she'd pushed him away once and would again.

"You know that I was badly hurt...the day I lost the baby."

"Fractured pelvis, femur, three crushed vertebrae," he said, cataloging those injuries he knew of. "I'm still amazed every time I see you walk so smoothly, let alone ride again..."

"There was more internal damage—with the placenta. They couldn't stop the bleeding. I'm told they would've surely lost me with the baby if they hadn't—hadn't done a…" Her eyes slid closed, her throat locking tight against the secret she had carried so long. "It's why I won't get pregnant, Hayden. Why I can't, not ever."

He slid his hand along her upper arm. "I'm so sorry. I had no idea."

She shook her head. "I made my parents promise—I begged them not to tell anyone. I was only seventeen, and I'd lost—I'd lost Riley Ann—"

"Our baby's name?"

"Not officially, but in my mind, I've always called her that," she said, her voice barely above a whisper.

"It's beautiful," he told her, sounding for all the world as if he meant it. "I'm only sorry I wasn't there to help you grieve her—and all of it."

"My parents barely acknowledged her. They couldn't wrap their heads around the fact that I'd been pregnant in the first place—but dealing with the trauma, the pain medication and—everything." She shook her head. "That surgery was just one more thing we didn't really speak of."

"I'm starting to understand, though, why your dad acted the way he did toward me, seeing you so devastated. But what I can't understand is why *you* kept me away."

"You have to realize, when I told them I didn't want to see you, I'd only just found out what they'd done—I was half out of my mind with drugs and grief and convinced my life was over. I was sure that you were better off without me. I almost thought the world would be a better place without me."

"You'd been through so much. You were upset, but Kate, that surgery wouldn't have made a difference in how I felt about you then, just like I swear it doesn't now," he insisted, not hesitating for a moment. "Nothing would have made any difference except for being with you. Can't you understand that?"

"I couldn't think any further than the pain." Convinced he didn't know what he was saying, she moved from his embrace enough to cover her body with the sheet. "And by the time I finally weakened and begged my parents to let me see you, I thought, after hearing what you said, that you were finished with me."

Cursing under his breath, he said, "So that's the day you started hating me."

Blinking back tears, she shook her head. "You have to understand. With my whole life shattered in a million pieces, you were just one more jagged shard that might kill me if I dwelled on it too long."

"I'd give anything, even my life, if I could change what happened to you back then," Hayden told her, thinking of all the years he'd lost to fantasizing about turning back time and doing exactly that, "but we both know how pointless it is, wasting whatever time we have left wishing for some do-over that's never going to happen."

"I do know that," she said.

"The only thing I can try to do about the past is try to learn from all my screwups, so this time, I swear to you, I'm not letting any damned misunderstanding get between us."

"But this isn't any *misunderstanding* this time, Hayden," Kate told him, wrapping the sheet more tightly around her. "It's me telling you that I'm not the woman you imagined when you proposed. So I'm letting you off the hook so you can find someone who can give you the family that you—"

"Would you please listen to yourself, Kate?" he

pleaded, racking his brain for something, anything that might get through to her. "And while you're at it, really think about your *mother*. Not the sorry excuse of a human being who was too wasted to give a damn that you were being literally tortured in the next room, but the woman we both know would give her *life* for you. Which one do you think of as your mom? And which one would you rather be?"

"But you deserve to have your own—"

"Whatever the hell ever gave you the idea that life's about *deserving* anything—or that one kind of family's any better than another in the first place? You think either of the McClaffertys could have loved you one bit more if you'd shared their DNA? Or that I'm incapable of loving a kid who doesn't carry mine?"

"I just *can't*—"

They startled at the unexpected sound from downstairs of the doorbell chiming. Almost immediately, it was followed, by an urgent-sounding knock.

Hurrying to the window, Hayden immediately reached for his pants—and cursed to realize that his phone wasn't in his pocket.

"Who is it?"

"That's Deputy Tomlinson's unit. They must be looking for me, but I guess I left my cell in the craft room and didn't hear it ringing down there."

Rising from the bed, she said, "Here, let me fix your hair," once he'd hurriedly pulled on his shirt, "unless you want everybody in the department to figure out we were doing more than discussing the case while they were out in the heat working."

He sighed, suspecting she wanted to keep their relationship secret because she had no intention of making it long-term. Though she'd clearly said as much before they'd made love, had nothing they'd shared, nothing he'd risked saying made the slightest bit of difference to her?

But none of that mattered right this moment, as another, harder rap followed. Hurrying downstairs, he spotted the round face of his most recent hire, Alice Tomlinson, pressed to a living room window. Her hands were cupped around worried blue eyes as the rookie deputy tried to peer inside.

Opening the front door, he called, "Right here, Deputy. What's going on?"

She stepped inside, a tall and slightly heavyset young woman who by all accounts was settling in well in her new position.

"Chief Deputy Yarborough asked me to track you down right away when he couldn't reach you by phone, and when I saw your unit was still here…" Her fair face went even paler. "I was afraid the man who attacked Ms. McClafferty this morning might've had another accomplice we weren't aware of, and that he might have even come back to—"

"I'm sorry to have worried you," Hayden said, bending the truth by explaining how he'd accidentally left his phone outside the room where Kate had been helping him conduct a remote interview online. "So what was it Clayton needed?"

"He said to tell you he's aware you're supposed to be convalescing, but under the circumstances, he really thought you might want to have me drive you out to the Old Meier Ranch River Crossing. You know the place?"

"Of course, I do," Hayden said, though the remote property, located along a road that had been washed out so often and received so little traffic, the county no longer bothered with its upkeep, was one that he doubted three out of ten people living in this county could still locate on a map. "What's there that's so important that I need to personally see to it?"

"It's a car, Sheriff, an abandoned car found just off the road, with the front driver's side door left standing open," she said, looking disturbed.

"We get abandoned vehicle calls pretty often, Deputy, so I don't understand. What's so urgent about this one?"

"Clayton says he recognizes it as the rental Tim Spaulding was driving when he saw him—and there are bullet holes through the side window and what looks like dried blood across the dash."

Hayden felt his heart sink. "Bullets holes and blood spatter? Why didn't you say so in the first place? What about a body?"

"No sign of one anywhere in the vehicle or the immediate vicinity—and the thing is, it wasn't a huge amount of blood in the car, so Clayton's working on the theory that Spaulding could've made a run for it after crashing the car into that culvert."

"Okay, I'll be right out to ride with you. Let me touch base first, though, with search and rescue on this."

Chapter 19

Once Hayden informed her what was going on, Kate offered to come with him and Deputy Tomlinson, who had gone out to wait for him back inside her vehicle.

Donning his sunglasses, he shook his head and reached out to help her with the top buttons of the shirt she'd pulled on before joining him downstairs. "Why don't you hang tight here? You can make a call to get a search and rescue team staged so we can have them ready if I need them. Afterward, you can rest up while you wait for me to phone you with an update."

"Rest up?" she asked, righteously indignant. "With a man missing and in danger—if he isn't dead already?"

"I hear what you're saying, but realistically, we both know that unless we catch the luckiest of breaks, this is likely to drag out for hours. It's bad enough I have to suck it up and go out there—and I definitely need to do this in person, at least long enough to get things rolling."

"I know I couldn't talk you out of it if I tried," she admitted.

"But, Kate, you were nearly killed this morning." He laid a hand on her shoulder. "You need to give your mind and body some time out to recover."

She wanted to argue that he should talk, but the truth was, she'd already begun stiffening up, aching everywhere—especially her healing hand—from her ordeal. Emotionally, she felt overloaded as well, still reeling from ways she'd exposed herself with Hayden.

"You don't know how it pains me to admit this, but I think you're right," she conceded. "So after I check on the animals, I'd like to decompress a little right here, without Mom in my face asking me a million questions about what happened."

"I get that. But promise me when you go back out to the barn again, you'll take the rifle, and call for help if there's the slightest sign of trouble."

She nodded. "You don't have to tell me twice. I'll be sure to lock up tight as soon as I'm back inside, too."

"Perfect." Leaning his head down, he gently kissed her forehead. "Promise me, too, you'll call over to the resort if you decide you want company after all. Or better yet, you can take my Tahoe. I'll leave you the keys, since I won't be driving it."

"Thanks, I'll do that," she agreed, accepting the key ring he'd offered. "And Hayden?"

"Yes?" he asked, what looked very much like hope unfurling in the deep blue depths of his gaze.

But there wasn't time to get into the discussion she already knew was bound to disappoint him, so she stuck with a safer subject. "I know you imagine it's a fate worse than death, showing any kind of weakness in front of your people, but please, take breaks when you need to. Ask for help, and bow out if you have to. If you don't, you're only going to end up dragging out your recovery longer."

His forehead furrowed, and when he opened his mouth, she was almost certain the bullheaded man was going to argue with her. Instead, he said, "I will try, and thanks for always caring enough to say the things I don't want to hear."

"I've been telling people stuff they don't want to hear for years," she reminded him, fumbling her way through a smile. "I have to admit, though, it's kind of nice to get thanked for it for once instead of the usual curses and eye-rolling."

As soon as Hayden left with the deputy, she called Simon as promised, to get the ball rolling on a possible search and rescue team deployment.

"We're actually stretched a little thin at the moment," he informed her. "We have all hands on deck looking for a missing autistic teen outside of Medina. Praying we get to her in time."

"I'll second that. Please keep me posted. And if you can't scrape together enough backup volunteers for here, try South Texas or even Texas EquuSearch," she said, naming other search and rescue groups in the region.

"I'll do that," he promised. "But I wanted to ask, how're you feeling since the surgery? You getting bored there out in the hinterlands?"

"The hand's fine," she said, "and you wouldn't believe how bored…"

"Well, boredom's good for healing," he said, clearly not catching the irony in her voice, "so I hope that means we'll be getting you back here soon. A lot of people miss you— and Jasper thinks my mule-sitting's a poor substitute for your personal TLC."

Smiling, she said, "Scratch those long ears for me, will you? I'm really missing my big boy something fierce."

After quickly wrapping up the conversation, she went out to see to the chickens and spent some time with Moonlight, stroking the mare's sleek neck and reassuring her.

"How about some apple slices, sweet girl?" she said, feeding the gray the fruit she'd brought out before carefully checking her hooves and legs. Once she felt reassured that the old horse had settled well and sustained no injuries from kicking at her stall, Kate headed back inside, her steps slowed by the aching stiffness that had settled over her body.

Knowing that an over-the-counter pain pill wouldn't cut it, she compromised by taking half of a prescription tablet in the hope that, even if she dozed off, she would at least remain responsive enough to wake up when Hayden called to update her on the Tim Spaulding situation.

Stretching out on the living room sofa, she said a quick prayer for the man's safety and that of his family before adding the missing autistic teen to her pleas. Then she thought, too, of Ada Kessler, who might at any moment be undergoing a surgery that could either save her life or take her forever from her precious daughters.

A lot of worry piled on top of her anxiety. In making love with Hayden again, she had crossed the line back into a territory she knew to be heavily mined with future heartache. Heartache she wasn't certain she could survive a second time.

As Hayden rode in the passenger seat, he felt every pothole on the washed-out ranch road as they traversed a rugged area where the soil was so poor and rocky, it was good for little more than wildlife habitat and beautiful mountain views. By the time they reached the Old Meier

Ranch area, the terrain sloped toward the river ahead and included a mix of trees and grassy swaths. In one of the latter, a herd of about twenty deer grazed in the distance, clearly undisturbed by any recent human activity.

"It'll be up here on the right," Tomlinson told him, as if he couldn't already see Clayton waving for their attention and directing her where to park.

Hayden wondered if he was trying to prevent them from driving over evidence, a theory his chief deputy confirmed the moment they climbed out of the rookie's unit.

"We've got a set of tire tracks right here," Clayton told them, pointing out a double lane of long-stemmed, crushed weeds. "Pretty fresh, and looks to have come from a full-size truck or SUV, judging from the track width. Could possibly belong to our shooter."

Given how seldom this mostly forgotten road was traveled, Hayden had to agree that was a decent working theory. But his attention was mostly on the abandoned black sedan, which he immediately started toward after briefly greeting Clayton and telling him, "Glad you rounded me up for this."

He thought, like Clayton, he recognized the sedan to be Spaulding's rental vehicle as well, a Lincoln Town Car that looked a whole lot worse for wear than the last time he had seen it. Nose down in a culvert not far from the riverbank, it had added a layer of thick dust to the pollen he remembered.

"That front end damage," Hayden said, "you think it's serious enough to keep a driver from backing out and trying to drive off?"

"Didn't look like a whole lot to me," Clayton answered. "But maybe our victim got stuck down there—or just plain panicked."

"Or there could be a broken axle or engine mount," Tomlinson suggested as they reached a rocky knoll above the culvert. When Hayden and Clayton looked back at her, she shrugged. "What? Don't you remember me telling you, I grew up in a family of mechanics?"

Hayden nodded, and told Clayton, "I really only hired her in the hope of scoring some free oil changes… Well, that, and that pesky 'most qualified candidate' stuff."

Both deputies smiled but the mood shifted when Hayden walked over and bent down to peer into the front of the car, where the driver's side door stood open, its side window perforated with at least three holes. Almost immediately, he spotted a reddish-brown substance splashed across the dash, and a larger smear across the back of the driver's seat. Though there wasn't enough to rule out hope that the victim had survived his injuries, Hayden knew very well that such signs could be deceptive. And of course, they would need to run a presumptive test to make certain the stains were human blood.

For the moment, he asked Clayton for a rundown of what he'd covered so far.

"I've walked up and down both sides of this road a bit, looking for shell casings or anything else suspicious," the chief deputy reported. "After that I climbed down that embankment to the river right here and checked for footprints, more blood or maybe drag marks, where somebody might've hauled a body to dump him in the water. There was only so much I could do alone, but so far, I've come up empty."

"And before I headed over to pick you up," Tomlinson chimed in, "I drove beyond this spot for a half mile before turning around so I could make sure we didn't have the shooter's vehicle parked nearby, with the guy out hunting our victim or disposing of a body on foot."

"Great work, both of you," Hayden told them. "Kate's getting a search and rescue team staged for us, too. Meanwhile, do we have any confirmation on our possible victim's ID?"

When he glanced over, he saw that Clayton was already nodding, his expression somber. "Unfortunately for Tim Spaulding, there's rental paperwork with his name on it in the console—along with a wallet with his driver's license, credit cards and several hundred in cash."

"Something a man doesn't leave behind unless there's the very devil on his heels," Hayden said grimly.

"Or he's dead already," Tomlinson suggested. "I mean, come on, with this blood and all…"

"Let's not get too far ahead of ourselves," Hayden cautioned. "For now, we're going to go on the assumption we're looking for a wounded survivor, because for his family's sake, if he still has a chance, we're damned well going to see he gets it. Understood?"

"Yes, sir," she said, blushing slightly, while the more seasoned Clayton nodded and murmured, "Absolutely, Sheriff."

"All right then," Hayden told them. "I'd like you to perform a more methodical search along the roadside, walking both sides fifty yards in each direction before we take on that riverbank in earnest. Meanwhile, I'll call out Deputy Gonzalez to handle the forensics on the vehicle and pull the trigger on getting that SAR team."

Just as he finished talking with Gonzalez, another call came through on his satellite phone from Lamar Robinson. The Memphis investigator barely let him get his own update out before saying, "I'm afraid I've got some troubling news here on Phoebe Spaulding as well. I'm inside the empty house."

"Please tell me she and the Spaulding kids haven't been—"

"There's no evidence they're dead, only that they took off in a hurry, after grabbing just a few clothes and valuables, as if something spooked them."

"Just like the Kesslers…"

"Maybe. Only they left a couple of cats inside. Looks like at least one of them got anxious because a candle left burning in there got knocked over, so the place was full of smoke when we drove up—"

"Giving you all the excuse you needed to force your way inside," Hayden said.

"Damned straight. The uniform riding with me had an extinguisher in his unit, and between the two of us, we put out a little fire and even saved both the cats."

"Good man," Hayden told him. "Now all you have to do is track down the missing family in time to save their lives, too."

"I've put out a BOLO on them. But I've got other news, too. I've got a lead on a woman from Ada Kessler's school matching the description of the attendance clerk there. According to the principal, she's pretty tight with Ada."

"Tight enough to loan her frightened friend a weapon?"

"That's what I intend to ask her when I speak to her this afternoon."

"Keep me posted," Hayden told him.

He ended the call and happened to look up to where a trio of black vultures circled in the near distance above an area dominated by scrubby mountain cedar. As he watched their gyrations, his chest clenched as the grim assemblage slowly grew in number.

Chapter 20

Lottie loved everything about the river resort where Miss Rita had brought them, and when they reached Miss Sara's house she'd been practically beside herself to learn their social worker had a friendly, fluffy cat, which she proclaimed was her second-favorite animal ever next to horses. Glancing over at Thunder, who'd come with them, she had hastily added, "Tied with dogs, of course!"

Hazel, however, being older and therefore naturally a whole lot smarter, had a big knot in her stomach, one that had started the minute Miss Rita had woken them this morning going on about some "extra-special surprise sleepover at a really fun vacation place right next door to Miss Sara's!"

After rushing them through dressing and then out to the Jeep without even stopping to make breakfast, Miss Rita had then done her best to direct their attention to Moonlight as the horse trotted along the pasture fence line as if to say goodbye. But, deeply suspicious of Miss Rita's overly cheery tone, which reminded Hazel too sharply of her mother's attempts at distraction after the crash, Hazel had instead looked toward the barn. Her heart had almost pounded its way up her throat when she'd spotted Miss Kate and Sheriff Hayden—who was holding a big gun—standing over a man. A man who had both hands cuffed behind him, like a criminal.

Remembering, Hazel started shaking, wondering if it had been one of the same bad men who had already taken away their dad forever and hurt their mom, too. Had he come back to try to get *them*? And what if there were more like him? Could she and Lottie really be safe here—or anywhere?

At the thought, Hazel felt her nose sting before her eyes threatened to spill over. Wishing she hadn't eaten the cereal Miss Sara gave each of them when they first got here, she put down the plastic spaceship model she and Lottie were putting together at the coffee table, in a room with a giant window overlooking the river below.

Miss Sara and Miss Rita went on quietly talking out in Miss Sara's kitchen. Lottie, who'd been sitting beside her on the rug, looked up from petting the cat, which had come out of hiding after Miss Sara's husband, Mr. Mac, had taken Thunder next door.

"What's wrong?" At the sound of Lottie's voice, an old black Lab who'd been resting in the corner looked up from her dog bed. "If you're getting bored, we can always watch a movie. Miss Sara says they have that one about kids with a pet dinosaur."

"I just—I just want Mom, that's all," Hazel lied, because she didn't want to scare her sister—or start bawling like a baby, either. Except the moment the words were out, Hazel realized that was exactly what she needed, her

Colleen Thompson

mother's arms around her as she assured them everything was going to be all right.

She wouldn't even care if Mom's voice sounded funny. Hazel would just hug her right back, tight as anything, and believe with everything she had in her. Maybe if they *all* believed hard enough, for long enough, things really might go back to the way they'd been in the days before their parents had started fighting about Uncle Cal with all his scary threats, or at least to before Dad had burst in that evening, only hours after Hazel had seen her mom so carefully bury that gun inside her big purse, and blurted, "Guess what, girls? We're all taking a surprise vacation, so hurry! Go get in the car."

With a slight whine, the big dog raised herself to wander over, her brown eyes warm with understanding as her thick tail gently waved. When the Lab lifted her gray muzzle to kiss Hazel's cheek, Hazel didn't try to stop her. She just sat there, stroking the black fur, and let the pink tongue wash her tears away.

Hours later, Hayden was still on the scene with the abandoned car, the nagging ache in his head wearing on him despite his best efforts to power through it. After the disappointment of learning that the circling vultures had found nothing more interesting than the furry remnants of some predators' meal of rabbit, he'd awakened a groggy-sounding Kate with a call about the SAR team before trying the nearest border patrol station to request a courtesy flyover of the area.

From there, he moved through a list of other tasks, trying all the while to ignore the dull thump of a headache. As long as he drank enough water and didn't do anything idiotic, he told himself he could push through the next hour and then the next one.

While Yarborough and Tomlinson continued their search for any sign of either their victim or a perpetrator, Deputy Gonzalez, who'd just arrived, confirmed that the stains on the dash and seat had tested positive for human blood. As the dark-haired and athletically built Gonzalez moved on to continue processing the vehicle for further evidence, Hayden left Lamar Robinson a voice mail once more, asking him to call back for another update when he got the chance.

Later, the Memphis detective hadn't yet reached out to him, but Kate did again.

Exasperated with his slow progress and losing his battle with the headache, Hayden told her, "Please don't say you're calling to tell me there's a hang-up with the SAR team because we haven't spotted a trace yet of Spaulding out here. If this guy's still alive at all, he's likely running out of time."

"You'll have a team there in about three hours from South Texas," she said brusquely, "but I'm calling to tell you, I'm afraid that we have bigger problems."

"Can you hold up, Kate? I have another call coming in from Mac." Hayden leaned against Tomlinson's Tahoe, taking advantage of the slim wedge of shade it offered.

"Just be quiet and *listen* to me, Hayden," she snapped. "I just got off the phone with your brother a few minutes ago, and yes, he's freaking out now, but I can give you a fuller picture."

"What the hell is going on?" Hayden asked, instinct warning him to fully focus on this conversation.

"My mother, both the girls and Sara are all missing. Or at least, neither one of us can reach them."

"*Reach* them? How is Mac not *with* them?" Hayden burst out. "He promised me he'd be keeping his eye on them."

"He *was*, until he got a call from the school. Cristo fell on the playground and broke a wire on his braces somehow. Mac had to go pick him up and take him over to the orthodontist, which I'm sure you know is a fifty-minute drive. Sara told him to go, of course. They had resort staff working, so plenty of people were around, and it's broad daylight…"

"So what on earth happened?" Hayden demanded, struggling not to picture bloodstains similar to those they had found inside Tim Spaulding's abandoned rental car inside of Rita McClafferty's Jeep.

Don't even think that. This has to be some misunder-standing—or maybe Kate's just messing with me. But even when she'd been at her angriest with him, he knew she would never joke about her mother's and the children's safety, much less that of a member of his own extended family.

"While heading home with Cristo, Mac drove through a little patch where there's no cell reception," Kate explained. "Not long afterward, he got an alert that he had a voice mail from Sara, saying she was taking my mother and the girls to the hospital in Kerrville right away."

"Why? Was someone hurt or—"

"The message said that Ada Kessler had taken an unexpected turn for the worse—and if the children wanted one more chance to see her, to say goodbye, they should get right in the car and hurry."

Alarm slicing through him, he said, "But I had an update myself a half hour ago, letting me know she'd made it through her surgery with flying colors."

Kate cried out, "I *knew* it had to be a lie! I knew it when I couldn't reach my mother's cell phone."

"Someone could've spoofed the hospital's phone number," Hayden speculated. "It's not that hard to do."

"And Mac can't reach Sara, either. That's when he called me to ask if I'd try to get a message through to my mom."

"Let's not panic, Kate. It's still possible we're wrong about this, and they're only out of range of a cell tower." Heaven only knew, communication issues were common in the mountainous, rural area—and Ada Kessler *could* have had a medical emergency after some hospital staff member had been asked to call him with an update. Wires sometimes did get crossed.

"Hold on—somebody's pulling up here," Kate said. "Maybe I can grab a ride and meet you out where you are, because I took pain medication so I shouldn't drive yet— Wait, it's Mac," she said, sounding startled. "And he's got a rifle."

Hayden cursed, because whatever the situation might be, the last thing he needed was his civilian older brother going off half-cocked. "See if you can calm him down enough to talk to me, will you? You aren't worried that he'd hurt you, are you?"

"Hurt me? *Mac?* Of course not. Hold on, and I'll put him on the line."

Though she must have partly covered the phone with her hand, he could still make out portions of their conversation as Mac tried to convince her that they needed to leave, right away. Instead, she talked him into taking a deep breath and speaking with Hayden.

"Just for a minute, okay?" she pleaded. "As the sheriff, who better to help us find Sara, my mom and the girls and bring them all home safely?"

Finally relenting, Mac came on the line. "I can't talk. I have to go find Sara. You don't understand."

"You don't have the twins there with you, do you?"

Hayden asked, worried about his niece and nephew around their father in his present state.

"They're safe at home with Frieda," Mac said, naming his resort's bighearted assistant manager. "But I'm trying to tell you, I know where Sara, Rita and her foster girls are. I looked up Sara's phone's location. We have that app because around our house, one of us or the other is always misplacing some expensive device."

"Good thinking," Hayden said. "Where is she?"

"The icon's grayed out on the screen now. That means the phone's lost contact with the network, but its last recorded location was about twenty minutes north of Leakey, on Highway 83, just past the Luna Roja," Mac said, naming the huge cattle operation where their brother worked.

"They might've gotten held up there by a wreck that was reported just a little while ago," Hayden told him, immediately thinking of the report he'd heard over Tomlinson's radio while making a call inside her vehicle. "Department of Public Safety's shut down the highway just north of there because a big truck lost its load and dumped lumber all over the highway. They're rerouting all traffic onto 39 until they can get it cleared."

"Cell service is practically nonexistent among those hills and ravines along the river," Mac said, "so if they did run into whoever lured them to that area—"

"It's possible that the person scheming to waylay them ended up cut off himself, on the other side of that detour," Hayden said, offering his brother what hope he could. "Sara could be getting back to you any minute, or maybe Rita took off without checking her fuel situation—"

"Sara would never let her do that. This is something serious. I damned well *know* it in my gut," Mac swore. "Even if they'd been out of cell range for a while, it's been well over an hour since I first tried my wife. And I know they aren't just at the hospital, too tied up to call me, because I spoke to a nurse on Ada Kessler's floor and explained this is an emergency. They haven't shown up there and weren't called, as far as anybody knows."

"All right." As worried as he was, too, Hayden made an effort to sound calm for his brother's sake. "I'm going to try reaching Ryan, see if he can go look for any sign of them, since he's out that way."

"Tell him Kate and I are headed there, too. We'll look for him."

"I'll have him meet *me*," Hayden said, infusing his voice with every bit of authority he could muster. "You need to go on home to your kids, either that or sit tight right there with Kate, until I call you with an update—"

"Forget it, Hayden."

"Listen to me, man. You have good phone service where you are, and you're safe—"

"Screw safe! I'm *not* losing another wife, you *understand* me? Hell—we weren't telling anybody this yet, but we only just found out, Sara's six weeks pregnant. If you had any idea what that means to her, to *us*—"

Hayden felt the air sucked out of his lungs. "I'll get her back to you, I swear on my life."

"I know you think you mean that, bro, but you can't control— Nobody can— I only came here to grab Kate, for backup." Voice muffled as he apparently turned from the phone, Mac said to Kate, "I need you to bring a gun, too. You're still good to shoot, aren't you, even with that injured left hand?"

"I can do what's needed," Kate assured him in the background.

"Listen to me, Mac! Don't do this!" Hayden shouted, an image flashing through his brain of his brother being flown off aboard that medevac helicopter last summer, when they'd come so close to losing him after an attack at the resort. He still had nightmares of Mac lying on that stretcher, pleading with him to take care of his children and Sara if he didn't make it.

Mac's voice came back on the line. "Meet us out there, Hayden. And you'd better bring some backup."

"Please, you're in no state to—" Hayden stopped himself when he realized the line had disconnected. He tried calling back his brother, but there was no answer.

After having the same results with Kate's phone, he cursed before dictating a brief text to her: "Heading out to have a look. Stay strong."

But in his heart, he feared that even Kate's strength might not be equal to what might await them when and if they found her mother's Jeep. He needed to beat them to it, to be there to greet them with a relieved smile if this really did turn out to be some easily explainable, if temporarily stressful, set of circumstances—

Or to physically hold them back if the truth was far worse than the small amount of blood inside the Lincoln.

Chapter 21

"These are the GPS coordinates, the last known spot where her phone's location was recorded," Mac said, his voice cracking under the pressure as he pulled over along the vacant roadside, at a place which overlooked a sunlit stretch of elevated rangeland dotted with the black shapes of grazing cattle. "Let me see my phone again, in case the app's updated her position."

"I've got it up right here, and it hasn't," Kate said, but she handed his cell over anyway since she knew that at the moment, Hayden's older brother, whose somewhat shaggy dark blond hair was a mess and handsome face was lined with worry, was incapable of listening. So far, she'd had her hands full convincing him to slow down enough not to get them killed on the way here, which would benefit neither Sara nor Kate's own family.

My family? Though Kate fully understood that Hazel and Lottie weren't hers and never would be, it hit her that she had still fallen hard for both girls, quickly coming to care for them in a way she'd never imagined would be possible for her. In a way that brought home what Hayden had been trying to tell her earlier, when he'd reminded her that a love that someone chose to give mattered every bit as much as one supposedly decreed by nature.

Blinking back tears, she looked over to where Mac sat frantically poking buttons on the phone's screen, as if sheer force of will would make the thing give up his wife's current location.

"I've used apps like that before in my search and rescue work," she told him, "and they can be wonderful, but things can go wrong with the connection—or the phone could've been powered off."

There were other possibilities as well, including the cell's deliberate wiping or even its destruction, but Kate didn't want to freak him out further by mentioning them aloud.

"Sara wouldn't have turned it off," Mac said, shaking his head, "not when she'd have certainly been expecting a call back from me. And if they'd just driven into another dead zone ahead, the app should have registered a new location for her by now, unless—"

"Come on," Kate said. "Let's keep driving. I'm betting we'll find them somewhere down along Highway 39, trying to change a flat or something."

"Do you really think this could all boil down to the two of them struggling with some frozen lug nuts?"

"We have to believe it's at least possible," she told him, "especially if my mom's gotten as far behind lately with the Jeep's maintenance as she has with the property's."

Handing her back the phone, Mac checked his pickup's mirrors before pulling back out onto an otherwise empty road. When they reached the intersection with Highway 39,

Kate saw that the roadblock Mac had told her Hayden had described had been cleared.

"Should I still take the turnoff?" Mac said, hesitating. "What if they reached the area earlier than we thought and ended up making it through on 83 after all?"

She shook her head. "That route's a lot more open and heavily traveled. I have to think that someone would've seen and helped them out if they'd been stuck there—or at least reported any issue that they'd spotted."

"Makes sense to me, too," Mac said as the truck's tires screeched on pavement, "but I pray we're guessing right."

"You aren't the only one," she said, wondering if Hayden was somewhere up ahead. Likely not, she realized, considering where he'd been when they had spoken. But if Hayden had managed to reach Ryan, as Mac had shared Hayden meant to attempt, they might certainly run across him. "We'll need to watch for Ryan's silver Ram truck."

"Or he could be in one of Luna Roja's pickups instead, a black Chevrolet with a red crescent moon painted on each front door. But, come to think of it, I believe he's off competing at another rodeo this week."

"He's still doing that?" she asked, thinking that most of the guys she'd known growing up opted to quit chasing after cowboy dreams long before they reached the age of thirty, discouraged either by the costs of remaining competitive or the toll on their bodies. "I'm surprised his boss still lets him take the time away."

"Are you kidding? Old Man Langley is just about his biggest fan—after the buckle bunnies, that is." Mac flashed a smile as he brought up his brother's ardent female admirers. "Besides that, between his winnings, his sponsorship and the horse he's been training on the side to sell, we're talking some serious money."

"Yeah, but if he ends up badly hurt—"

"I've told him the same thing, Kate, but he won't listen—and the worry's killing me, along with the guilt."

"The *guilt*? I don't understand," she said. "What on earth would you have to do with his refusal to give up rodeoing?"

"He's absolutely obsessed with restoring the legacy my legal battles cost the family. He means to buy the ranch back, or die trying."

Kate blinked, thinking that the price tag for the property, if the new owners would even be willing to part with it, could easily run to seven figures. She realized, too, that the loss of their family's ranch—its pride for generations—had left far deeper scars on all three brothers than she had imagined.

"First off, it wasn't your fault that your wife died and your kids were stolen. You had to do everything you legally could to get them back. I'm sure both Hayden and Ryan understand that."

"They claim they do, but I'll never forgive myself for not doing a better job of keeping them in the loop about the costs." As the terrain began to grow more rugged and more heavily treed, they started heading downhill. "It's—it's the whole reason things are still so off between us."

"I hope you know how much Hayden loves your kids. And how absolutely thrilled he is for you and Sara."

"She's our life," Mac said simply, sounding so bereft that she reached over to touch her old friend's arm.

"We'll find Sara. We'll find all of them," she said as the road narrowed and became more winding. In some spots, rocky hillsides hemmed it in tightly along one side, while in others, they caught glimpses of greenish water—the first signs of what she recognized as the Medina River.

As they continued, the area became more scenic, and homes and the occasional small retreat began popping up along the river's edge or on the hillsides overlooking the water.

"Not a lot of safe places along here to pull over if they happened to have car trouble," Mac commented as they started over a bridge crossing the river, where she had a brief glimpse of cypress trees lining the banks, along with someone's rope swing over the sun-dappled water.

"No, but—*slow down!* Was that Ryan's work truck we just passed, parked way back off that pullout just past the river?"

Her heart thumped wildly at the glimpse of the dark, two-door pickup, just beyond the cypress trees, within walking distance of the water. Possibly it was only some random person parked there to go fishing, but her instincts were screaming as they drove farther from the spot.

"I don't know. Did you see anybody?" Mac said.

"I didn't, but we'd better check," she told him, her stomach tightening as her pulse picked up speed.

"Let me find a safe place to turn around."

Once they did, he approached slowly, clearly unwilling to pass up the spot again before making a left to pull in behind the pickup, which had been parked at a haphazard angle and had a badly damaged right front bumper and quarter panel.

"That's definitely not Ryan's truck." In a voice steeped with disappointment, he gestured toward the plain, dark blue door. "And anyway, looks empty."

But Kate, who had noticed the front door standing open, was already unbuckling her seat belt anyway, eager to look inside the Chevy Silverado. "There was a truck like this one used in a related crime," she said, grabbing her father's rifle, which she had tucked by her right side, to go and have a look. "It could just be a coincidence, but wait in here a minute, will you?"

She wasn't surprised when she heard him get out of the truck to jog up behind her. But a moment later, she heard him shout, "Forget the truck, Kate! Look, down by the river!"

When she did, she saw what they'd both missed earlier, from the more elevated bridge crossing. Her mother's Jeep was angled sharply downhill, its front end dug into the riverbank's mud and several sapling trees snapped off just behind it and beneath its wheels. As Kate shrieked and started running toward it, she could see that the passenger-side back door was open—and someone, a woman in the front seat, was struggling to escape the billowing clouds of deployed airbags.

"Sara!" Mac shouted, barreling past her toward his wife. "Don't try to move! Are you hurt?"

"I—I'm *stuck*!" Sara cried, lowering the Jeep's window. "My legs are trapped, not hurt—the metal's twisted underneath here. But forget that— You have to go and find them, help them, before the girls' uncle—"

"It's their uncle Cal?" Kate asked. "Which way did they go?"

"I don't know the name," Sara cried, her cheekbone abraded and her green eyes bloodshot, most likely from the airbags. "I only know that they went running down along the river, that way—" she pointed away from the bridge "—with a man after them. He definitely had a handgun."

Thrusting her satellite phone toward Mac, Kate said, "You stay with your wife, and call for rescue, an ambulance and law enforcement backup. This should get a signal, even down in here. I'm going after them."

"You can't—"

"Listen to me—as a civilian, the best thing you can do is keep Sara safe, make sure she's not bleeding somewhere and then flag down help when it arrives."

"I'll get help. I swear it. Just—be careful, Kate," Mac said, his blue-gray eyes intense. "Hayden might not know it, but I swear to you, he needs you."

"Well, right this minute, my mother and those two girls need me more."

Just past a crossing on the Medina River, Hayden shouted to Gonzalez, "Hold up! That's my brother!" as he saw Mac frantically waving at them to pull off the road.

Gonzalez barely had the car stopped before Hayden was out the door.

"The Jeep's over the bank, down by the river, and Sara's trapped inside! I've called 911 for help," Mac shouted, gesturing wildly beyond a dark blue, two-door pickup. "But Sara can wait for now—Kate can't. She took off running that way, after the girls' uncle. Sara says he was chasing them and Rita!"

"What the—"

"Down through those trees," Mac repeated. "Hurry!"

Hayden didn't hear the rest, his heart nearly stopping as he heard the crack of a single gunshot from downriver.

As Gonzalez caught up, Hayden told him, "Follow me—and keep your head down. Cal Thorley's after his nieces and Rita."

"I heard the shot," his deputy told him.

"And Kate went after him." *If she's still alive to help them.* But Hayden shoved the thought out of his mind, telling himself she had already proved she could handle herself even in desperate situations.

But with the lives of her own mother and the children

that he knew she'd come to care for at stake, could she have gotten careless this time and paid the ultimate price?

God help us all, he prayed, struggling to lock down his emotions before hearing Gonzalez, just behind him, cry out sharply. Turning, his saw his deputy clutch his ankle, which he must have turned on the uneven ground.

Struggling to get back to his feet, Gonzalez took a limping step, then vowed, "I'll catch up!"

Wishing he'd been able to reach Ryan—or any other backup—Hayden continued, attempting to mind his own steps more carefully. But with vision blurring from his exertion and pounding headache, he could only grit his teeth and charge ahead.

His lungs burning, he heard an echoing male voice, coming from the direction of the river. Carefully picking his way among the trees, Hayden huffed his way downslope, only to slip on loose rock and end up clattering on his rump, sliding noisily down the incline.

While his heart thumped wildly in his chest, the voice cut off midsentence, the speaker shouting, "What the hell was that? Who's there? You come any closer, and I swear I'll pull this trigger."

Barely able to focus, Hayden blinked hard, peering through a screen of trees and the dark haze that obscured his vision. When he could finally see again, his blood froze at the sight of a man standing in knee-deep water—pressing a gun to the head of a woman he held in front of him like a shield, a hank of her long silver hair knotted in his left fist.

Rita McClafferty's mouth was open in a silent scream, her face white with terror.

"Let her go—*now*," ordered Kate from farther down and higher up the bank. "Or so help me, I will put you down like the mad dog that you are, Spaulding!"

Spaulding? Blinking again, Hayden was shocked to recognize the thin build of a man he'd imagined murdered back near Old Meier Ranch River Crossing, Nicolas Kessler's supposed friend and boss.

"I only want to take the girls—take them to join their mother!" Spaulding shouted, his tone abruptly turning oily. "Hand them both over and I promise, you and your mother will walk free."

"Don't you dare, Kate! You know he's lying!" Rita screamed, twisting desperately and jamming back a sharp elbow into her attacker's ribs. Her body pitched backward, a hand flying back as if for balance.

Impossibly loud, another gunshot echoed. Hayden caught a flash of Rita's silver hair before her head splashed down in the water. Then came his own shot, followed by Kate's—and Tim Spaulding dropped into a river that bloomed with crimson streamers.

Chapter 22

Kate raced toward the darkening water, a desperate prayer on her lips. *Let her be alive! Please!*

A soaked head broke the surface, her mother crying out in fear or pain—Kate didn't know which. She only knew that Hayden, who was closer, reached her first and helped Kate drag her mother's surprisingly light body to the bank.

"The girls! Where are my girls?" was her mother's first question, as Hayden ran back to the river for the collapsed gunman.

"Right over there," Kate said. "I had them hunker down behind that fallen tree, where they're safe and out of sight."

She felt a stab of pride for how incredibly strong they'd been, particularly Hazel, whom she'd spotted literally burying her little sister in the leaf litter to try to shield her from the horror. But Kate would definitely talk to

Sara about seeing that both were offered counseling, no matter where they ended up once this was over.

But her mother's pained cry, as she tried to move, drew Kate's full attention.

"What is it? Did he hurt you?" she asked, squeezing her mother's cool hand.

"It's—it's my hip," her mother said, shivering in her damp clothes. "When I—when I twisted away from that monster, I slipped on a rock and hurt myself."

"We'll get you all checked out. Don't try to move." Kate looked over her shoulder to Deputy Gonzalez, as he limped his way downhill. "My mother needs medical attention!"

"I'll be glad to check on the ambulance's ETA, but first, let me help Hayden here before he—"

At the sound of a splash, Kate saw that Hayden had slipped and gotten dripping wet attempting to maneuver Spaulding's body in the water. When he came up cursing and spitting water, she ran over, along with Gonzalez, to help Hayden drag the limp form to the bank.

Gonzalez squatted down to check near the man's throat for a pulse. Considering the neat hole Kate had spotted in the girls' "Uncle Tim's" cheekbone and the larger wound on his side, she wasn't surprised when the deputy shook his head and told them, "This one's definitely gone. Let me head back up now and check on those medics. I'll grab an emergency blanket out of my unit for you, too."

"After faking his death earlier and then taking off in the truck used by his hired goons, this is pretty much poetic justice," Hayden said, still staring at the lifeless body. "I'm figuring Tim Spaulding must've been in on that whole scheme Mrs. Singh—and of course Nic Kessler before her—uncovered. Feds'll have to figure out if he had coconspirators, but it could be he was the mastermind from the start."

"Do you think Kessler realized he was in danger from his own good friend?" Kate asked.

"Maybe he did or maybe he didn't—but Spaulding must've worried that Ada and the children either heard him say or saw him do something that would link the man they knew so well to Nic's murder. Otherwise, he'd never have gone to such lengths, especially once his hired thugs failed." Hayden shook his head. "But what about you? Are you all right? And the girls?"

"I'm fine, but I need to go see to them, and my mother's injured her hip somehow. She needs a hospital."

Hayden stepped over to where her mother sat, her head drooping and her body trembling. Much to Kate's surprise, when he squatted down, the two of them embraced each other tightly, both so soaked that their relative wetness didn't matter.

"You could've gotten yourself killed with that fool stunt," he scolded her. "What were you thinking, attacking him like that?"

"I was thinking I'd rather die than let that monster use me to endanger my three girls, that's what," her mother said, sounding so scrappy that fierce pride twisted in Kate's heart.

"Well I, for one, am damned glad that you didn't die." Hayden ducked his head down before confiding, "Great mothers-in-law don't grow on trees, you know."

Rita looked up at him sharply. "*Mothers-in-law?* Just how hard did you crack that skull of yours last week, Hayden?" Brown eyes sparking with suspicion, she looked from him to Kate. "Or is there something you two haven't been telling me? *Kate?*"

"Let's not do this here and now, Hayden," Kate said,

furious that he would put her on the spot like this, when she practically had adrenaline popping out of her pores, "and certainly not with two frightened children and everything else needing our attention."

Pushing dark, dripping hair from his deep blue eyes, he gave her a chagrined look. "Of course, you're right. I'm sorry. But don't expect for me to care that your mother here—or the whole world—knows my intentions toward you, Kate McClafferty, because the days of my pretending that you don't own my heart—that you haven't since the two of us were kids—are over."

After making the biggest fool of himself in the state of Texas, Hayden did all he could to coordinate the scene as more emergency responders began arriving. Though Mac had managed to free Sara from the damaged Jeep himself, she ended up being transported by ambulance to be checked out at the hospital, mostly as a precaution due to her pregnancy. With a suspected hip fracture, Rita's situation was more serious, and Mac ended up driving Kate, along with the girls, to Kerrville while Hayden stayed for hours longer to deal with the death investigation, until his river-soaked clothes at last dried on his body.

It wasn't until early evening that he finally borrowed a clean—if somewhat tight—shirt from Gonzalez and caught a ride to the hospital with a Kerr County deputy, who had come to inform him that Cal Thorley had been apprehended without incident earlier that afternoon and was being held for questioning at his convenience.

"Hold him overnight if you would, and I'll talk to him in the morning." Hayden no longer believed that Ada's brother had anything to do with the attacks against her family, but he intended to make certain the surviving Kesslers would be safe from him before releasing the man—or advising him to return to his home state if his sister, quite understandably, decided she didn't wish to see him.

"I'll pass along the message," the deputy promised before dropping Hayden off at the hospital entrance.

He skipped the emergency department, since Mac had contacted him hours earlier to let him know that Sara had been released. Though she'd been advised to take it easy for a few days to recover from minor bumps and bruises, she had nonetheless insisted on taking charge of the Kessler girls, who were allowed a brief visit with their mother.

Ada Kessler had been quite groggy following her surgery, but Mac had reported that the girls had spoken of nothing else but their excitement over hearing her voice and getting to carefully embrace her, along with their plans for returning home with her to Tennessee as soon as she was well again. "But for at least for the short term, they'll be safe at our place, with Silvia and Cristo, since Sara's certified as an emergency foster."

Hayden had been more than grateful, knowing that Hazel and Lottie would be well cared for. He felt hopeful, too, that with Sara's guidance, they would begin to recover from the horrors they had suffered.

After learning that Kate's mother had been admitted, Hayden stopped at the gift shop on impulse before heading up to her room. After settling on a basket containing various magazines, puzzles and a balloon with a get-well message, he was paying when Lamar Robinson called with one last update.

"Don't you *ever* go home to your family?" Hayden asked by way of greeting.

"Man, I get enough of that from my wife." Lamar laughed. "You want to hear what's got me sleeping in the doghouse for missing another dinner tonight or not?"

"I'm definitely listening," Hayden said as he nodded his thanks to the clerk and took his purchase to an out-of-the-way spot in the lobby. "So what's the verdict on Phoebe Spaulding? Is she another victim or a coconspirator?"

He'd been leaning toward the latter since Lamar had called earlier to tell him that she and her children had been picked up entering the airport—with one-way tickets that would eventually take them to an island nation with no extradition treaty with the US.

"After being brought in, she panicked at the thought of being separated from her children and sent to prison. Since then, she's been talking her head off, claiming that it was her husband who called her this morning to tell her he'd transferred millions in investors' money into offshore accounts under his name and instructed her where to find a set of tickets he'd left for them, just in case things went to hell."

"With one of the goons he's hired dead and the other spinning off on some kind of mad vendetta of his own, Spaulding must've realized he had only the slimmest chance of keeping his scheme from breaking open."

"So why risk going after the Kessler kids, if he was about to skip the country?"

"Maybe he imagined the girls could name and stop him," Hayden theorized. "Or maybe wiping out the entire Kessler family was, in his mind, the only way to erase the stain of his original betrayal, in the killing of his own friend and the shooting of Ada Kessler."

"Or he might've been trying to keep it from getting back to his own family," Lamar suggested. "I definitely know that the *instant* I made it clear to Phoebe that we had hard evidence that her husband was behind what'd happened to the Kesslers, that woman was completely done with him. You could see it in her eyes."

"Have you broken the news to her yet that her husband's been killed?"

With a sigh, the investigator said, "About to handle that now. I don't much like the woman. She definitely knew more about her husband's financial schemes than she's pretending, even if we can't prove it—*and* she abandoned the family cats to starve inside that house—or burn in it. Still, I like breaking this news even less."

"Good luck with that."

"Thanks—and there was one other thing. One of my colleagues let me know that Ada Kessler's friend, the attendance clerk, must've heard from her principal because she came and gave a statement. Claimed that Ada told her she was really worried about Nic booking the family into some shady-looking vacation rental he'd found online at the last minute. So the friend offered to loan her her handgun to take along, just so she'd feel safer."

"So Ada lied to get a gun without a waiting period, one that wouldn't be traceable? Your colleague buy that story?"

"Judging from how upset the woman was, he did."

"Will this friend be charged, you suppose?" Hayden asked, though he wasn't up on current Tennessee gun laws.

"She certainly could be, as could Ada Kessler, since the transfer happened on school property, but under the circumstances, I seriously doubt the DA's going to pursue charges. I doubt very much that this clerk's ever going to be loaning anybody guns again, though."

"I'd certainly hope not. How about if we talk again tomorrow?"

"Finally calling it a day yourself, are you?" Lamar asked. "I'm honestly surprised you've hung in as long as you have, considering that concussion."

"To tell you the truth, the head's feeling better," Hayden

admitted, pleasantly surprised to realize that, since he'd eaten a take-out sandwich on the way here, the ache had faded to a distant murmur, and his vision was far clearer than it had been in days. "But I'm definitely overdue for getting off my feet. Hope you find your way home soon, too."

After ending the call, he headed upstairs. He found Kate alone in her mother's semidarkened room, where she stood looking out the window, wiping at her eyes with a tissue.

"Hey, there," he said quietly, walking up beside her. "Is your mother—"

He was afraid to finish the question, so he set down the gift basket on a rolling bedside table and opened up his arms.

"They took her for one more scan," Kate said, slipping into his embrace and hugging him. "I guess the surgeon wanted another view before he goes in to repair that hip fracture."

"She's going to pull through this," Hayden said, laying a kiss on top of her head. "I know she will. And afterward, whatever she needs—"

"I'll be there to help her," Kate vowed, taking a step back to look up at him.

"And so will I, Kate. Whatever you need from me, I promise you, you'll have it…even if you won't have me."

She looked up at him, studying him intently. "You really are a good man, aren't you? Even if you don't at all fight fair."

Realizing she was referring to his dragging her mother into his campaign earlier, he fought back his own low chuckle. "No, ma'am, I don't and I don't intend to. Not when the stakes are as high as this. Even if that means buying out the gift shop and putting up with your mother's cranky comments while I tend her after surgery myself."

"As generous as that offer is, you definitely won't be doing it alone. I'm moving back home, permanently, because according to the doctor, this will be more than a short-term rehab situation. Honestly, I should've seen before now how much my mother needs me. And how much I want to be close with her."

"But what about your job with search and rescue?"

"What my role is going forward depends on the organization. There's a lot I can still do, working remotely, as far as training and logistics and spearheading their fundraising. If they're on board with the idea, maybe I can work out some sort of job-sharing arrangement with Simon Corbett. But if not—my life's in the Hill Country…"

"With your mother?"

"With my mother…" Her lips curved upward, her beautiful eyes warmed by the smile she offered. "Plus her future son-in-law—and whatever kind of family you and I are brave and bold enough to build together."

He stared into her face, barely able to fathom what he heard. "So you—you're really serious about this?"

"I'm serious when I say I've never loved another man, Hayden, and I never will because there's been no room in my heart for anybody but you…even if we had some serious growing up to do before we made it to this point."

"I know you're right," he told her, "but from this moment forward, how about if the two of us just concentrate on growing old, and growing whatever happiness we can, together?"

"I can't imagine anything more perfect," she said before sealing the bargain with a kiss that vanquished all lingering traces of his pain.

* * * * *

COMING NEXT MONTH FROM

HARLEQUIN
ROMANTIC SUSPENSE

#2195 COLTON'S BABY MOTIVE
The Coltons of Colorado • by Lara Lacombe

A one-night stand might have led Hilary Weston and Oliver Colton to a pregnancy, but when Hilary's brother is snatched from the restaurant she works at, Oliver will have to find him—while proving to Hilary that he can be the involved father their baby needs.

#2196 CONARD COUNTY PROTECTOR
Conard County: The Next Generation
by Rachel Lee

Widow Lynn Macy has no idea that her brother-in-law will do anything to gain possession of her house. Marine master gunnery sergeant Jax Stone learns that a killer is on his tail. When the killer teams up with Lynn's brother-in-law, Jax ends up in a race against time to keep Lynn and himself alive.

#2197 HOTSHOT HERO ON THE EDGE
Hotshot Heroes • by Lisa Childs

Firefighter Luke Garrison is in danger of losing his wife and someone's trying to kill him. Willow Garrison doesn't want a divorce, but after multiple miscarriages, she's not sure how to continue their marriage. But then the killer sets his sights on Willow, and Luke will have to do everything he can to save her—and their baby!

#2198 TRACKING HIS SECRET CHILD
Sierra's Web • by Tara Taylor Quinn

When Amanda Smith's teenage daughter goes missing, she calls the girl's father for help. But Hudson Warner didn't even know he *had* a daughter. Now they're in a desperate search to find their daughter before their worst nightmare happens.

Hudson wasn't turning pages anymore. He was just sitting there, staring at the book. Then he was looking at Amanda, his steely eyes topped by brows furrowed in disbelief. "Hope is mine?"

She wanted to glance away but didn't. Forcing herself to look him straight in the eye, she simply repeated her earlier assurance. "Yes."

"You were pregnant when I left."

"Only about a month. I didn't know." The fact seemed important to her. "I wasn't begging you stay with me, crying about my lack of a part in your plans, because I was pregnant. I was just being the immature, selfish, privileged girl you said I was."

"I was…" He shook his head. They'd already been over all that. Couldn't change who'd they'd been.

"And all the years since…" He shook his head. "I can't… It doesn't matter right now. We have to find her." A strange glint covered that dark brown gaze then. It wasn't pointed. More like…awash with tears.

"I know," she said. "And I didn't intend to tell you until afterward, so you weren't distracted. But with your friends coming…looking into things you wouldn't find on her computer…I didn't want you to hear from them." She'd made the decisions she thought best. Maybe they hadn't always been.

Or maybe there just hadn't been any easy answers.

He still held the book open between his hands. Kept shaking his head. She so badly wanted to comfort him.

But she was the one instilling the hurt instead.

"I find out I have a daughter only to know that she's… out there… That I can't…"

Helplessness weakened her again. She slumped, feeling his despair and sharing it in silence. And yet, completely apart from him, too. Unable to find him. Minutes passed.

She remained still. Just there. Prepared to be there all night.

Don't miss
Tracking His Secret Child *by Tara Taylor Quinn,*
available September 2022 wherever
Harlequin Romantic Suspense books and
ebooks are sold.

Harlequin.com

Get 4 FREE REWARDS!

We'll send you 2 FREE Books plus 2 FREE Mystery Gifts.

KENTUCKY CRIME RING
JULIE ANNE LINDSEY

TEXAS STALKER
BARB HAN

UNDER THE RANCHER'S PROTECTION
ADDISON FOX

OPERATION WHISTLEBLOWER
JUSTINE DAVIS

FREE Value Over **$20**

Both the **Harlequin Intrigue®** and **Harlequin® Romantic Suspense** series feature compelling novels filled with heart-racing action-packed romance that will keep you on the edge of your seat.

YES! Please send me 2 FREE novels from the Harlequin Intrigue or Harlequin Romantic Suspense series and my 2 FREE gifts (gifts are worth about $10 retail). After receiving them, if I don't wish to receive any more books, I can return the shipping statement marked "cancel." If I don't cancel, I will receive 6 brand-new Harlequin Intrigue Larger-Print books every month and be billed just $5.99 each in the U.S. or $6.49 each in Canada, a savings of at least 14% off the cover price or 4 brand-new Harlequin Romantic Suspense books every month and be billed just $4.99 each in the U.S. or $5.74 each in Canada, a savings of at least 13% off the cover price. It's quite a bargain! Shipping and handling is just 50¢ per book in the U.S. and $1.25 per book in Canada.* I understand that accepting the 2 free books and gifts places me under no obligation to buy anything. I can always return a shipment and cancel at any time. The free books and gifts are mine to keep no matter what I decide.

Choose one: ☐ **Harlequin Intrigue Larger-Print** (199/399 HDN GNXC)   ☐ **Harlequin Romantic Suspense** (240/340 HDN GNMZ)

Name (please print)

Address   Apt. #

City   State/Province   Zip/Postal Code

Email: Please check this box ☐ if you would like to receive newsletters and promotional emails from Harlequin Enterprises ULC and its affiliates. You can unsubscribe anytime.

Mail to the Harlequin Reader Service:
IN U.S.A.: P.O. Box 1341, Buffalo, NY 14240-8531
IN CANADA: P.O. Box 603, Fort Erie, Ontario L2A 5X3

Want to try 2 free books from another series? Call 1-800-873-8635 or visit www.ReaderService.com.